MEGAN HART

BLACK WINGS

This is a **FLAME TREE PRESS** book

Text copyright © 2019 Megan Hart

FLAME TREE PRESS
6 Melbray Mews, London, SW6 3NS, UK
flametreepress.com

Distribution and warehouse:
Baker & Taylor Publisher Services (BTPS)
30 Amberwood Parkway, Ashland, OH 44805
btpubservices.com

Thanks to the Flame Tree Press team, including:
Taylor Bentley, Frances Bodiam, Federica Ciaravella, Don D'Auria,
Chris Herbert, Matteo Middlemiss, Josie Mitchell, Mike Spender,
Cat Taylor, Maria Tissot, Nick Wells, Gillian Whitaker.

The cover is created by Flame Tree Studio with
thanks to Nik Keevil and Shutterstock.com.
The font families used are Avenir and Bembo.

Flame Tree Press is an imprint of Flame Tree Publishing Ltd
flametreepublishing.com

A copy of the CIP data for this book is available from the British Library
and the Library of Congress.

HB ISBN: 978-1-78758-117-3
PB ISBN: 978-1-78758-115-9
ebook ISBN: 978-1-78758-118-0
Also available in FLAME TREE AUDIO

Printed in the US at Bookmasters, Ashland, Ohio

MEGAN HART

BLACK WINGS

FLAME TREE PRESS
London & New York

CHAPTER ONE

There hadn't always been something wrong with her.

As a baby, Briella had been the most beautiful thing Marian had ever seen. Premature by a few weeks, but nothing the doctors had been concerned about. No stay in the NICU or anything like that. She'd been too small for all of the clothes Marian had been given for her baby shower, even the newborn sizes. Tiny, but beautiful and perfect. A little living doll. Ten teensy perfect fingers and toes. With her father's pale gray eyes and her mother's dark, spiraling curls, her skin the color of sea-wet sand, Briella had always been a perfect blend of Marian and Tommy. There'd never been a second's doubt that the kid had inherited the best features from both her parents, even if she'd been an 'oops'.

A late night, too many visits from the tequila bottle. Marian and Tommy had been thinking about reconciling, stalling the divorce each had threatened at one time or another. High school sweethearts, eight or nine years together, on and off, neither of them willing to give each other up. A baby was the worst way for them to make things work, but who thinks about that when you're young and made stupid by love?

The pregnancy had seemed like a miracle, after all the trouble Marian had had keeping one before that, the babies they had tried for. Seemed like a sign they ought to try to work it out one more time. Young. Stupid. In love, or what had passed for love between them, at least.

Not that she would have chosen anything different, even if anyone could have convinced her then how hard it was going to end up being. How beautiful babies become recalcitrant, tantrum-throwing toddlers, who grow into elementary school kids with attitude, who morph into pre-teens who think they ought to rule the world.

She and Tommy had stayed together long enough for Briella to be born, and after that Marian had kicked Tommy out for the final time. It had been rough at first. Tommy as her husband had been prone to unreliability. Tommy as not-her-husband felt even less obligation. They got along okay now, for the sake of their daughter. There were still times when Marian could look at him and remember how much she'd loved him, and there were plenty of times when she had no trouble remembering why she didn't anymore.

From the start, Briella had focused on the world around her in a way that Marian hadn't realized was unusual in a newborn until the pediatrician had commented on it, suggesting they check the baby's vision. Briella had been able to see perfectly fine. She just paid more attention to the world than other infants her age.

Briella had been born tiny and had stayed small. Maybe that was part of the problem. Always a little bit behind the other, bigger kids, never able to catch up in some ways, but so far beyond them in others. She'd been sorted into a series of supplemental gifted programs since kindergarten, when the teacher realized Briella was falling behind on her reading work because she was spending too much time devouring the copy of *Gone with the Wind* she'd begged Marian to buy her after they'd watched the movie together. The shortest kid in her class, but the smartest.

It had never seemed to matter until the last year or so, when they started sorting the kids into classes according to ability level, when they all started to get taller as they headed toward puberty, when friendships that had been in place since preschool started to shift and change right along with them.

In her own elementary school days, Marian had been best friends with two girls in her class. Jody Evans and Angela Heller had lived next door to each other since birth, more like sisters than simply besties. Marian had become their third, happily a bridge between the two strong personalities. Sometimes closer with one, the next week with the other, Marian had been devastated the summer after middle school, when they all moved into the new high school building, to discover Jody and Angela had been placed in a different set of classes to Marian. They had drifted apart after that, although sometimes Marian still bumped into Jody in town. They always promised to get together, but they never managed to find the time. She'd made other friends since, some even better, but there'd never been any who were quite the same.

What was happening to Briella seemed a lot more deliberate. Kids who'd been her lunch buddies for years were sitting at different tables. The ones in her gifted classes stopped inviting her to their birthday parties. Briella had told Marian it was because they didn't like her anymore, but she wouldn't say why. When Marian wanted to know if Briella was being bullied, the school guidance counselor had assured her that she was not.

"Some children simply aren't popular," the counselor had said. "Not being liked isn't the same thing as being bullied."

"Briella…Bean…are you doing something to make them not like you? If you are, why don't you stop doing it?" Marian had asked later.

Briella's answer to that had been a shrug. "Why should I be a different person just to make people like me? You can't *make* people like you if they don't, Mama."

Wise words from a little girl, words that Marian knew were true and yet…something about them had seemed off. She'd spent hours sobbing into her own mother's arms about the loss of her friendships. If Marian had raised Briella to have enough self-esteem that she didn't worry about the judgment of her classmates, that was supposed to be a good thing, right? Why, then, did it seem to bother Marian so much more than it did her daughter?

Briella didn't get into trouble at school. Her grades were above and beyond anything Marian could have asked for, academically. At home, Briella was her usual bright and talkative self, except for an occasional rise of temper that showed itself in ways that Marian wondered might have something to do with the other kids' opinions of her. Nobody liked to be reminded they weren't as smart as someone else, and Briella's go-to insult when she was frustrated about something usually ended up using the words 'stupid' or 'dummy', no matter how many times Marian scolded her for it.

The kid had inherited that trait from her dad. Tommy had always been at the head of the class and not afraid to point that out. Teachers had loved him despite his smart-ass attitude, so at school he'd gotten away with a lot of crap nobody else could. At home, he'd been and remained his parents' golden child, unable to do any wrong – except when it came to Marian, of course. His mother had hated her from the start for 'taking her baby away,' an attitude that had not improved with the addition of a grandchild Nancy Gallagher had once called 'an embarrassment'.

Unlike Briella, Tommy had always been able to make and keep friends. Even if he was an arrogant son of a bitch, he worked that clichéd Irish charm in ways Marian had to admit that their daughter had not inherited.

Tommy traveled a lot, and when he was gone it mostly seemed like Briella was out of sight, out of mind. He couldn't be counted on to send a regular check, but when he came home he threw his money around like he'd printed it. He'd promised Briella he would take her to Disney World for her birthday, but instead he'd taken her to the Disney Store and gaslit her into believing that was what he'd originally said. The kid had come home with a stuffed Pluto dog that was bigger than she was. Briella always acted like her daddy could do no wrong, so if she was resentful about the obvious bait-and-switch, she never said a word about it.

Still, didn't that have to be at least part of the reason Briella had started acting out so much more frequently? An absentee dad with feast-or-famine affections was bound to mess with a kid's well-being, even if she had an amazing step-father like Marian's husband, Dean. *But then so could anything else*, Marian thought, knowing it was easier to blame Tommy for not being around than it would be to take a good hard look at herself and how bad *she* might be screwing up.

She did the best she could, Marian told herself now, watching her daughter bent over a large, battered notebook at the computer desk. Marian had picked up the five-subject monster at the thrift store back when she'd considered keeping a journal again. Two entries into it, Marian had realized she was never going to do anything or even think anything important enough to write about. She'd torn away the used pages and tucked the book itself into the drawer where she put things she didn't know what to do with. A year later, Briella had found it there and taken it for her own.

The best she could. What more could anyone expect out of a mother? Marian paused in the den doorway with the plate of apple slices and peanut butter she'd put together for Briella's snack. The kid came home from school starving almost every day and usually demanded her snacks in the kitchen while she swung her little feet and told her mother all about her day in the fifth grade. Today, though, she'd gone straight to the ancient desktop set up in the den's back corner, beneath the window. Marian and Dean had talked about upgrading, but a new computer wasn't high on the priority list, not with the mortgage upside down and Dean's overtime being cut back every time they got even a little bit ahead.

"Hey, Bean, whatcha doing? Homework?"

Marian had been floored to realize they gave elementary kids so much homework. Not the bullshit kind she remembered from her days at Southside, either. These kids got full-on assignments that counted toward grades, even in the regular classes that weren't part of the gifted program.

Briella didn't turn to look at her mother. She was hunched over her 'idea book'. Nobody was allowed to look inside it. She'd taught herself to write at the age of three and a half, only shortly after she'd learned to read. In the beginning, concerned at her preschool kid's obsession with the heavy, thick notebook she seemed barely able to lift, Marian had sneaked a peek in the notebook a few times. She'd kind of hated herself for doing it because it reminded her of the times her own mother had violated her trust and read her teenage journal.

There hadn't been much to snoop on. Scrawled in a nearly illegible hand, it showed that Briella might be *able* to write, but she wasn't very good at it. Anyway, at that age, what could Briella be writing in there that was anything for Marian to worry about? She'd stopped checking it after that. Studying her daughter's intent expression now, Marian wondered if she ought to sneak another look. It might give her at least a tiny clue into what had been going on with the kid since the end of the last school year.

"Aren't you hungry? Briella," Marian said sharply now to get her attention. "I brought your snack."

Briella closed the battered notebook with a snap and looked at her mother with an expression Marian couldn't figure out, only that she didn't like it. Marian held up the plate. Briella slid off the chair and reached for it.

"Yum, nom nom nom," she said. "Thanks, Mama."

"How was school today?"

Briella shrugged and turned back to the computer monitor. "Fine."

"Anything good happen?" Marian asked.

"No."

Marian hesitated, bracing herself as she thought of the end of fourth grade. Fifth had barely begun. "Anything bad happen?"

"No."

Briella's fingers danced on the keyboard. The desktop was so slow that any kind of internet search became a chore too taxing for Marian to have the patience for. If she wanted to look something up, she did it on her phone. Briella had a tablet that Tommy had given her last year for her birthday, but no phone yet. She might have tested into a gifted-level IQ, and could read at a college level, but she was still only ten years old.

Marian watched the screen fill with text. Pages of it. Tiny font, hard to read. It looked scientific. "What are you looking at?"

"Did you know that ravens can recognize human faces?" Briella twisted in the chair and stuffed an apple slice into her mouth. She chomped noisily.

Messily. Peanut butter gathered at the corners of her lips in a way that had Marian itching to wipe it away.

She looked for a tissue on the desk and snagged one from the box. "I didn't. C'mere. Get the schmutz off."

Briella squirmed out of her grip before Marian could take more than a couple swipes. "They can. They remember people who hurt them. Sometimes, they'll even attack them!"

"Sounds scary." Marian grabbed her daughter firmly by the arm, almost pinching. "Stay still."

The school had sent home a letter to parents about how it was common for kids this age to slack off in personal hygiene, and Briella had been acting like the perfect example of that. Nightly showers were a constant battle, as was keeping up with her head of springy natural curls. All of her clothes had stains. She had to be reminded repeatedly to brush her teeth.

Briella shook her head to keep it away from the tissue and yanked her arm hard enough to dig Marian's fingers in too deep. "They will remember you if you treat them good, too. They'll bring you treats. Some can even talk! Better than parrots, even."

"Briella! Damn it, you have peanut butter all over the place. If you can't eat it neatly, you'll have to do it at the kitchen table. You can't be getting—" Marian cut herself off with a sigh at the sight of her daughter's sullen glare and drew in a breath to calm her tone. "Sweetie, I told you before. We can't afford to replace the keyboard if it gets too messy to use. You promised me you'd be more careful."

"Dean could get a second job," Briella said.

Marian stopped swiping at the girl's face. "What?"

"If he really wanted to, he could get another job so he could buy me a computer. Anyway, Daddy says he's going to get me a laptop. He's not poor, like we are."

Marian bit the tip of her tongue. Dean worked third shift at the local potato chip plant. He was a supervisor, but that meant instead of working a single line, he often had to take turns at several different jobs when people were out sick or took vacation. There'd been cut-backs and no raise for the past two years. Add in the half-hour commute, and he came home exhausted every morning. He made decent money, but he'd taken on a lot of Marian's debts when they got together. She'd had some old medical bills from her emergency appendectomy, and not all of them had been paid off yet. They didn't live hand to mouth, but there was often very little left over from each paycheck.

"We aren't poor, Briella. Did your daddy say we were?" Tommy might have money now, but he hadn't grown up with it. Marian wouldn't have put it past him to try to make himself look better in Briella's eyes, though.

Briella shrugged. "He didn't have to say it, I just can tell by our house and stuff."

This gave Marian pause. They'd moved into Dean's childhood home when his parents moved to Florida. The house was old, true, and needed some repairs, but old houses always did. Their cars were also old, but paid off. She shopped with coupons, had a budget, saved for things rather than putting them on credit, when she could. They didn't have the best of everything, but they also didn't lack for much. She couldn't recall ever talking about money with or around Briella, and the thought that her child believed they were poor, especially in comparison to Tommy's unreliable generosity, stung.

"Your daddy says a lot of things he doesn't...he can't.... Briella, Dean works very hard to support us. We told you that maybe for Christmas, Santa might—"

"I *don't* believe in Santa," Briella said flatly. "Ruthie Miller doesn't either, and *she* told me he's not real."

Ruthie Miller was Jewish, something Marian didn't feel qualified to explain to her kid, since she wasn't sure exactly what Jews believed, other than they didn't celebrate Christmas or believe in Jesus. Truth was, Marian herself had stopped believing in him a while ago, right around the time she'd lost her mom. Prayers hadn't done anything to save June Taylor when she'd stepped into the crosswalk with the right of way, and the drunk asshole with two prior convictions ran her down. Mom had been on her way to church.

"Well, then, if it's not Santa, Dean and I might be able to get you one for Christmas." Marian had been researching refurbished Macs. Even the used ones cost more than she thought they'd be able to spend, but Briella had been adamant about getting an Apple.

"That's three months from now. I need my research sooner than that." Briella squirmed out of Marian's grip.

Marian looked over Briella's shoulder at the computer screen. "What are you researching? Birds? Is it something for school?"

As part of Southside's gifted program, Briella had done a bunch of projects on her own. They called it independent study. Marian thought it was more like busywork for smart kids who'd be bored without something extra, but Briella had always seemed to love the additional work and spent a lot of her time on voluntary projects. Briella had been working steadily on something since the end of school last May, spending hours scribbling notes in her notebook without sharing anything. She'd also been tinkering with bits of metal and wire she scrounged from the garage and sometimes from the trash, but lately Marian had seen all the tiny, twisted pieces tossed into the garbage can in her room. Whatever the experiments had been, apparently they weren't working out.

Briella shook her head. "No. Not for school. I just wanted to learn about them."

"Is it the same thing you've been working on all summer?"

"I quit that project. It was stupid," Briella said with a shift in her gaze that told Marian she was being more secretive than honest.

That was another of those recent developments. Along with the loathing for personal hygiene and lack of friends, Briella had taken up lying. Much like her father, she wasn't really very good at it.

"I'm sure it wasn't," Marian said. "Nothing you do is stupid."

Briella's lip curled. "It's too hard to do anything without the right tools. It never left the theory stage. I wanted it all to work, but I don't have the right equipment to make it to the practical applications of it. I need better supplies, and if you can't get me a new computer, you sure can't get me the other stuff I'd need."

"What are you trying to make, a robot?" Marian had meant it as a joke, but seeing the look on Briella's face, she sobered. "Is that it?"

"It wasn't going to be a *robot*," Briella said disdainfully.

Not for the first time, Marian was reminded of how little she could relate to her own daughter. So instead, she fell back on something she did understand. She put her hands on her hips and gave Briella a stern look.

"Did you do the rest of your homework before you started on your project?"

Briella sighed and kicked a small foot against the leg of the rickety desk so that the entire setup shook. "Yeah. It was all stupid. The teacher is stupid, too."

"I've told you about calling people stupid. And I thought you liked Mrs. Jackson," Marian said, feeling like she was losing this battle before it had even begun.

Again, she was reminded of Tommy and how single-mindedly obnoxious he could be. But Briella was still a kid, Marian's kid as a matter of fact, and there was still plenty of time to make sure Briella didn't end up like her father as an adult. Marian tried again.

"Tell you what. Why don't you bring your snack into the kitchen with me while I cook dinner, and you can tell me about your bird project. Then, when you're finished, you can get back to it. Sometimes, taking a break on something that's frustrating you can help you get a fresh perspective."

Dean would be up in about an hour, hungry for what would be his breakfast. Marian had a package of chicken thighs thawing in the sink. She was going to use up the last of the boxed potato flakes and do an oven bake. She wouldn't be able to get to the store until next week, after payday.... With her mind stuck on dinner and the chores and a thousand other things, she didn't notice at first that the kid hadn't budged.

"Briella. Let's go."

At first it looked as though Briella was going to protest, but then she nodded and hopped off the chair. Marian took the plate with its smears of peanut butter all around the rim – how had she managed to make such a mess in so short a time? Both of them went into the kitchen. Marian set the plate on the table.

"Briella," she said again, this time to turn the girl's attention from the window next to the back door, overlooking the yard.

Her daughter turned with a gap-toothed grin. "He's out there, Mama. I saw him on the way home from school today, but now he's in the backyard!"

"Who?" For a second, Marian's heart froze with visions of a white van and a man offering ice cream to little girls.

"The raven from near my school. His wife raven got killed. She was dead by the garbage cans. I gave him a treat from my backpack, and he followed me home," Briella said in that tone she'd taken on lately. As though Marian was dumber than a dog's foot.

If that was in fact how Briella talked to the other kids at school, no wonder they didn't like her anymore, Marian thought, then immediately felt guilty. Childhood was hard enough without even your mother not being on your side. She looked out the window, tweaking aside the faded yellow curtains that had belonged to her mom's Scandinavian grandmother. Her fingers skated on the soft material, tugging at the hem. The backyard, little more than patchy grass and a fire pit ringed with battered metal lawn chairs, edged up to the pine forest and the mountain beyond. She didn't see any birds, much less a raven.

Briella didn't seem to notice that the bird, if one had been there at all, was gone. She turned, beaming, to the table and slid into her seat. "I'm going to name him Onyx."

CHAPTER TWO

This was that sweet, brief stretch of the morning between the time Briella left for school and Dean arrived home from work that was all Marian's. She'd never been an early riser by nature, but that had all changed after having her daughter. Briella hadn't slept through the night until she was almost three, and even now would get up on her own around five thirty in the morning, no matter what time she'd gone to bed. And that could be late. With Dean leaving for work by ten p.m., sometimes a little earlier if he had to stop along the way, Marian had fallen into the habit of letting her daughter stay up long past what most parents would consider a proper bedtime, rather than fighting with her to stay in bed when she clearly wasn't ready to sleep.

This particular morning had dawned with the fresh, sweet hint of autumn in the coolness. Sure, in September it could still be eighty degrees by the afternoon, and Marian would be sweating and cursing the fact they didn't have central air, but for now she could sit on the back stoop with the single cigarette she allowed herself every morning, her mug of coffee, and nothing else but the silence.

She drank, wincing at the bitterness of the black coffee. She'd run out of creamer a couple days ago and thought it might be a good time to wean herself off it. Flavored creamers were full of junk and chemicals, and they cost a fortune. It was hard to justify that indulgence when she was also trying to save for a laptop.

Briella's comments about being poor still stung. Maybe it was time Marian talked to Dean about going back to work. Briella was in school all day. Dean was usually still asleep when she got off the bus, but at ten, wasn't she old enough to manage herself until Marian got home?

Marian had quit her job at the dentist's office when she and Dean got married. Briella had been two, and it made sense to stay home rather than keep paying for daycare. They'd talked about having another baby, so staying home made even more sense, but two more losses had ended those conversations.

Dean had said he wanted to take care of them both. He always had and still did. Marian had no complaints about that. The past couple of years had been leaner than they both liked, but their bills were always paid, and they never went hungry. Still, Marian could surely pick up some hours here or there, no more than part-time. It would ease the pinch, give them some money toward a new computer and other things Briella was going to need. College. It would be here before they knew it.

A job would also get her out of the house. Dean used a white noise machine and a floor fan to block out sounds so that he could sleep, but even so, she still tiptoed around while he was sleeping to make sure she didn't wake him. There were days, stuck in the silence all day, when Marian thought she was going to lose her mind.

Marian drew deep on the smoke, letting it sear the back of her throat. Her eyes stung. Moments later, the head rush tickled the spot between her eyes. She'd been a heavy smoker before Briella but had quit the minute she found out she was pregnant. She hadn't taken it up again until a couple years ago, and now restricted herself to that single cigarette per day so she could keep her tolerance low and still get the buzz. She'd promised herself the first time it took more than one to get her there—

"Holy shit," Marian yelped as a black shape dive-bombed past her and flew toward the wild tangle of tall green pokeweed and the deer feeder on the edge of the woods.

Her hair, which had been pulled into a messy topknot, now had several curls tickling her cheek from the force of the bird nearly clipping her ear. Marian pushed it away from her face and stood, shading her eyes to watch the black-winged shape strut around the edges of the wooden trough. It squawked loudly as though it were scolding her, then dove into the pokeweed to strip the purple berries off the stems and gobble them down.

Marian put a hand to her heart, which was thumpa-thumping, and stubbed out her cigarette in the glass ashtray she kept on the back porch railing. There wasn't any food in the feeder. Dean would fill it later in the fall to bring the deer in so he could make noises like he planned to shoot them for venison, not that he ever did. The bird flapped. It looked like it had the wingspan of a turkey buzzard, but that was impossible, wasn't it? Ravens didn't get that big. Did they? Marian tried to remember some of the facts Briella had been spouting about birds, but couldn't think of any.

"Hey, babe."

Marian shrieked, twisting and grabbing the wrought iron railing. "Holy hell, Dean. You scared the shit out of me!"

Dean, dark green eyes twinkling, shook his head with a chuckle. "I already know you smoke."

"Not because…no. I mean, I was, but…" Marian burst into a flurry of giggles and waved a hand toward the deer feeder. "That bird scared me."

He looked past her. "What bird?"

"It's at the feeder." Marian looked, but it had gone. Probably flew off into the woods, which was where birds belonged, as far as she was concerned. Not shitting all over her house and dive-bombing her when she was just trying to grab a smoke. "Well, it was there a minute ago."

"Okay, Tippi Hedren. Are you going to come inside and have something to eat with me?" Dean reached for her hand and tugged Marian up against him as they backed through the doorway and into the kitchen. He nudged the door closed with the toe of his boot. "And I don't mean whatever it is you had on the stovetop when I got home."

All thoughts of the bird flew out of her mind as Marian lifted her face to Dean's for a long, slow kiss. She linked her fingers behind his neck, loving the brush of his thick black hair against her knuckles. He was going gray at the temples, but the rest of his hair was dark as pitch and bristly as a boot brush, such a contrast to her own natural curls. He rubbed his prickling beard against her cheek, then lower, against her throat, until she giggled and pushed out of his grip.

"What's got into you today?" she asked.

Dean grinned and shrugged. "Can't a guy come home from work raring to get some from his sexy-as-hell old lady?"

"Oh, sure." Marian rolled her eyes and gestured at her worn T-shirt and sweatpants. A job, she thought, would give her an excuse to wear real clothes. "All this. So sexy."

He kissed her again, a little harder this time. The laundry and floor mopping could wait until he was asleep, she thought as she gave herself up to his embrace. He'd just started to lead her down the hallway to their bedroom when the phone rang. Neither of them tried to answer it, and the machine picked up. When the caller started leaving a message, though, Marian pulled from Dean's grasp with a groan.

"It's the school," she said. "Shit, it's the nurse."

CHAPTER THREE

The car ride home from school was tense and quiet. Marian glanced a few times in the rearview mirror, but Briella stared steadfastly out of her window and didn't meet her mother's gaze. The bandage on her forehead had been clean when they left the nurse's office, but now sported a pinprick of crimson.

"We could stop for ice cream, if you want?" Marian offered in a light tone of voice.

Briella shook her head.

"Are you sure?"

"I'm not hungry. My belly hurts." Briella made a face without pulling her gaze from the window.

"How bad? If you're going to throw up—"

"I'm not. It just hurts."

The school nurse had told Marian she didn't think there was anything more than a simple bump to worry about, but to watch for dizziness, nausea, sleepiness. So far, Briella just seemed grumpy. Still, the school had seemed to think it was important enough to send her home, so Marian was at least a little worried.

"You want to talk about what happened, Bean?"

"No."

Silence for the rest of the car ride, until they pulled into the driveway. Marian turned the car off and twisted in her seat to look back at her daughter. "Dean's sleeping, so you have to be quiet, okay?"

"I know." Briella looked at her, then, with a frown. "Can I watch TV?"

When Marian was a kid, the television had been on around the clock, a constant background hum of noise and distraction for her and her older brother, Desmond. Her dad still kept it on all the time, even when he wasn't watching, maybe especially then, to cover up the quiet her mother's death had left behind. Briella hadn't grown up in a world with Saturday morning cartoons and *Gorgeous Ladies of Wrestling* and late-night infomercials. She got all her media content via streaming, on demand, parental control locked. She'd never been much of a television watcher, preferring to read or scribble in her notebook.

"My head hurts," Briella said when Marian didn't answer, like she knew what her mother was thinking. "I just want to lie down and not think too hard about anything."

"Sure, kiddo. Of course. I'll make some lunch and you can just get comfy on the couch, okay?" Marian wanted to hug her, but she couldn't reach across the backseat to do it. She settled for reaching so Briella could squeeze her fingers. "Just keep the volume low."

As it turned out, Dean wasn't asleep when they got inside. He looked tired enough, eyes heavy-lidded and the scruff of his beard standing out even more thickly than it had an hour or so ago when he got home. He greeted them both with a smile from his seat at the kitchen table.

"Hey, kid," he said. "Heard you had a little accident at school."

Briella nodded and hung back behind Marian for a few seconds. "Yeah."

"She's going to lie down on the couch for a bit and watch some TV." Marian kissed the top of his head. "Did you eat anything? I can make you something."

Briella disappeared into the living room, and Dean snagged Marian's wrist when she started to move toward the fridge. He tugged her closer to put his hands on her hips. She looked down at him, her hands on his shoulders.

"What happened?" he asked in a low voice.

"Apparently a bunch of the kids were playing outside at morning recess, and Briella was taking a turn on the monkey bars when she slipped off and fell." Marian hesitated. "The nurse said that the kids aren't supposed to go on top of the monkey bars, but a few of them might have been up there and that's why she fell. I asked her if she thought any of the kids had pushed Briella, but she said all the kids on the playground swore nobody had."

"What's the kid say?" Dean settled her on his knee, a big hand tucked between her thighs.

She rested her cheek on the top of his head. "She wouldn't talk about it. The nurse said the playground monitors didn't see anything, either."

"You think it's more of what happened last year?" Dean sounded concerned.

A quick glance toward the hallway showed they were still alone. Marian could hear the drone of the TV. She shrugged and threaded her fingers through his hair, pulling until he looked up at her.

"The teachers this year were all made aware of the problems from last year, and they're supposed to be monitoring it," she said. "Briella hasn't mentioned any bullying, and the girls from last year who gave her such a hard time aren't in her class this year."

Dean frowned. "Doesn't mean they weren't on the playground."

"I don't know." Marian's mouth twisted. "We can't just accuse anyone of pushing her, Dean. Especially if she says she fell."

The pack of mean girls who'd stopped being friendly to Briella because they said she was 'weird' had made her kid's life miserable for months before Marian found out anything about it. The school counselor hadn't been any help, and because there'd been only exclusion and no active bullying that anyone could prove, nothing much had been done. *You can't make people like you if they don't*, Marian remembered now with a frown and a pang in her heart.

"You want me to call the guidance counselor again?"

She shook her head. "Let's just see what Briella says about it. It really could have been an accident. She's clumsy, you know?"

There'd been a brief period of time, right before Dean, when Marian had been certain the pediatrician was going to call protective services on her. Bumps, bruises. Not only had she been prone to throwing herself to the ground in tantrums, she'd also had a healthy sense of inhibition. The kid had leaped from the top of the stairs once, convinced she could fly, and split open her eyebrow. She still bore a scar.

"Do you think she'd tell you the truth?" Dean nuzzled her throat for a second. "She was pretty adamant last year that those girls were still her friends, even when we found out they weren't."

The shit had hit the fan when Marian discovered that Briella hadn't been invited to Pamela Morgan's birthday party. The girls had been in the same classes since preschool. Marian and her mother had been friendly but not friends, and the awkward conversation between them when Marian called her, convinced the invitation had been lost instead of simply not offered, still made Marian cringe when she thought about it. Cringe and also fume.

"I don't know." Marian sighed. "Shit. I was really hoping this year would turn things around for her. She doesn't seem as bored in school.

They're pulling her out of class half a day three times a week instead of only once to do that gifted stuff."

"Which only makes her stand out more as being weird."

Marian's nose wrinkled. "Smart doesn't have to equal weird, Dean."

"Yeah, but…" He trailed off, wisely unwilling to say aloud what she knew he had to be thinking.

The kid was simply hard to like.

"She'll grow out of it. All of it," Marian said.

"Sure, baby. Of course." Dean yawned so wide his jaw popped. "I really got to get to sleep."

She slid off his lap. "Of course. You didn't have to stay up until we got home."

"Sure I did. Needed to make sure everything was okay."

Marian cupped Dean's face in her hands, tipping it up so she could look into his eyes. "You're a good dad. You know that, right?"

"Sure." He laughed and cut his gaze, maybe embarrassed with the praise. He shrugged and added in a much lower voice, "She doesn't even call me Dad."

"But that's what you are to her. You've been in her life longer than you haven't. You've been a better father to that kid than her own's ever been." Marian kissed him, slow and sweet and with a promise of more for later.

About five minutes after Dean left the kitchen for the bedroom, Briella appeared in the doorway. "I'm hungry now."

"I have tomato soup and a grilled cheese." Marian turned from the counter, where she was doctoring the heel of the bread loaf to make the sandwich. Nobody in the house liked the heel, including her, but it was the last of the bread and she still hadn't made it to the store.

"I don't want grilled cheese. Can't I have the ice cream now?"

Marian shook her head. "We don't have any here. That's why I asked if you wanted to stop on the way home."

Briella's sigh was so long and loud it lifted her shoulders. She buried her face in her hands. She looked so distraught that Marian went to her at once to put a hand on the back of her neck.

"Bean. Are you sure you don't want to talk to me about what happened? Was it…" Marian cleared her throat and pulled the chair out next to her daughter's. She braced herself for bad news. "Did someone push you off the monkey bars?"

"No. I fell all by myself. But they laughed." Briella looked up then. "Pamela said I was being stupid, because I was trying to show them how birds do it. I mean, I know I can't really fly like a bird, Mama. I'm *not* stupid."

"No. You're definitely not." Marian pushed the hair off Briella's forehead and wondered if she ought to take off the bandage. The gauze looked even whiter against the sandy tones of Briella's skin. The small red spot on the bandage had turned brown. "You're very, very smart. And sometimes, other people who aren't as smart don't like that. So they laugh or make fun."

"You don't, and you're not as smart as I am."

Marian's eyebrows rose, and she pressed her lips together for a moment before answering. "That might be true, Bean, but it's not really nice to say so. And if that's what you say to the other kids…"

"Yeah, I know. Nobody likes a smartypants." Briella muttered something else under her breath, too low for Marian to hear.

"What?"

"I said, Dean's not smarter than me, either. And he's *not* my dad. I heard you say he was a good dad. But he's just a step. Not a real one."

"That doesn't mean he doesn't love you, Briella."

"Daddy loves me," she said in the stubborn tone that grated on Marian's nerves worse than the scratch of teeth on a fork.

"It's not a bad thing to have lots of people in your life who love you," Marian said. "You love more people than just Daddy, don't you? You love Grandpa and me and Dean and Auntie Theresa and Uncle Desmond and Dilly and Caitlin, right?"

"I love my family."

"Dean *is* your family, Briella. You'll hurt his feelings a lot if you don't think so," Marian said and added after a pause, "and you'll hurt mine, too."

Briella frowned and crossed her arms, but didn't make any other protests. She slid into the chair at the kitchen table and slumped with her chin in her hands. She huffed a loud, dramatic sigh.

"Do you want some baby aspirin for your head?" Marian asked.

"No. It feels better. Ice cream would make it even better, though." Briella gave Marian an adorable grin, all sunshine, the grumpiness of literally only moments before vanishing.

Marian pressed her lips together, but didn't scold. Truth was, the idea of the soup and sandwich didn't thrill her, either. Besides, the kid had fallen off the freaking monkey bars. She deserved at least a little treat.

Marian hugged her kid. "All right. Let's go get some."

CHAPTER FOUR

Using her credit card at the grocery store was not a habit Marian wanted to get into, but she'd be able to pay off the bill with Dean's next check, and the bare cupboards had depressed her. At home, she sent Briella out back to play along with the last of her ice cream cone, so she could put the groceries away. It didn't take long, since she hadn't fully stocked up. What stopped her, though, was when she looked out the window over the kitchen sink to make sure Briella was still all right.

The backyard was empty.

Irritated now but not yet worried, Marian went to the front door to look out. Briella stood on the sidewalk, the last of her cone in her raised hand. She giggled wildly as the bird from earlier made swooping passes at it. It had to be the same one, right? Marian couldn't remember ever seeing a single raven that size, much less more than one.

Marian went out onto the concrete front porch. "Don't do that, Briella!"

"Mama, he likes it." Briella squealed as the raven again dived at her hand, laughing aloud as it nipped the cone from her fingertips. "Yowch!"

Marian was down the front porch steps and crossing the tiny front yard in a heartbeat. "Did he peck you? Birds are dirty. Let me see."

"Human mouths are dirtier than a bird's mouth," Briella said but allowed Marian to take her hand and inspect it. "And you kiss me with yours."

Marian stopped to stare at her daughter with a frown. If she'd spoken to her own mother that way, Mom would have done more than give her an irritated look. People didn't spank anymore, though. New age parenting.

"And you can watch yours, Briella. You've had a rough day, but that's not a reason to get an attitude."

"Sorry," Briella muttered insincerely.

"Come inside, now."

"I want to play with Onyx." Briella gestured at the raven, which had settled in the middle of the sidewalk across the street with its prize. The cone fragmented on the pavement, and the bird pecked it swiftly.

The bird looked up, tilting its head like it was staring at them. Marian pressed her lips together in distaste. The late afternoon sun slanting off the inky wings made them look somehow oily. Ravens were bad luck, she thought. Weren't they?

"Here, Onyx! Here!"

"Don't do that," Marian scolded.

From the end of the lane came the familiar rumble of the pickup truck belonging to Hank Simpson, who lived next door. His was the last house on the cul-de-sac, and his property also backed up onto the edges of what eventually became state game lands. He liked to drink too much and drive too fast on this otherwise quiet street. He kept to himself except when he was complaining about his neighbor's grass being too long, or the kids who took the path along the edge of his property to get to the small frog pond beyond in the woods.

He was driving too fast now, one beefy arm hanging out the window. Even at this distance, Marian could see the glare of the dropping sun on his windshield. He had to be half-blinded by it, and instinctively, she grabbed Briella's sleeve as though the girl might tear off and run straight for the road.

"Here, Onyx, c'mere!"

Marian shook Briella's arm. "Come on, let's go inside."

The bird squawked and jerked its head back, swallowing the last of the ice cream cone. It took several exploratory flaps of its wings and began to rise into the air. Incredibly, it started toward them – right into the path of Hank's truck.

Briella shrieked and yanked her arm loose. "*Onyx!*"

Marian swiped for her daughter's sleeve, but missed. The girl was already on the sidewalk. The bird cawed as the truck bore down on them.

"The bird will fly away, Briella, don't – Oh my God. Oh my God...." Marian, breathless with terror, stumbled after her daughter.

At the last minute, before Briella could step off the sidewalk and into the street, the bird swooped. It dove at her, driving her back with flapping wings and screams. Briella tripped and fell, blessedly backward and not into the street. The raven whirled. The truck's side mirror clipped the bird and sent it tumbling wings over tail onto the grass.

Hank drove on past, oblivious to anything that had just happened. Marian collapsed next to Briella on the sidewalk. She gathered the girl close, too relieved to shout or scold. She pressed her face to Briella's hair, which smelled faintly sour and damp.

"You can't run into the street," Marian choked out.

Briella struggled free of her mother's grip and knelt next to the bird. She looked up with tears sliding down her cheeks, cutting a path through grime and leftover ice cream. "He's hurt."

"Don't touch it!"

Too late. Briella had gathered the injured raven into her lap, where it shuddered and cried out in low, plaintive squawks. She stroked the feathers, wincing in sympathy as she folded the clearly messed-up wing back into place.

"We have to make him better, Mama."

"I don't know anything about birds, and we don't have the money to take him to a vet, Bean. He's a wild bird, he'll be fine." Marian's breath had returned, but now her stomach churned in the aftermath of what had almost happened.

Briella shook her head. She could be as stubborn as anything when she set her mind to it. That, Marian had to admit, came from her.

"I'll look it up on the internet. How to fix his wing. I have to. It's my fault he got hurt. He was trying to protect me!"

Marian didn't believe that for a second. "It's going to bite you!"

"He won't bite me. I'm going to keep him in my room."

"Absolutely not," Marian said, but looking at the determined set of Briella's jaw, she knew the only way to prevent this was going to be with a fight Marian also knew she didn't have in her.

"I'll keep him in the den. In a cage," Briella said.

The kid would pout and whine and wheedle and beg until Marian gave in, and Marian *would* give in, eventually. It was easier that way. Not for the first time since losing her, Marian wondered if her mother would have been disappointed in the way she was raising her granddaughter.

"Fine. But you take care of him. He stays in the garage, in a cage, and you're responsible for him."

Briella was already nodding as she got to her feet with the bird cradled to her chest like it was a baby. Marian was sure it would fight, peck or try to fly away, but the thing seemed content to let Briella carry it. Hell, maybe it was already half dead and they'd wake up tomorrow to find its cold, stiff corpse.

This idea sent a shiver down Marian's spine, especially when the bird fixed its unblinking gaze on her before Briella moved too far ahead of her for it to keep looking at her. In the garage, Marian pulled out an old guinea pig cage that had been there when she moved in. It had belonged to Dean's younger brother, decades ago. It was dusty but otherwise clean, and she helped line the bottom with shredded circulars and watched as Briella settled the bird inside it.

"He'll need food and water," Marian said. "Do you even know what they eat?"

"Ravens eat anything. Bugs, worms, hamburgers. They've totally adapted to both suburban and urban environments," Briella told her, for once not in a smart-ass way. Simply providing the information. "They can eat even garbage. Usually they eat dead things. Like roadkill."

"Stay out of the garbage *and* the street," Marian said sharply.

Marian bent low to peer into the cage. The bird hadn't made a sound since they brought it inside. It shifted into a pile of shredded paper and then went still. "It looks better now. Maybe it will be fine on its own."

"He got hit by a *truck*." Briella made it clear that Marian's statement was stupid. "I'm going to fix him and make him better. Even better than he used to be."

"Just don't—" Marian stopped herself for a second before continuing firmly, "Don't be upset or disappointed if you can't, Bean. Okay? If something should happen to it, it won't be your fault."

Briella's grin seemed sudden and harsh, more a baring of those gapped teeth than a true grin. "I won't let anything happen to him. I'm going to protect him, the way he protected me."

Again, Marian imagined the bird's corpse, stiff and cold, and Briella's screams upon discovering it. She straightened. "Sometimes things happen whether you want them to or not."

But Briella was already heading into the den through the garage door to set herself up in front of the computer. Marian bent again to look into the cage. The raven's eyes had closed, but it didn't seem to be in pain or anything. She sighed.

"Don't you die," she whispered with a quick glance to see if Briella had overheard her. The kid didn't seem to, but the bird had. It looked at Marian as though it understood her every word.

CHAPTER FIVE

"Go, bird, go!" Dean's guffaw rang throughout the house.

Marian peeked around the doorway to the den, watching Briella demonstrate to Dean how Onyx gobbled up the platter of worms she'd dug up from the backyard. The bird was delicate about it, taking each squirming bit of flesh directly from Briella's fingers while she giggled. Frowning, Marian came into the room, torn between keeping her distance from the bird and moving close enough to rescue her daughter if the thing decided to bite. Somehow, the cage had moved from the garage into the den, but she didn't know if it had been Briella or Dean who moved it.

"Be careful. Don't let that thing nip your fingers."

Dean looked up at her with a wide grin and a light in his eyes. "Don't worry, Mama, she's got this."

Marian's frown didn't ease. She crossed her arms over her chest and stayed a few steps away. She watched as Briella held out a spoonful of dry oatmeal, which Onyx pecked at. The girl had spent an hour or so researching on the internet to find out how to care for an injured raven, and Marian had to admit she was proud of her daughter's commitment to making sure she was doing it right. How far that commitment would go once Briella realized how much work it was going to be, Marian didn't know, but she'd made it clear that she wasn't going to take on the tasks herself.

"My pappy had a pet crow," Dean said now. "It would say 'hello, Ward' when he came into the room."

"No way, he did? Really?" Marian had heard a lot of stories about Dean's family, including Pappy Ward, but never that one.

Briella looked over her shoulder. "Ravens and crows are called corvids. But ravens and crows are not the same thing, even if they look a lot alike. This is a raven, he's a *Corvus corax*. Isn't that right, Onyx?"

She tickled the bird under its ebony chin. It let out a low, croaking groan and closed its eyes, seemingly in bliss. Briella stroked its head next.

"Why Onyx?" Dean asked.

Briella shrugged. "That's his name."

The kid's research had pulled up a bunch of different advice on how to bind the bird's wing, but ultimately, she'd decided that without being able to set it properly, she should leave it alone. They couldn't be sure anything was broken instead of merely sprained, Briella had told her mother seriously. So they couldn't risk doing something that would cause permanent damage. Now the bird seemed to be sleeping in the nest Briella had made from some old towels.

"Wash your hands," Marian said. "Both of you."

Briella closed the door to the guinea pig cage and stood. "I'm going to teach him to talk. He's going to be my best friend. Better than that, even. He doesn't have anyone else. His wife got killed."

"His wife?" Dean snorted soft laughter.

Briella gave him a solid, icy stare. "Yes. Ravens mate in pairs. Onyx had a wife raven. They used to both fly around together at the school, but one day she was dead by the garbage cans."

"That's sad," Dean said, chastened.

"So he's all alone now. And I'm going to keep him here with me."

"Bean, we can't keep it. Once its wing is better, it has to go back outside," Marian said.

Briella frowned and put her hands on her hips. Her voice dropped as she scowled. "But I *want* to keep him here, with me. You never let me have *any* pets."

Every carnival fish had gone belly up within days of bringing them home. The hamster had escaped and disappeared. The hermit crab had drowned in its water dish. Animals had never fared very well in this house, but that didn't mean they'd never had any.

"Not true," Marian said. "And anyway, a wild bird is not a pet."

"It's probably against the law to keep it inside," Dean added, although the glance he gave the caged bird was edged with disappointment.

"You said your pappy had a pet crow!" Briella gave him a pleading look.

Dean shook his head. "That was a long time ago, and I'm not saying that it wasn't also against the law then. The game commission probably has information about it. We should look it up."

"No," Briella said stubbornly. "I want to keep him, especially after he's better. I'm going to teach him to talk! He's already learning. Listen." She cooed at the bird, "Say 'hello, Briella'. Say 'hello!'"

The raven gave a muttery, whispery caw that sounded nothing like words but definitely seemed in response to Briella's urgings. The chill tickling up and down Marian's spine centered at the nape of her neck so fiercely that she cupped a hand over it. Her nails dug into her skin for a moment before she forced herself to relax.

Briella gave her mother a triumphant glare. "See?"

"I don't make the laws, Briella. If the law says we can't keep it, then we can't keep it."

"It's a him," Briella corrected with that same irritating tone of condescension. "Not an *it*."

"Don't talk to your mother that way," Dean admonished. "You know better than that."

Briella stomped a foot and left the room. The pound of her feet on the stairs and the slam of her bedroom door a moment later had Marian sighing. She laughed after a second, though, and gave her husband an apologetic shrug.

"Tell me it's not going to get worse when she's a teenager," she said.

Dean laughed, but after a pause. "I hope not. Were you a pain in the ass when you were a teenager?"

"Of course not," she said with a grin, because she knew she'd given her parents their share of her attitude. This sobered her after a moment, though. Testing curfew and wearing too much eyeliner was different than Briella's rapidly swinging moods and backtalk. "Why don't kids come with instruction manuals?"

"That would be too easy." Dean stood and looked into the cage one last time. The bird didn't move or make a sound. He tapped the wire bars for a second and got no reaction. "Hello, Onyx. Say 'hello'."

The raven said nothing. Marian scowled. "Don't encourage it. It's creepy."

"They mimic sounds, babe. That's all. Nothing to be creeped out about." Dean looked at Marian. "Maybe the kid should have a pet. She's old enough to learn how to take care of something, and it's a good responsibility. I always had dogs growing up."

"You know I don't like dogs."

"I know a dog bit you when you were small, and you're afraid of them enough that you've made sure to never talk to Briella about why you don't like them," Dean said calmly.

"I don't want her to be afraid of dogs," Marian said, defending herself.

Dean nodded. "Right. But what about you?"

"I do *not* want a dog," Marian said, which wasn't really the answer to the question he'd asked, but she was going to pretend it was. "And you're allergic to cats. Anyway, we've had fish. We had that hermit crab."

It had died and fallen out of its shell, its rear end a horror of stumpy, segmented flesh with tiny flipper things that had made Marian shriek as she dumped it into the trash. Thinking of it now made her nose wrinkle. Dean laughed, but under his breath.

"I'm just saying, Marian. I know we can't keep the bird. But we could get the kid something. It would be good for her to have something to take care of. Might make her a little less…umm…self-absorbed."

Marian gave him a sharp glance. "Is that how you'd describe her?"

"Yes," Dean replied evenly. "It is. She's an only child who's never really learned to share, first of all. She's obviously been having some trouble making friends, or rather, keeping them. Whatever she's going through, babe, it's probably related somehow to that."

"You think having a pet would change that?"

Dean shrugged.

Marian sighed and looked into the cage. "Is it really illegal to keep this?"

"Yeah, I think so. So we'll give it a week or so to get back on its feet, or its wings, I guess. And then we can take it out back and release it. Hey, don't worry," Dean said when he saw her expression. "We're not going to get in trouble."

From upstairs came a dull thud. Marian looked at the ceiling. "What the hell is she doing up there?"

"Being pissed off because we told her she can't keep the bird."

She frowned. "I'll go talk to her."

"Kiss me first," Dean said.

"Oh, like that's a hardship."

"I'll show you something hard," he said, "and it's not a ship."

Marian burst into a flutter of laughter, her heart swelling with love for the man in front of her. He'd taken on every burden she had, and in the eight years they'd been together, had never let her down, not even once. She didn't deserve him. She thought that often. But she was really grateful to have him.

"Later," she promised him. It was his night off, and then he had the whole weekend, too. "I'll even do that thing you like."

"Baby, I like all the things you do," Dean replied with a waggle of his eyebrows and a sexy smirk that sent a rush of heat through her.

Upstairs, her mind still on the night ahead of them and how much she was looking forward to it, Marian stopped abruptly at Briella's closed door. The kid never shut her door. She still slept with a night-light on in the bedroom and one in the hall. Marian raised a hand, then thought better of it and pressed her ear to the door for a moment to listen.

She didn't hear anything at first. Then, the low mutter of a voice. Not Briella's. Masculine, British, droning. She must be watching nature videos on her tablet.

Marian knocked. After a second, the male voice quieted. Briella didn't answer, so Marian knocked again and turned the knob to let herself in.

"You're supposed to wait until I say come in," Briella said from her spot on the bed, where she sat cross-legged with her tablet on her lap.

Marian hesitated. "You don't usually have your door shut. Can I come in?"

"May I," Briella said.

Marian's temper snapped. "You want to watch your mouth, Briella. You're the kid. I'm the grown-up. You best remember that, if you don't want to face the consequences."

"But I don't want to watch my mouth," Briella said. "I mean, I can't even see my own mouth!"

She burst into tears, loud and braying and hoarse. Surprised, then worried, Marian went to the bed and sat next to her. She stroked the girl's hair, curly as Marian's but unwashed and tangled. Marian worked her fingers through a knot at the base of Briella's neck. It had been easier, when Briella was young, to keep her natural curls soft and well-kept, but she'd been fighting all of Marian's attempts at grooming. The girl needed a shower in the worst way, but now wasn't the time to tell her so. Instead, Marian hugged her daughter and stroked her messy hair off her forehead.

"Bean, what's going on?"

"My head hurts." Briella buried her face against Marian's chest. She hitched with sobs. Her tablet fell to the side, sliding off the comforter so that Marian had to grab it before it could hit the floor.

"I'm sorry. I can give you something to make it feel better." The nurse had been adamant that there was no suggestion of a concussion, but Marian was suddenly unsure if she ought to let the girl sleep.

Briella pulled away, her eyes red and wet, her nose leaking a bubble of snot. "More ice cream?"

"Not any more tonight, no. It's bedtime."

Briella frowned. "I want to see Onyx."

"You can see it in the morning," Marian said firmly.

"I want to bring him up here, with me. He's going to get lonely. What if he needs something in the night? You're not going to take care of him!" Briella's voice rose almost to a shriek, hysterical and desperate.

Marian pulled Briella close again, trying to soothe her. "I take care of you, don't I?"

"You don't know how to take care of Onyx. You'll probably put him out in the yard!" Briella lashed out, one small fist catching the underside of Marian's chin.

"Dammit, Briella. Watch what you're doing. That hurt!" Marian rubbed her tongue along her teeth. She'd clipped the tip of it and tasted the coppery flavor of blood.

"Sorry," Briella said.

Marian shook her head. "You know what? Saying sorry only matters when you mean it, and when you don't keep doing the same things over and over again. You've been getting a very bad attitude lately, and I've had it. I'm not going to argue with you any more about this. It stays in the den. In the cage."

"Him. You keep calling him an it, but he's a *him*!" Briella drew in a shaky breath and added in a whisper, "I'm sorry, Mama, I didn't mean to hurt you. My mad feelings just want to come out so much."

Marian sighed, but didn't hug her again. "It's okay to be mad. Or sad. But it's not okay to hurt someone else because of it."

"I know that." More icy derision.

"It's a bird, Briella. How do you even know it's a boy bird? How can you tell?"

"I just can," Briella said.

Marian fell silent for a moment before grabbing a tissue from the box on Briella's nightstand. She wiped away the snot and the tears and then took her daughter's face in her hands to look into her eyes. Lots of people commented about the kid's pale gray eyes, the same as her dad's, and how striking they looked against her darker skin. Now, though, they were red-rimmed and dim from all the weeping.

"Animals are not the same as people," Marian said.

Briella frowned. "Why not?"

"They just aren't." Marian had stopped going to church years before her mother was killed and never missed it. They did Christmas and Easter with a Santa and the bunny, but that was it. She didn't want to get into a discussion about the existence, or not, of a soul. She had no idea how to even start a conversation like that.

Briella shook her head stubbornly. "Did you know that ravens are as smart as dolphins or chimpanzees? And they are almost as smart as people. Some of them are even smarter than people like, you know, retards."

"Briella! Oh my God!" Marian recoiled, revolted and stunned. "Where did you learn that word?"

Silence.

A memory sliced her. In the beginning, Tommy's mother had tried hard to make her golden child's daughter her own, stomping every boundary Marian had constructed from bedtimes to snacks. That had ended when Briella was a toddler. Marian had left her with Nancy and Ed Gallagher for an evening. Briella had been prone at the time to periods of what the pediatrician had called "self-entertaining". Singing to herself, conversations with imaginary friends, sometimes so focused she would ignore anyone who tried to interrupt her and throw tantrums, holding her breath to be left alone.

"That retard is an embarrassment."

Marian had never forgotten the disgust in Nancy Gallagher's voice when she'd said it. Marian had never forgiven that bitch for it, either. It had been the last time she'd asked her ex-mother-in-law to help with childcare.

"Did you hear it at school?" Marian's lip curled, and she tasted sourness. "That's not a nice word. We don't use it, ever. If someone at school is using it, they shouldn't, either."

"You think *they're* human, though, right? You'd call someone like that a him or a her, not an it."

Marian swallowed convulsively. She drew in a breath to keep her voice calm. The kid was barely ten years old. Marian, in her recollection, had never used that word, and neither did Dean. She might be able to blame it on Tommy, but even so, Marian couldn't excuse it by saying Briella didn't know what it meant – she clearly did.

"People are human. No matter if they're smart or not. Animals are not the same. I don't want you to use that word ever again, do you understand?

It's…" Marian trailed away, uncertain what to say it was. "It's gross."

Briella huffed and eased away from her mother to push herself back against the satin pillowcase. "Is it because of the dog?"

"What dog?" Marian asked after a moment, carefully. Warily.

"The dog that bit you on the face and made you hate dogs. And all animals," Briella added.

Marian kept herself from recoiling again only by clutching the comforter in one fist. She pressed her lips together. She studied her daughter's expression, but Briella's face was impassive, scarcely even curious.

"How did you know about that?"

"I just found out sometime." She shrugged as though it made no difference.

It shouldn't have. The dog attack wasn't a secret, although Marian had kept it from Briella for the exact reason she'd told Dean. She hadn't wanted her kid to grow up terrified of dogs the way she was. Something in the way Briella said it, though, clenched Marian's jaw.

"I don't hate animals, Briella."

Briella might favor a lot of her dad's expressions, but the look she gave her mother now came purely from Marian herself. "Yes, you do. But you shouldn't hate all animals just because a dog bit you in the face a long time ago. And you sure as hell shouldn't hate Onyx."

Marian stood, unsteadily. She shifted, planting her feet firmly on the bare wooden floor. "That language is not for you."

"Sorry," Briella said sullenly.

"I don't hate anything, okay? Go to bed now."

To her surprise, Briella settled into the fluff of the pillow, turned on her side and closed her eyes. Her breathing slowed. Suspiciously, Marian peeked at her face, but the kid really seemed to be asleep. Marian waited a minute longer, to see if Briella would wake up, but she didn't.

Downstairs, she found a glass of red wine waiting for her on the kitchen table, along with a slice of cherry pie. It had come from the basement freezer, left over from the Fourth of July. She almost burst into tears at the sight of it, but she kissed Dean instead.

"Sit," he said.

"I have to take care of the dinner dishes—"

Dean shook his head. "I did them. Sit down. Drink the wine. Eat the pie."

"And then what?" Marian asked as she slid into the hard-backed kitchen chair with a grin.

Dean laughed. "We'll see what happens after that."

"I love you," Marian told him, serious, her voice a little rough. "How did I get so lucky?"

"No clue. But we both are."

She sipped the wine, the rush of warmth welcome. She'd get buzzed pretty fast if she kept going that way. She eyed the pie.

"Only one piece," she said.

Dean smiled. "That's all that was left."

"Share it with me."

"You eat it, baby."

Marian shook her head and got up to grab another fork. On the way back to the table, she paused again to kiss him. The embrace lingered this time. The flavor of his mouth mingled with the red wine, and she sighed into the kiss. Her fingers threaded his hair as Dean looked at her.

"I love you," she said again. "It's crazy how much, Dean, do you know that?"

His gaze became shadowed for a second, his ready smile fading as he looked concerned. "I know it. C'mere."

He tugged her onto his lap and cradled her. Marian tucked her face against his neck, letting herself melt against him. She breathed, her eyes closed, relishing his touch.

"Briella accused me of hating animals," she said after a bit of silence. She hesitated, then added, "And upstairs, when we were talking, she used the word 'retards'."

"Yowch. Why?"

"She said that I should call that bird a him, not an it, and that I'd call a…special-needs person…a him or her and not an it. Then she said I hated animals." Marian pulled herself from the comfort of his neck to look at Dean's face. "I want that bird gone, Dean. I don't feel right about it. She's already too wrapped up in it."

"She wants to take care of it. She's never really had a pet. And you know how she gets focused on things." Dean shrugged. "It will fade, and by then Onyx will be ready to fly on his own, and we'll set him free. We can see how you feel about getting a pet then. Okay?"

Marian grimaced. "You're doing it, too. Calling it by name, like it should even have one. It's a wild bird. Not a pet. And I don't like it in the house. It was supposed to stay in the garage."

She could tell by the way Dean didn't answer that he didn't agree with her, but he was trying not to argue. Marian puffed out a breath and leaned to snag the wineglass with her fingertips. Red liquid sloshed as she pulled it closer and sipped. Better to fill her mouth with wine than to keep ranting like a crazy person.

"It can stay until it's better," she said after a few sips, with Dean not saying anything. "But then it's out."

CHAPTER SIX

Marian hadn't dreamed of the dog in a long time. Maybe it was the half bottle of red wine she'd polished off, or the sugary pie. Whatever it was, she woke, sweating, from a nightmare in which she couldn't fight off the bite. Her stomach rolled as she sat up in bed, and she put a hand over her mouth, unsure if she was going to be sick.

Everything settled in the bathroom, where she splashed cool water on her face and the back of her neck. She hadn't turned on the light, not wanting to wake Dean, so she couldn't see her reflection, but she felt better once she'd sipped a handful of water from the tap. She wasn't going to be able to sleep, though, so she pulled on a housecoat over her nakedness and headed for the kitchen.

She'd meant to make herself a mug of peppermint tea to settle her complaining stomach, but a sound from the den turned her toward that room instead. As quietly as she could, Marian crept to the doorway and looked into the room. As she'd guessed, Briella was crouched near the cage, the door open, the bird outside of it on the table.

It was singing. A low warble, an unnamed tune. Marian's stifled an anxious, horrified giggle when the bird caught sight of her and cawed. Briella turned. She didn't look the least bit guilty at being discovered out of bed.

"Hello, Mama."

"Hello," the bird said.

Marian screamed, or tried to. All that came out was a sputtered gasp as she recoiled. Her heart thundered. She shook her head to get the sound of it out of her ears.

Briella laughed. "I told you he could talk!"

Still shaking her head, Marian stepped fully into the den. "You shouldn't be out of bed."

"I couldn't sleep. I came down to make sure Onyx was okay." Briella stood and turned, holding out an arm that the bird hopped onto.

Marian's upset stomach returned at the sight. "Put it back in the cage now."

Briella murmured something to the bird, too low for Marian to hear it. The bird reproduced the sound, also low and incoherent. It hopped into the cage, and Briella shut the door. She turned to her mother with a smug and somehow victorious grin stretching her small mouth.

"I told him I'd be able to play with him all day tomorrow, cuz it's Saturday." Briella skipped past Marian, stopped when her mother took her by the shoulder as she passed. "What?"

"You're going to stay with Grandpa tomorrow afternoon, remember? While Dean and I have a date? Anyway, if its wing is hurt, it probably needs to rest. The more you fuss with it, the longer it's going to take for it to heal. You might even make it worse." Marian looked over at her shoulder, but if the bird was monitoring this conversation, she could see no sign of it listening. "C'mon. Let's get you back to bed. You have a few hours left before it's time to wake up."

"I'm not tired," Briella said belligerently.

"Then read quietly in your room," Marian snapped, immediately regretting her loss of temper.

If Briella was offended, she didn't show it. She waved at the bird in the cage. "Goodbye, Onyx."

"Goodbye," the bird called after her.

Marian shivered with distaste and guided Briella toward the stairs. She was going to walk her up to her room, but Briella stopped her. "I can do it myself."

"It's dark," Marian began, but Briella waved a hand.

"I'm fine, Mama. I'm old enough to go by myself."

Marian watched Briella mount the steep and narrow stairs until her shadow blended with the darkness at the top of them. She thought about going back to bed herself, but knew she was still too unsettled to sleep. She'd make herself that peppermint tea and snuggle back into bed with Dean, who didn't have to work again until Monday night. They could sleep in at least a little bit.

She hovered over the electric kettle until the water finally boiled. The tea steeped while she sorted through some bills, but, too impatient to let the liquid cool, she added an ice cube and sipped. From the den came the unmistakable sound of her daughter's murmuring voice.

Irritated, Marian swept into the room, only to find it empty except for the damned raven in its cage. She looked around, thinking the girl might be hiding so she didn't get in trouble. "Briella?"

"Briella," the bird mimicked, sounding so much like her that Marian would have sworn it was her daughter.

Marian backed out of the room without another word. Upstairs, Briella was sound asleep in bed, or at least giving the impression that she was. Marian stood and watched her for a very long time, but the girl didn't so much as shift beneath the covers, and her breathing was soft and slow.

By the time Marian got downstairs her tea was cold, but that was okay because she no longer wanted to drink it.

CHAPTER SEVEN

Briella wouldn't get out of the car. Marian opened her door and gestured, but Briella was too busy scribbling in the notebook to pay attention. With a sigh, Marian tapped the book.

"C'mon, Bean. Grandpa's waiting."

Briella looked up, her gaze distant and cloudy before clearing. She unbuckled her seat belt and got out of the car, clutching the notebook tightly. In the house, she set it carefully on the small table by the front door before going to greet Marian's father, who'd barely made it out of his recliner by the time they got into the living room.

"Hey, little princess," Marian's dad said as Briella gave him a hug and a kiss on the cheek. "So good to see you. Where's Dean?"

"Waiting in the car. I can't stay long, the movie starts soon. You're sure you're going to be okay for a few hours, Dad?" Marian hugged him, feeling how brittle he'd become.

He'd been losing weight, despite denying that he wasn't eating enough. Today he felt a bit sturdier than he had for a while. She hugged him harder for a moment, eyes closed, hating the knowledge that her father was getting older. He was fading, and had been since her mother died. Marian was going to lose him, too, no matter how much she tried not to think about it.

"Of course. My favorite princess and I are going to have a great time. I got out the Scrabble board, and we're going to have grilled cheese sandwiches." Dad grinned, his dark skin creasing at the corners of his eyes. "Isn't that right?"

"You be good," Marian reminded Briella before she left, one eye already on the time. She and Dean would only have a few hours, long enough to grab the matinee of the movie they'd been wanting to see and maybe a quick bite after. She didn't want to be late.

The movie was a bust, but the early dinner date with her man made up for it. As they pulled into her dad's driveway half an hour later than she'd said they'd be, Marian waited until Dean had turned off the ignition. She turned in the front seat and kissed him.

"Your dad's going to see us," he said but kissed her anyway.

"Won't be the first time he's caught me kissing a boy in the driveway," she teased him for a second before kissing him once more. "I wish we had more time."

"We have our whole lives," Dean said.

Marian shook her head. "I meant today. Right now. I wish we'd told him we'd be back later. But I don't feel right leaving her with him for so much longer. I know he gets tired out. I just…damn, Dean, I just love getting to spend time with you alone."

He didn't answer her right away, but the corners of his mouth curved upward for a second or so. "Yeah. Well, that's what being a parent is about, I guess. Before we know it, she'll be able to stay on her own. Anyway, she loves spending time with your dad, and he loves having her."

"I know. It's just…" She trailed off, then decided to open up about her recent feelings of isolation, her decision to look for part-time work, hell, even her anxiety about doing a shit job as a mother, but before she could, the front door opened.

"Caught," Dean said with a grin.

Marian got out of the car. "Hey, Bean. What's up?"

"Is it time to go home?"

"Yes. Where's Grandpa?" Marian didn't see her father behind Briella.

"He's sleeping." Briella hopped down the front porch steps and headed for the car, with her notebook clutched beneath one arm. "He's been sleeping all day. I was so bored."

"All day?" Alarmed, Marian pushed past the girl and went inside. She was convinced she was going to find her father dead in his recliner, but he was blinking owlishly and pushing himself out of it when she got to the living room. "Dad. Oh, God. You're up."

"I'm up. Just had a little nap." Her father tilted his head. "What's wrong?"

"Nothing." She wasn't about to tell him she'd had a panic attack that she was going to find a corpse, this time human and not a bird.

Dad frowned. "Where's Briella?"

"She went out to the car already. Dad, are you feeling all right? She said you slept all day." Marian moved toward him to help him steady himself as he finally got up.

"I did take a nap, but only for the past, oh," he checked his watch, "maybe twenty minutes or so. We had a nice lunch and played a game or two. She wiped me out in Monopoly. I suppose twenty minutes might feel like all day to a child."

Marian hugged him. "Thanks for having her."

"Any time. You and Dean come around for dinner once in a while too, you hear me?" Her father shook a finger at her, then hugged her again.

"We will." Marian kissed his cheek. It had the same bristly feel she could remember from childhood. His cologne sent another rush of nostalgia through her. "Love you, Dad."

"Love you too, girly. Is everything okay with you?"

She nodded. "Yes. Of course."

"Good, good." Her father hesitated. "That little girl's a smart one, all right. Is she okay?"

"She's...fine, Dad." Marian had never liked lying to her father, not about sneaking in after curfew, and not now. "Why? Doesn't she seem fine?"

"Well, now," her father said after a second, "it would seem to me that she's in need of church."

"Dad. You know I don't go."

"I know, I know." He waved a gnarled hand. "I'm not saying it because I want to change you, Marian. I respect your beliefs, or lack of them. I say it because that child has a lot of questions about God and heaven and the other place, and I couldn't believe she'd gotten to be the age she is without any kind of religious learning."

Marian bit her upper lip for a moment before saying, "What did you tell her?"

"Not much." He shook his head. "Didn't want to step on your toes. I know you've had your issues with the Lord."

"It's not the Lord I have issues with. It's the people who try to speak for him."

Her father chuckled. "Well, now, I don't claim to do that. But I did tell her that I believe in heaven and also hell, and that I was certain your mother was waiting for me to join her in the good place, not the bad one. She wanted to know how I could believe in something that nobody could prove. Like I said, she's a smart one."

"Too smart," Marian said.

"I might have said the same about you, when you were her age."

She shook her head. "Not the same. Briella is…"

"She's special," he father told her gently. "You were blessed with a little girl whose mind is bigger than she's ready to handle. She's got a lot of questions and no way to process them, Marian."

"And you think talking to her about Jesus will help?"

"I'm saying that she might have the brainpower of an adult, but she's still a child in need of guidance. She could end up in her adulthood without a speck of faith," her father added with a significant look at her, "but if she has no place to start from, how can you expect her to choose anything?"

Marian hugged him again. Her mother would have had a lot more to say to Briella about religion than he did, and Marian supposed she was glad her father respected her wishes. At the same time, she couldn't stop the feeling that she'd disappointed him. Maybe not as much as she would have her mom. But enough.

"I can talk to her," Marian said. "But I'm not going to start taking her to church."

"You do what you think is best, of course. Talking to her about the questions she has is the best way to handle it. You're her mother. You'll figure it out."

If only it were that easy, Marian thought.

CHAPTER EIGHT

"I told him you'll take care of him," Briella said as Marian tried her best to get the girl into her jacket and out the front door Monday morning. "You'll have to make sure to feed him and that he has water. You can put the TV on for him to keep him company. Or the radio. He likes music, he likes to sing."

Marian wasn't about to leave the squawk box on for a bird while Dean was sleeping, but she didn't say so. She hefted the girl's backpack and got her to the sidewalk, then down to the end of the street to wait for the bus. Briella was the only kid her age on this street, so Marian always waited with her at the bus stop. Today, Amy Patterson from across the street stopped by with her little boy Toby clutching at her hand. His other held a Thomas the Tank Engine figurine that had seen better days.

"Hi, Briella," Amy said brightly. "Toby, say hi."

Toby, blond like his mother, didn't say anything. He was two? Three? He might be as old as four, but it was hard to tell because he didn't speak. He did hold up the toy for Briella to inspect, but she wasn't interested. She had her head bent over her notebook, busy scribbling, and the bus arrived in the next minute. Without so much as a backward look, she got on.

Marian stepped back from the curb to watch the bus leave. Guilt poked at her because of how relieved she felt at the idea of having a few hours without Briella in the house. She loved her kid, she reminded herself. But it was better for Briella to be in school, where she could be kept busy. Better for both of them. Reminded that she wanted to start scanning the want ads for possible part-time jobs, Marian turned to go.

"I'm so not ready for that," Amy said conversationally as the bus disappeared around the corner, so that Marian had to stop and acknowledge her. "School, I mean. I love having Toby home with me all day. I can't imagine what it will be like to send him off. Maybe I'll homeschool him."

More guilt. When had motherhood become such a damned competition? Marian gave the other woman a thin smile. She could remember the days when it had seemed impossible for her to send Briella away, but they felt really long ago. Being at home all day with a kid whose IQ had outpaced her mother's by the age of three had led to long, frustrating days that often ended in tears, and not just for Briella.

"I wouldn't know what to do with myself all day long at home alone," Amy continued as she bent to scoop Toby into her arms and hold him on one hip. He seemed too big for that but didn't protest. Amy snuggled him for a moment before adding, "I love being a mom more than anything else. It's like what I was born to do."

"Yeah. It's great." Marian nodded.

Amy's older brother had gone to school with Marian, a grade or two below her. Marian remembered her as a freckle-faced kid tagging along when big groups of them had hung out at the local pool. It was hard to relate this supermom to that little girl. Hell, it was hard to relate to Amy at all.

"He's my best little buddy, aren't you? Mommy's best little guy." Amy hefted the kid higher onto her hip and kissed his fat rosy cheeks. "If I sent him off to school, I think I'd just go crazy, waiting around all day for him to come home. I mean, what would I do with myself?"

"I've been thinking of going back to work," Marian offered. It was the first time she'd said it aloud. It sounded scary, but she laughed, also strangely unburdened by making what had been only thoughts at least a little more real.

Amy's eyebrows rose. "Wow. That's exciting."

"We'll see." Marian eased away, eager now to get home and start searching.

"Hey, is Briella all right?" Amy called after her.

Marian turned with her smile fading. "What do you mean?"

"I saw what happened. Hank driving too fast. It looked like it could have been bad," Amy said. "I just wanted to make sure she was okay. I was thinking of going over there and asking him to remember we have little ones on this street, and he should slow down."

Marian had lived next door to Hank for years without either of them saying more than a few words to each other, and most of them had been disputes over the property line and whose tree was shedding leaves onto whose grass. He'd been the same with Dean before she moved in, and with Dean's parents before that. Amy'd only lived in the neighborhood for a couple of years. She'd learn. Maybe.

"You can try, I guess? But don't be shocked if he says no and runs you off his lawn." Marian shrugged, watching as Toby stuck the train in his mouth and gnawed. What would it be like to have a kid like that, she wondered absently. A normal kid? Kind of…dumb?

The second she thought it, she felt bad enough to bend down to Toby's level and give him a smile she hoped made up for it. "You like Thomas, huh?"

Toby grunted and chewed the train. He then offered it to Marian, who laughed but didn't take it. She straightened as a dark gray sedan drove past them. Because the street was a dead end, the only traffic on this road belonged to the residents, delivery drivers or guests. Marian watched the car slow and turn into her driveway.

"Oh, shit," she said aloud, then apologized at the sight of Amy's stricken face and the way she automatically shielded Toby's ear with her free hand. "Sorry. That's my ex."

Amy turned, eyes wide, then looked back at Marian. "Oh. Wow. You'd better go."

"Yeah. I'll see you."

Tommy and Dean had been friendly in high school, but not friends. Since then, they'd never seemed to have a problem with each other, but Marian had always been sure to be the buffer between them. She didn't think Dean gave a rat's ass about what Tommy might think or say, but Tommy had been known to go out of his way to push buttons when he could. By the time she got to the house, Tommy had already knocked at the front door and been let inside.

Shit.

Marian found both men in the den, bent over the cage. Before she could say anything, Tommy had flicked the latch and opened the door. The raven hopped forward. If its wing was still hurt, it wasn't showing signs of any pain. It looked at Tommy with one bright eye, then the other, but didn't come out of the cage.

Tommy laughed. "See if you can get it to say 'hello, Ward'."

"It's not the same bird, man." Dean shook his head and saw Marian in the doorway. He straightened. "Hey, b— Marian. Look who's here."

"I see." She noticed that Dean had very obviously cut himself off from calling her 'babe' or 'baby'. She lifted her chin. "What's up, Tommy? Don't you know how to call first?"

Tommy had been laughing and poking at the bird, but he looked at her now. When his attention moved away from the bird, it hopped close enough to peck him firmly on the hand. With a yelp, Tommy yanked his hand out of reach.

"Damn thing. Shit, that hurt." He stood, shaking his hand.

Dean closed the cage door. "You probably scared it."

"What's going on, Tommy?" Marian said firmly, trying to get them both back on topic. Her ex showed up on his terms and schedule, and it never ended up benefiting Marian, even if she did appreciate the fact that Briella went crazy for her dad's visits.

"Between gigs, thought I'd come back home to see the folks. And Briella, of course."

"Of course. Make sure you give them my best."

Tommy grinned. "You sure you don't want to come over and give it to them yourself?"

"Briella's at school," Marian said, refusing to react to Tommy's teasing. He knew that she hated his mother. "You can come back around three thirty if you want to see her."

Tommy's grin faded. He shoved his hands into his jeans pockets and rocked on his heels. "Sure, yeah. I figured she might be. I guess I didn't really pay attention to the time."

"It's not even eight in the morning," she said flatly. "On a Monday. Where did you think she'd be?"

Dean coughed into his fist. Tommy looked from Marian to Dean, then at the bird. It muttered something in Briella's voice. Then it spoke louder.

"Goodbye. Goodbye."

Maybe the raven wasn't so bad after all. Marian laughed silently, pressing her lips together, at Tommy's expression. She caught Dean's gaze over her ex's shoulder, and they shared a look. Her irritation didn't disappear, but it faded. That's what Dean did for her. He made her calm.

Her phone buzzed from her jeans pocket, and she pulled it out. She rarely got calls on it. Her brother always texted first, and Dad didn't even own a mobile phone, although she'd been after him to get one for safety reasons. When she saw the name and number, she groaned, but swiped to take the call.

It was the school.

CHAPTER NINE

"First of all, let me say how nice it is to see a coparenting relationship working out." The school guidance counselor, Mrs. Cuddy, wore her reading glasses pushed on top of her curly, graying hair, the chain dangling down on either side of her head. She had lipstick curdled in the corners of her lips, but her smile was broad and kind.

Marian remembered her from her own days at Southside Elementary. Mrs. Cuddy had been one of only two black teachers in the school. She and Marian had never talked about it, what it was like to be one of a few dark faces in the sea of white, but there'd been a silent understanding between them anytime they had to interact. By the time Briella came to this school, the diversity of the population had expanded, but Mrs. Cuddy was still a familiar and welcome face.

"It's about what's best for the kid." Tommy sounded sincere.

The hell?

Marian shifted in her chair, ignoring him. She cleared her throat, trying but failing to keep her voice from shaking. "So, if you could please tell us what's going on...?"

Mrs. Cuddy folded her hands on the desk in front of her. "I think it might be best if I just...show you. But I don't want you to be alarmed, all right? Briella's not in any kind of trouble."

"Is she hurt?" Marian blurted. "Did something else happen on the playground?"

"I think you'd better just tell us right now what's going on." Dean took Marian's hand. Squeezed her fingers tight.

She squeezed back.

Marian did not look at Tommy, on her other side. She'd taken the middle seat to keep a distance between her ex and Dean, but now she felt like a bridge she didn't want to be. Tommy shouldn't have been there, acting like a father, like he somehow had anything to do with Briella beyond providing the sperm and then coincidentally being there when Marian got the school's call. She wanted to spit. Dean had been the one to acquiesce, to say that it was fine for Tommy to come along. He was the one who never felt threatened by Tommy's periodic appearances.

"Briella's always been a bright girl. She's been part of our gifted program since kindergarten." Mrs. Cuddy stopped, clearly struggling to be diplomatic. "We've never had any problems with her, academically. But… there have been some behavioral problems."

Tommy sat up straighter. "Huh? What kind of behavioral problems?"

"She's had some difficulties getting along with some of the other students."

"Only recently. She used to get along with everyone." Marian lifted her chin, meeting Mrs. Cuddy's gaze without flinching, as though she could somehow make this true. It wasn't, not quite.

Mrs. Cuddy's smile wasn't as soothing as she probably meant it to be. "Now's about the time when we start seeing a lot of…changes…in the kids. They're about to head into middle school. Some of them are entering puberty, while their peers haven't yet caught up. It's a tough time, even for kids without Briella's special gifts. But I really should just show you. Please come with me."

She stood. So did Marian and the others. Mrs. Cuddy nodded as she passed them, gesturing in the doorway for them to follow. Tommy pushed his way first. Typical. Once again, Marian found herself sandwiched between the men as Dean hung behind, his hand on her lower back as they walked. Today that comforting touch irritated her, and she shrugged it off.

Mrs. Cuddy took them down a long hall, away from Briella's classroom, past the library and then around a corner. The rooms here were spaced farther apart, but unlike the rest of the doors they'd passed, these were all closed. The door Mrs. Cuddy put them in front of had a large glass pane, threaded with wire inside the glass.

"We won't go in just yet. I wanted you to see, first."

Marian knuckled Tommy aside, her breath held. She didn't know what to expect, but whatever it was had to be bad, right? They didn't just call you down to the school this way for anything good. She looked into the window, hesitantly at first, not wanting Briella to see her watching. She didn't have to worry. The kid was at the chalkboard, scrawling away at a bunch of numbers and equations, too intent to see if she were being observed. Her mouth was going a mile a minute, too, as she looked over her shoulder at someone else in the room. Marian peered to see who it was.

"That's not Mrs. Jackson." She looked at Mrs. Cuddy.

"Bill Spector is the district's special-needs coordinator, and he's also a psychiatrist."

"A shrink? F— no." Tommy blurted the words, taking a step toward the door like he meant to fight it. At least he'd managed to keep his cursing under control.

Marian let out a huff of surprise and stepped back so Tommy could muscle his way in front of the window. "Special needs? Psychiatrist? I don't understand."

"My kid's not a retard," Tommy said.

Well, that explained everything about where Briella had heard it, and of course Tommy had learned at his dear old bitch of a mother's knee. Marian's teeth snapped shut on the tip of her tongue, but she refused to bite it. She pushed at him to get him away from the window so she could look in again.

"You're a pig, Tommy."

Tommy gave her a wide-eyed look of surprise. "What? Why?"

"We prefer not to marginalize our students with special needs by using derogatory terms," Mrs. Cuddy said, then added with a look at Marian, "or calling each other derogatory names."

Marian frowned, feeling scolded. "You don't call people that, Tommy."

"Sorry for not being 'PC,'" he said, using obnoxious air quotes and not sounding sorry at all.

Dean stepped in, tugging Marian gently away from the window and turning her to stand at his side, facing the guidance counselor. "We know Briella's really smart and gifted. And we know about the issues with her attitude, too. We've been trying to work with her on it."

"As I said," Mrs. Cuddy paused to look at Tommy with disdain, "our *special-needs* students receive guidance not only from myself and the other counselors at their individual buildings, but also district-wide. I asked Dr. Spector to come in today because over the past couple weeks, Briella's been having some difficulties at school that have become untenable for her teachers."

"What's that mean? Kids not talking to her, not paying attention to her, not wanting to be her friends is *now* important? We were told last year that she wasn't being bullied, so what's going on now, and why haven't I heard about it before?" Marian demanded, her arms crossed. Her breath snagged in her throat, hurting. She swallowed hard, but everything was so dry, scratching like sand.

Mrs. Cuddy gave her a calm smile. "At the time we spoke last year, there was no evidence of bullying. That's true. This year, as I said, it's the time when many of our kids here are undergoing changes. Sometimes they spark out in behavioral issues. Even well-behaved kids can start to get into trouble. Friendships that have been in place since preschool can break, while others form. It's a very tumultuous time in children's lives right now."

"It's Pamela Morgan, isn't it? She's the one giving Briella such a hard time," Marian said.

"We are not having any issues with Pamela, no."

"Is Briella in trouble?" Tommy asked.

Marian shot him a glare. He sounded almost proud, but of course he would be. Tommy'd been a bad student and a troublemaker, even if he'd always been charming enough to get out of it. He'd been voted most likely to serve time, but the school hadn't allowed that in the yearbook, so he'd ended up as class clown.

Mrs. Cuddy shook her head. "No. Not exactly. But I called you to come in today because…well. Let me have you speak with Dr. Spector. All right? Shall we go in?"

Marian almost said no. Whatever was going to happen inside that room was going to change everything. She knew that somehow. At the squeeze of Dean's fingers in her own, she gave him a grateful smile. Whatever was going to happen, she thought with relief, they'd be in it together.

Plus Tommy. Marian frowned again. It wasn't so much that he wanted to be involved as the way he pretended he *was* always involved, like he had the slightest clue about what happened on a normal basis. Like he ought to get a trophy and a parade for showing up once in a while, when every time he did, all he managed to do was disrupt everything.

At least he had the decency to hang back and let Marian and Dean go ahead of him. At first, Briella didn't turn from the board. The chalk in her hand snapped as she finished an equation, and she grabbed another from the tray. She scribbled what looked like gibberish to Marian, then turned with a triumphant grin. Her eyes were alight, her tawny cheeks flushed. Strands of tangled dark hair clung to her sweaty forehead.

"That's it," she said in a calm voice at odds with her frenzied appearance. "That's how it's going to work."

"Interesting, Briella. I want to hear more about how you figure you'll implement it, but first, let's say hi to your parents, okay?" Dr. Spector turned a smile toward the adults and stood to hold out his hand, first to Marian. "Mrs. Blake. I'm Bill Spector."

"Marian. This is my husband, Dean." She took the man's hand but dropped it immediately to gather Briella into her arms as the girl hugged her. Marian stroked the hair off Briella's face and cupped the girl's cheeks in her hands. Briella's skin was feverish. The tiny wound on her head had almost, not quite, healed. "Hey, Bean. What's going on?"

"I'm talking to Dr. Bill about my ideas. He doesn't think I'm crazy," Briella said.

Marian looked apologetically at the doctor. "Nobody ever said you were."

"Kids in class did." Briella pulled away from her mother and squealed. "Daddy!"

Tommy hugged her, then rubbed at the top of her head with his knuckles. "Hey, kiddo."

"Mrs. Cuddy, did you call my real daddy to come in?"

Mrs. Cuddy looked surprised and shot a glance at Dean, who, as usual, didn't look offended by Briella's blatant dismissal of his role in her life. "No, honey, your dad happened to be around when I talked to your mom and stepdad."

Briella looked at Dean without expression. Then she turned back to Tommy with a broad grin. "Look at my stuff that I'm doing, Daddy."

"Looks like a bunch of numbers to me, kid." Tommy let her take him by the hand to appraise the chalkboard.

Briella explained animatedly what she'd been doing, while Dr. Spector turned to Marian and Dean. "Mr. and Mrs. Blake, I'm sure you're both well aware that Briella's a very special little girl."

"Yes," Marian said faintly, watching her daughter's sweeping gestures at the work she'd scribbled on the board. "That's what everyone keeps saying. But what is she doing?"

Dr. Spector's lips pressed together. "Well…I'm not quite sure. But I can tell you this. There's a lot going on inside her head, and she's having a hard time not only getting it out in a language she can understand and explain, but in a format that she can utilize. She's very frustrated. Has she been acting out at home?"

"Yes," Dean said before Marian could answer, "sometimes."

Marian sighed and rubbed the spot between her eyes. It felt shameful to admit that to this guy. That she couldn't keep her kid under control. "She's been a little mouthy. Yeah. But she's a good kid, most of the time. Has she been causing trouble here at school? I mean, I'm going to say it again: if she's been mouthing off to teachers or getting in fights, why is this the first I'm hearing about it?"

Dr. Spector and Mrs. Cuddy shared a look Marian couldn't interpret.

"What?" she demanded. There was way more going on here than either of these two were saying. She felt it low in her belly. Maternal instinct.

"We feel that Southside Elementary has done all we can for Briella," Dr. Spector said.

Marian gaped, then snapped her jaw shut. She turned to Mrs. Cuddy. "What the he— heck is that supposed to mean? You've done all you can for her? Are you kicking her out? She's ten years old!"

She'd almost shrieked those last few words. Too loud. Briella stopped her chattering and turned, her hand in Tommy's. He turned, too, and Marian was so upset she couldn't even take satisfaction in his confused expression.

"I think we should let Briella tell you what she's been working on," Mrs. Cuddy said. "It might make all of this more clear."

Dean stepped up, because Marian found herself unable to do more than shake her head. "Yeah, that sounds great. Briella, why don't you show me and your mom and your dad what you're writing on the board? Can you explain it to us?"

"Probably not," Briella said. "None of *you* are smart enough to understand it."

Marian began to scold, but Dean waved her to silence. "We know that, honey. Could you try to give us some idea?"

Briella sighed and put her tiny hands on her hips. The piece of chalk still clutched in her fist smudged at her dark blue shirt. "Well, basically, I'm trying to work out the technology to capture memories."

"Isn't that what a video camera does?" Tommy joked.

Briella, who normally ate up every single word Tommy said like it was ice cream, instead gave him a look of such pure disdain that he stepped back like she'd pushed him. Briella gestured at the chalkboard. "I'm not talking about pictures, *Daddy*. I mean like, memories, your real memories and your real self. The stuff that's inside your brain. Not just what you see, but what you feel.

"Bean, nobody can do that," Marian said.

Briella didn't look a bit bothered. "I can. If I can figure this out, I can do it."

Mrs. Cuddy reached for Briella with a small gesture. "Hey, Briella. It's lunchtime, and it's pizza day. I know you don't want to miss that. How about you and I head for the café and let Dr. Bill talk to your parents?"

"Pizza day!" Briella clapped and grinned and gave a little fist bump to the guidance counselor.

Briella followed Mrs. Cuddy out of the room without a second glance, but the older woman paused in the doorway to give Marian a nod. It looked as though it was meant as reassurance, but it did little to make Marian feel better. Mrs. Cuddy closed the door behind her.

Marian turned to the doctor and drew in a slow breath, trying to keep her voice from quivering. She didn't quite make it. "Is there something wrong with her? With her brain, I mean? Mentally? She just had a head injury…"

"She mentioned the bump on her head. Yes. And it's true, there have been cases in which traumatic brain damage can cause abrupt changes in personality or mental acuity. There have even been cases of people experiencing enormous leaps in skills they previously had not had. Playing the piano, speaking another language…" The doctor trailed off, probably at the look on Marian's face. "Sorry. Briella's bump, I'm sure, has nothing to do with what she was doing today, certainly nothing negative."

"Is this the first time she's gone off like that?" Dean gestured at the chalkboard.

"She keeps a notebook," Marian said hoarsely. "I stopped looking in it, but she writes things down all the time."

Dr. Spector looked at the board. "Yes. Today she came into class and was excused to attend her gifted tutorial. She started with this immediately, and her teacher called me in to take a look. I thought it was extraordinary."

"So…there's nothing wrong with her?" Marian asked.

"With Briella? No, I don't think so." The doctor laughed, shaking his head. "If anything, there's so much right about her. Your daughter is one of the brightest kids I've had the pleasure of working with for a long, long time."

"She's scary smart," Tommy agreed, pride evident in his voice.

Marian glared at him. "Like you know anything about it."

"She can't be serious, can she? About the memories thing? You can't record memories. Can you?" Dean scratched at his head. He'd taken off his ball cap out of respect at being inside the school, and he looked surprised that it was missing.

"There've been studies that monitor brain waves as memories are being made. They've been able to determine the sections of the brain that make different kinds of memories. As far as I know, there's no way to actually record the memories themselves, or to play them back," Dr. Spector said. "I'll be the first to tell you that. But Briella has tested off the charts for math and cognitive abilities, and her scores are also at gifted level in language comprehension and a whole long list of other things. The bottom line is, whether or not the technology she's trying to create works, for a girl of her age to even be able to articulate what she wants to do, much less make any efforts at all…well. It's an extraordinary brilliance, to be frank."

Marian had calmed a bit, but she leaned against Dean for comfort. None of this was making total sense to her. "So what does this mean?"

"It means," the doctor said, rubbing his hands together, "that we are going to recommend Briella leave Southside and start attending a smaller, private school."

"Parkhaven," Tommy said at once. "You want us to send her to the mutant school."

CHAPTER TEN

"A full scholarship," Dean said when neither Marian nor Tommy had spoken for a full sweep of the clock's second hand. "There's that. Right? That means something."

The three of them sat around the kitchen table in Dean and Marian's house. Marian got up to bring the coffee carafe to the table. She filled Dean's cup first. Then her own. Tommy waved her off when she offered him some. She put the carafe on a small, lacy hot pad her mother had crocheted. Marian had always meant to ask for lessons in how to crochet, but Mom had been killed before she ever had the chance.

"Of course they're giving her a free ride. She's a genius. They want kids like her going there, so they can show off to the rich assholes who can afford to pay the tuition. They're going to use our kid to prove Parkhaven's got what it takes. How else would they get anyone to attend that freakfest?" Tommy shook his head, then sat back in the chair hard enough to rock it a little. He ran both hands through his dirty blond hair, scratching at his scalp. "Shit, Marian. You can't be thinking this is a good idea. You know the kids who go to that school are weird as fuck. And yeah, Briella's got her… quirks…but…you know what I'm saying."

Tommy gave Marian a steady, fierce look that she met evenly, without flinching.

"No, Tommy. What *are* you saying?"

"I'm saying that she's weird. But she's not *that* fucking weird."

She frowned at his language, and at the suggestion their daughter…no, fuck that. *Her* daughter was anything close to not being normal. "You heard the doctor. Briella is brilliant."

"And strange," Tommy said. "Brilliant and strange. But she's still not weird enough for Parkhaven."

"Have you ever even met anyone who went to school there?"

Parkhaven had been founded sometime in the early 1920s as a private boarding school for orphans who'd been lucky enough to find benefactors, but it had not always been a school. The massive pseudo-Victorian building had been added to over the years without much thought toward matching the architecture, resulting in a sprawl of several wings and additions off the main building, along with other outbuildings on the property. In the fifties and sixties it had become a private hospital, taking care of mostly special-needs children whose families didn't want to or could not care for them at home. By the seventies, lack of private funding had turned the hospital into a state psychiatric facility. It had been shut down in the mid-eighties and left empty until about fifteen years ago, when a board of trustees had renovated and reopened it as a private boarding school.

Marian, Tommy and Dean had been kids in the early nineties, when Parkhaven took on the role that any old house does in the neighborhood – rumors that it was haunted, the scene of serial killings, that the crazy people who lived there had not gone on to homes or other places when the government defunded it, but instead were holed up in the attics and basements. Kids dared each other to break in and wander the rooms, abandoned but not empty. Marian had never done it, but she wouldn't have put it past Tommy to have gone in with a couple cans of spray paint and a few joints to get stoned and mess the place up.

"I had a cousin who married a guy who went there," Dean said quietly.

Tommy and Marian both looked at him. Tommy laughed, shaking his head, but it sounded more like he was mocking than amused. Marian ignored him. She did that a lot.

"And?" she asked.

Dean shrugged. "Seemed like a decent enough guy. Quiet."

"They're all quiet," Tommy said, "until they turn out to have jars of teeth in the basement."

Marian exploded. "You shut the fuck up, Tommy. This is your kid we're talking about, and I get it, you have no fucking clue who she is or what it's like living with her…"

She broke off with a gasping, choking cry and got up to get herself a glass of cool water from the sink. She shrugged off Dean's touch from her shoulder, hating herself for it but grateful that he knew her well enough to let her push him away without getting butthurt about the rejection. She gave herself a second or so to turn, expecting to have to tell Tommy to get his skinny ass out of her house, but she found him looking contrite. Almost believably so.

"You're right. I'm an asshole," he said.

Her anger deflated, a pinpricked balloon. Marian leaned against the counter and crossed her arms over her chest. "We all know Briella has always been different. Special. You heard what Spector said. Southside has done all they can for her. Going to Parkhaven will be good for her. And if they're going to give her a free ride, provide her with an education that could get her into a really good college.... The opportunities she'll have from this are so much more than we could possibly ever give her."

From the corner of her eye, Marian saw Dean flinch, and she felt worse about what she'd just said than when she'd shrugged off his comforting touch. Still, she lifted her chin. Money wasn't everything, but damn it, money was always something, and it was no secret that she and Dean sometimes struggled with the basics, much less being able to afford anything above and beyond.

"I don't want my kid to be a charity case," Tommy said in a low voice.

"I would rather take charity than hold on to my damned pride, if it means I can see my daughter go to the best school and have the brightest future possible. And unless you plan to fully fund her way through her college education, Tommy, it's not going to be up to you whether or not we turn this down. Buy her a laptop, buy her a new one every year, if that makes you feel like a hotshot. But in the end, Briella deserves whatever chances we can give her." Marian finished with her hands on her hips, glaring, but kept her voice low.

Tommy had the grace to look ashamed. "If you really want to send her away to school, Mare—"

"I don't," she interrupted. "I don't *want* to send her away."

But she did, didn't she? Maybe just a little bit? Wasn't there a bit of shameful comfort in the idea of someone else taking on the burden of the constant questions, the temper tantrums? The derision? Hell, just the general burden of having a kid at all, much less one like Briella.

"There are other places to send her," Tommy finished as though she hadn't spoken. "We could look into it, that's all I'm saying. If you think she needs to go to private school, we could find another one."

"And once again, who's going to pay for it? You?" Marian shook her head.

Tommy cleared his throat and hitched forward in the chair. "I could. Yeah."

"I can't trust you, Tommy. You'd get her settled in some school and then all of a sudden I'd be getting notices that the bills aren't paid, and we'd have to bring her home. I won't do that to her."

Dean, wisely, had been staying out of it, but now spoke up. "She's too young to go away to school, anyhow. Even Parkhaven will only take her as a day student until she's twelve, and then they'll have to assess her to see if she's ready for full-time."

The look Tommy gave Dean was level and considering. "So you think she ought to go there?"

"I think that we should do whatever is best for her," Dean said.

The front door opened and, startled, Marian looked at the clock on the soffit above the sink. They'd been talking about this for so long, she'd forgotten Briella would be getting off the bus. Her small figure appeared in the doorway to the kitchen, and they all turned to look.

"You didn't come to the bus stop to get me, Mama."

"I know, honey, I'm sorry. Me and your dad and Dean were talking." Marian gestured for the girl to come closer. "You want a snack?"

"Yeah, but I'm going to see Onyx first. Daddy, do you want to see Onyx? I'm teaching him to talk."

That bird. That damned bird. It was a disgusting reminder of everything Tommy had said that Marian didn't want to hear – that her daughter was and had always been…odd.

Tommy's laugh was strained. "No way. I gotta go hear that."

Marian gave him an impatient wave and waited until he'd gone into the den to say to Dean, "This is a good thing. Right? Isn't it? Parkhaven, I mean."

"A free scholarship to a private school that can let her learn at her own pace, where she'll have access to computer and science labs? The paperwork said she'd even get a laptop to use at home for her assignments." Dean shook his head, holding out his hands, palms up. "Babe, I don't see how we can refuse. I mean, what should we do, keep her at Southside, where—"

"Where they make fun of her," Marian said as she pulled out the jar of peanut butter from the cupboard and an apple from the small basket in the corner of the kitchen. "Where she struggles to fit in, where she's bored. I know she said she fell off the monkey bars all on her own, but the other kids laughed at her when she did. And her teacher said they can't do anything more for her in that school. They can't just say that, can they? To get rid of her? They're not allowed to do that, Dean, are they?"

She heard the rising sound of her own hysteria and tried to fight it back, knock it down, but her hands were shaking and there was no way for her to keep them still. Her stomach twisted, churning, and her throat closed so that she had to swallow over and over. Faintly, she heard the sound of that damned bird squawking, along with the rise of Tommy's laughter. Her shaking fingers curled over her palms. "They can't just kick her out of Southside because she's too smart, can they?"

"No, baby. They're recommending Parkhaven because they really believe Briella would do well there. And she will. And, if she doesn't like Parkhaven, we can always see about transferring her somewhere else." Dean held up his hand to stop her from talking. "We'll find the money."

Marian burst into tears she stifled behind her hands. Dean was at her side in an instant, and this time, she didn't push him away. She clung to him for a moment, letting him be her rock. She swiped at her face, aware that Tommy and Briella could be back in the kitchen at any moment.

"You took us both on," she said against his chest. "You didn't have to."

"Of course I didn't have to. I love you," Dean told her with a small laugh as he stroked his hand over her hair. "I love both of you, Marian. So if the kid needs to get into a school that's going to help her, then we make that happen. Whatever it takes. Okay?"

A small breath of relief eased out of her. She raised her face to his for a damp kiss, then laughed and swiped again at her eyes. "Sorry. You know how I get around this time of the month."

Dean kissed her again and squeezed her, hard. "It's all going to be okay, baby. I promise."

Briella showed up in the doorway, the raven on her shoulder. It was easily twice the size of her head, and Marian couldn't stop the grunt of disgust that slipped past her lips. Briella didn't seem to notice her mother's discomfort.

The girl beamed. "Look, Mama. He's so much better now."

"Mama," the bird said in Briella's voice.

Marian shook her head, her lip curling. "Get it out of the kitchen. I told you not to take it out of the cage. If it's that much better, it can go back and live outside."

She expected a fight, but Briella nodded as she reached to stroke the bird's feathered back. "I know. Onyx has to live in nature. He doesn't want to stay in a cage. That's not fair. Nobody would want to live locked up forever, right, Onyx?"

The raven didn't answer with words but gave a muttered, rasping caw. It tugged a strand of Briella's curly hair and flapped its wings as though it meant to take off. Marian pointed at the back door.

"Out. Now."

Briella went out the back door to the small concrete stoop. "Go on, Onyx. Go fly!"

The bird did, taking off from Briella's shoulder with a huge swoop, then circling back to dip low in front of her before wheeling off and heading for the woods. Briella waved, calling goodbye.

The girl looked up at Marian with a frown and a glitter of tears. "He'll come back, though. Won't he?"

Marian smoothed the strands of her daughter's hair that the bird had pulled. "It's a wild animal, Briella. It can take care of itself, and it'll be fine. It's meant to live out there in the wild. Not to come around people."

"But will he come back to visit me?"

Marian cupped Briella's cheeks in her hands and found a smile for her. "I guess we never know what might happen. How about we go inside now and get that snack? There's some stuff we want to talk to you about."

CHAPTER ELEVEN

The tour of Parkhaven was supposed to take only an hour, but with the fifteen-minute drive on each end of it, Marian had insisted Dean stay home and go to bed. He had enough trouble working nights without losing more sleep, and he'd be wrecked without it. She had not intended for his place to be taken by Tommy, who'd insisted on attending.

An older student had taken Briella to show her around. Dr. Garrett, the Parkhaven school psychologist, gave Marian and Tommy the tour. The school, a massive, looming building, had been renovated with every modern school convenience.

"Still looks like a looney bin," Tommy said under his breath as Dr. Garrett excused himself to duck into the restroom.

Marian scowled. "Shut your mouth. This place is…it's…"

"Admit it. It's creepy as fuck," Tommy said.

Marian would not admit it. The library, auditorium and computer labs had all impressed the hell out of her. Southside had been a fine school, one of the better ones in the district, but Parkhaven stood all on its own.

Tommy wouldn't let up. "You know it's haunted. You *know* there's been some bad shit that went on in here."

"Do you want your kid to thrive and succeed?" Marian snapped at him. "Or do you want to keep being a giant asshole about this?"

He looked chagrined. "I'm just kidding around."

"Don't," she told him. "This could be a really big deal, a great thing for her. Don't you ruin it."

"I'm not going to ruin anything for her. Shit, Mare. You think I'd do that? Really?"

Dr. Garrett, an amiable man who wore a tie adorned with smiling sunny-side up eggs, returned from the restroom. "Sorry about that. Shall we continue?"

The rest of the tour took only another fifteen minutes or so, ending at the science labs, where they met Briella. She was bubbling over with glee at the facilities, talking the ear off of her tour guide. At least the older kid looked amused and not put off.

"Is she going to fit in here?" Marian bluntly asked the psychologist.

Garrett smiled. "I think so. Yes."

"You can't promise that," Tommy interjected, earning a sour look from Marian.

"Of course not. But I can promise you both that Parkhaven's going to treat Briella very well. I've seen a lot of kids go through this school, and not many like her."

Briella had caught sight of them. "Mama! Guess what! They have an organics lab here! And I might be able to use it!"

"The organics lab is a live experiment facility. We've got students working with hydroponics, genetics work on plants, that sort of thing. Nothing contagious or with animals," Garrett added hastily, maybe at the sight of Marian's expression. "But it's state of the art. We're very proud of it."

Briella took one hand from each of her parents, swinging them back and forth. "I'm going to like it here."

★   ★   ★

Briella had asked Tommy to stay for dinner and then to play some games with her after that. He'd never been one for games except the kind you played in casinos, so Marian expected him to shrug it off and head out. Tommy, however, seemingly oblivious to Marian's hints that he probably wanted to get on the road, stayed. Dean had left for work early to cover part of a shift for someone who'd gone home sick.

This left Marian, Tommy and Briella alone. Marian couldn't remember a time when that had ever been the case. Maybe once or twice, long ago, when Briella was an infant, but even back then it had never been with Marian cooking dinner while father and daughter played a card game at the table. The three of them had never been a family like this, and the easy, casual normalcy of it left Marian unsettled.

"You want to play?" Briella held up the pack of brightly colored cards.

Marian usually enjoyed playing games, but she didn't particularly want to play with Tommy. "I need to get these potatoes peeled, Bean."

"You should take a break. Come play with us." Tommy shot her an old familiar grin, the sort that had always been meant to turn her knees to jelly. It was that smile that had ended up with her pregnant with Briella, and there was no way Marian was going to let herself be anything close to seduced by it ever again.

A rapping at the back door window had them all turning toward it. Briella cried out in delight and got out of her chair to cross to the door. The raven was so big it could stand on the rail and tap its beak on the glass window in the door's center. Briella flung it open before Marian could stop her.

"He wants to come inside," Briella said with a glance over her shoulder.

"Absolutely not!"

Briella turned her attention back to the bird. "Sorry, Onyx. My mom says you have to stay outside."

"It's almost dark out. Shouldn't it be nesting for the night or something? Roosting?" Marian took a few cautious steps toward the door.

"Maybe he thinks he lives here now," Tommy said. "You know, like a homing pigeon or something. Awww, Mare, look. He wants to come inside." Tommy's tone had gone wheedling. He thought he was being charming.

Marian frowned at him. "Terrific, but no. It's not happening. Briella, close the door. C'mon, now."

"Mama says no, Onyx. You have to stay outside. But you can come play with me tomorrow, after school. Okay? I'll be home in the afternoon. Okay? Did you understand me?"

Marian looked around the girl at the oversize bird. "What's it got in its beak?"

As if it understood her, the raven tilted its head to look at her with that unblinking eye. It dropped whatever it had been holding in its beak onto the railing with a soft *plop*.

Before Marian could warn her not to, Briella had grabbed it. "Oh! He brought me a present. How cool!"

"Don't touch that, it's poison." Marian moved fast, snagging the cluster of purple pokeweed berries out of Briella's fist. "Go wash your hands."

"Give that back. It's mine. He brought it for me. Ravens bring little gifts to people who help them—"

Marian tossed the berries out into the yard. "Those are poison berries. Go wash your hands, Briella. Now. They'll make you sick."

"Goodbye. Goodbye." The bird croaked and flew off, becoming one with the darkness so quickly it was almost easy to pretend it hadn't been there in the first place.

"Goodbye," Tommy imitated and flinched as though Marian was going to hit him, even though she hadn't done so much as glance in his direction.

"He brought them for *me*," Briella said with a scowl.

"They'll make you very sick," Marian snapped. "Do you want to get very sick?"

"No, Mama."

"Anyway, it's time for bed. School in the morning."

"The new school?"

"No," Marian said after a hesitation.

The packet from the school had included every possible piece of information Marian could have needed. Instead of taking the bus, Briella would be getting a ride in the school van that would come right to the house to pick her up and drop her off. She'd be wearing a uniform. There'd been a voucher for the new clothes in the package of information Mrs. Cuddy had given them, and a list of local stores and online sites that would honor it. There was paperwork to fill out regarding the lunch program, the school-provided health insurance, the lease of a laptop. Briella was going to get a free ride, but before she could, a lot needed to be done.

"Tomorrow you'll go back to Southside to finish up the rest of the week," Marian finished.

"I thought I was going to the *new* school." Briella crossed her arms, a storm brewing in her pale gray eyes.

Marian knew that look, and she meant to cut off a tantrum before it could start. She kept her voice light, her smile bright. "You will be. Next week. This week, you get to finish up at Southside and say goodbye to all your friends there. Mrs. Cuddy said you could take in cupcakes. Have a little going-away party."

"I want to go to the new school tomorrow. I don't want to go back to Southside. I don't want to bring in cupcakes, I don't care about any of those kids. None of them are my friends!" Briella's voice rose, up and up, ending in a teakettle scream that cut off abruptly as she ran out of breath.

Tommy shifted in his seat. He stared very pointedly at the floor, his mouth in a thin, grim line. When Briella stamped her foot, he shot Marian a hard look she ignored.

Marian kept her voice calm. "I'm sorry, but you're not set up to start there until next week. It takes time to get everything settled."

"Okay, Mama," Briella said, her voice brightly brittle, plastic, but expression still stormy. "I'll just stay home, then. With you."

For a second, Marian flashed to the conversation she'd had with Amy at the bus stop. She was not that kind of mother, the sort who put everything into her kid, and although a ripple of guilt tickled up and down her spine at the self-confession, she shook her head. "No, you won't stay home. You're going to school tomorrow the way you always do. Next week, you'll go to the new school."

"Hey," Tommy broke in, taking Briella's attention, and for once Marian was grateful he was there to stop the showdown before it started instead of exacerbating it like he'd been known to do in the past. "Tell you what. You don't give your mom a hard time about this, and I'll tuck you in so you can tell me all about your bird. Okay?"

Half an hour later – and that seemed early, considering how long Briella could be known to drag out bedtime – Tommy was back in the kitchen, where Marian had settled at the table with a mug of tea and a book of sudoku. She motioned to the empty chair opposite her. Tommy sat, shifting and looking awkward.

Marian enjoyed his discomfort for a nice few minutes before finally saying, "What?"

"So…she doesn't do the…thing, anymore?"

"She was a toddler, Tommy. She had tantrums. She's older now. No. She doesn't do 'the thing' anymore."

"You were right, earlier. About me not knowing her."

"I know I was," Marian answered.

Tommy didn't rise to her snark, and that was a first. "I want to be better about it, Marian."

She put down her pen and closed the soft, pulpy book with a finger in the pages to mark her spot. "Why now?"

"My mom," he said after a second. "She's got breast cancer."

There was no love lost between Marian and her former mother-in-law, but this was not something Marian could take joy in learning. "I'm so sorry. That's rough."

Tommy shrugged. "It made me think about how, you know, we should pay attention to the time we have now. With the people who are important."

Marian wanted to make a joke about asking him if he was high or drunk, or where the class clown Tommy had gone, but his face was too serious for that. "So, what are you going to do about it?"

"Try to spend more time with her, I guess. Get to know her better. If it's okay with you."

"Of course it is. If you can promise me that you'll actually follow through with it. You can't just show up when you want to, Tommy. You've done that too often."

"And not just with the kid, huh?"

She didn't say anything at first. They'd never had a heart-to-heart, no kind of closure, no apologies. They'd both behaved badly in the past, and maybe she'd been mistaken in thinking she'd put it behind her, because now the idea that Tommy might be trying to say he was sorry closed Marian's throat up so tight she couldn't speak.

Another set of raps came at the back door. Tommy looked past her. "I'll be damned. It's that bird. Who does he think lives here, Edgar Allan Poe?"

"Don't open the door," Marian said at once, although Tommy was already getting to his feet.

Tommy shot her a glance over his shoulder. "I'm just looking."

He flicked on the back porch light and bent close to the glass, shielding his eyes so he could see out. He jumped back with a startled, embarrassed laugh at another series of taps. Marian got to her feet, not moving toward the door, but straining to see.

"Make it go away. It creeps me out," she said. "What the hell is it doing here?"

"You fed it. It's going to keep coming back." Tommy shrugged. "Like a bad ex-husband."

She rolled her eyes at that, but couldn't help laughing. She wouldn't trust his charms, she'd learned that lesson long ago, but it did feel much nicer not to be irritated with him. "Turn off the light. Maybe it will go away."

Tommy did, still looking out the door with his hand to his eyes. "Still there. It's sitting on the railing."

"Ugh." Marian moved next to him and also looked out. The bird was hard to see in the darkness, although she could make out the shape of it.

On impulse, she grabbed a dishtowel from the counter and then yanked the door open as she swung it with a low holler. The bird squawked and took off, the sound of its beating wings getting farther away until she couldn't see or hear it. She turned to see Tommy shaking his head.

"You're being ridiculous," he said.

Another time she might have taken that as an insult, but now Marian only shrugged and tossed the towel back on the counter. "Isn't it time you went home?"

"Fine, fine," he said with a conciliatory gesture. His expression turned serious. "I do mean what I said, Mare. About being closer with the kid. I know I let you down in the past. And her. I'm not saying I'm a changed man or anything, but I do want to try. Okay?"

"Yes," she said. "But I swear to you, Tommy, if you screw this up and let her down, if you can't keep your shit together...I will..."

She didn't know what she'd do, only that she intended it to be bad. Tommy nodded. For a weird, strained moment, Marian thought he was going to hug her, but thank God for both of them, he didn't. He just nodded again and headed out. In a minute, she heard the front door close.

The sound of tapping on the glass stopped her. Marian turned to the window, but could see only darkness outside. She waited, holding her breath, but the tapping didn't come again.

CHAPTER TWELVE

Marian had promised Briella she would pick her up from Southside this last day, rather than have her come home on the bus. They would go for ice cream one last time before the local parlor closed for the season. Spend some mother-daughter bonding time. As Marian got out of her car into the late September heat, she lifted her hair off her neck with a sigh. Ice cream was going to be the perfect end to the day, and later they'd have spaghetti for dinner and popcorn for a snack while they stayed up late watching movies. They had an entire weekend before Briella had to go to the new school.

Marian went in through the school's propped-open front doors. The janitor mopped the tile floor in slow swipes. Straight back from where she stood, Marian could see the back doors leading to the courtyard and playground, and the sun shining in through them was bright enough to cast everything else into a deep gloom. The front office was still lit, but everything else was dim and quiet, almost disturbingly so.

Marian didn't bother checking in at the office. With school hours over, any kids left waiting to be picked up would be in the gated playground. When she went through the back doors, though, the courtyard looked empty.

Marian shaded her eyes against the late afternoon sun to look around. It wasn't a huge space, although it had been broken into segments. A large square of asphalt painted with four square lines. A smaller, mulch-filled rectangle toward the back of the courtyard featured the jungle gym equipment.

Slowly, two small figures came into focus in the shadows beneath the bridge part of the jungle gym. Calling Briella's name, Marian headed for it. When the girl didn't answer, Marian called again, just as Briella came into full view.

"Hi, Mama," Briella said brightly.

The girl next to her had a guilty look on her face and chocolate smeared around her mouth. Marian recognized her at once. Pamela Morgan. Briella seemed to have forgotten they had stopped being friends last year, when Pamela decided to take sides with some of the other girls against her. Marian definitely remembered.

"I was just sharing my candy with Pamela," Briella said. "Is it time to go?"

"Yeah. Hi, Pamela."

"Hi," the other girl said. "Did you see my mom waiting for me?"

Before Marian could answer, a woman's voice called Pamela's name, and the girl gave Briella a nod and headed toward her mother. Marian slung an arm around Briella's shoulder. Her daughter linked her arm around Marian's waist as they walked.

"Are you and Pamela friends again?"

Briella shrugged. "No. But since I'm not going to Southside anymore, I figured it would be nice if we could say goodbye to each other like we used to."

"That's very nice of you, honey." Marian thought she might have held a longer grudge.

By the time they got to the parking lot, Pamela's mother, hysterical, was kneeling over Pamela, who was convulsing on the pavement. Mrs. Morgan was screaming, clutching at her daughter. Marian muttered an exclamation, but she didn't have the chance to do more than that before a man got out of another car parked in the lot and knelt next to them. He started shouting out instructions to Mrs. Morgan as he dialed his phone, clearing calling 911.

"Stay back here," Marian said, holding Briella by the shoulder. "Out of the way."

"Is Pamela sick?"

"It looks like it," Marian said. "Let's just keep out of the way, okay?"

"What happened?" a new voice asked.

Marian turned to see the school secretary, whose name she'd forgotten. "I'm not sure."

"Are they calling the ambulance?"

"Yes, I think so," Marian said.

By now, Pamela had stopped convulsing. She lay still and silent on the pavement. The school secretary moved forward, kneeling by her still sobbing mother. Marian could not hear what they said. Moments later, the ambulance arrived, and Marian tugged Briella toward their own car.

"C'mon, Bean. Let's just get home."

"Don't you want to see what happened to her?" Briella asked, straining against Marian's touch as she tried to keep watching.

Marian's fingers pinched deep into Briella's shoulder. "No. The people on the ambulance will take care of her. We'll just be in the way. And besides, how would you feel if people stood around and watched you being sick?"

Buckled into the backseat, Briella said, "Something bad happened to Pamela's brain."

"How do you know that?" Marian glanced into the rearview mirror as she pulled out of the lot, going in the opposite direction of the girl and the crowd gathered around her.

Briella shrugged. "She was having a seizure."

"How do you know what a seizure is?"

"I know things," Briella said.

*　　*　　*

Briella had showered and allowed Marian to condition and fingercomb out her hair without much fuss. She'd gone to bed all on her own at what anyone would have considered a reasonable time. Dean had gone off to work with a kiss for Marian and a reminder that everything was going to be all right. She'd waited until his car left her sight before she went back inside and climbed the stairs to Briella's bedroom.

The door was closed again. Marian paused before knocking, thinking of the last time she'd come in without it. She listened for noises inside. Briella might be asleep already.

She took a chance and turned the knob, cracking open the door and sneaking a peek. Briella's bed was empty, but opening the door a little wider revealed that she was sitting at the window. The attic bedroom had a built-in seat with cushions Dean's mother had made for him when this sloped-ceilinged room had been his, but Briella had tossed them aside. She toyed with the window's crank handle.

"Hi, Mama," she said, although Marian hadn't said anything or even opened the door the whole way. "I'm not sleeping yet. I was just saying goodnight to Onyx."

"Is it out there now?" Marian went over to the window, but saw nothing.

Briella uncurled her legs from beneath her and shook her head. "No. He flew away, back to his nest. I wish I could fly, Mama."

Marian took a seat next to her daughter and pulled her close. "That would be fun, wouldn't it?"

"I'd fly away," Briella said.

Marian hugged her a little tighter. "You would? Where would you go?"

"Just away. Way up into the sky, I guess, as far as I could go."

"So long as you come back," Marian said.

Briella looked at her. "I wouldn't be able to if I flew up to heaven."

"Why would you say that?" Marian shook her head with a frown, then added, keeping her voice calm, "Are you worried about what happened at school today?"

"No."

"You know..." Marian struggled to find the words to express what she'd been thinking all day, since first seeing the two girls together. "It's okay to have mixed feelings about what happened to Pamela."

"I don't have mixed feelings about her."

Marian studied her child. "No?"

"Nope. She's had seizures before." Briella said this confidently.

Marian didn't know much about what could cause seizures. "Does she have epilepsy?"

"Something like that," Briella agreed. "But lots of things can cause seizures. Sometimes pills and stuff."

Alarmed, Marian sat on the edge of Briella's bed. She didn't ask how her daughter knew this, since she already knew Briella had a wealth of information in her little noggin, more than Marian thought she should but could not prevent her from knowing. Fifth grade seemed too soon for kids to be popping pills, but hell, what did Marian know? Even as their parents shielded them more than Marian's parents had her, in lots of ways Briella's generation was exposed to way more than Marian had been at the same age.

Tommy had been a big stoner, and Marian had dabbled a few times. She knew, too, that he'd done harder stuff, though never with her. She wouldn't have said he had a problem with addiction, but stuff like that could still be hereditary, couldn't it?

"Was..." Marian coughed lightly into her fist, trying to find the right words. "Was Pamela taking pills she shouldn't be?"

Briella shrugged.

Marian tried again. "You know we've talked about drugs and what kinds of things are bad, right?"

"Yeah."

"You shouldn't take medicine that's meant for someone else, and you shouldn't take it from anyone else except me or Dean, right?"

Briella made a snorting laugh sound, although she didn't look as though she were laughing. "*I* wouldn't take *any* pills. Taking drugs is bad for you."

"Good. I'm glad to hear it. Something seems to be upsetting you, though. Do you want to talk about it?"

Briella sighed, long and hard, sounded desolate. "I just don't like the way my brain works sometimes. That's all."

"Are you worried about having a seizure? Because—"

Briella's face twisted into a grimace. "No. But it hurts."

"Your head hurts?" Marian's mind raced, thinking of the bump from a few weeks ago. Remembering the sight of Pamela convulsing and the sound of her mother's wail. Her heart clenched. What did any parent fear the most but an inexplicable illness in their child?

"Not like a headache. My thoughts," Briella explained. "I think so hard, and it hurts my brain sometimes. Because there's so much to learn and know, and I want to fit it all in there, but I just can't."

"You don't have to know everything, Briella. You're just a kid. You have the rest of your life to learn." Marian kissed her forehead, trying to look into Briella's eyes to reassure her, but the girl shrugged away from her grasp and went to her bed, where she climbed under the blankets and lay flat on her back, staring at the ceiling.

Marian pulled the covers up to beneath her daughter's chin. "Sleep tight. Tomorrow's going to be a great day. And next week you get to start your new school, and that's going to be even better. Okay?"

Briella closed her eyes. A tapping at the window had Marian cursing under her breath. She strode to the window, intending to scare the bird away again, but stopped herself at the last second. From inside, all she could see was her reflection in the glass, overlaying the night outside.

She turned to see Briella watching her.

"Goodnight," Marian said. "No more talk about flying away up to heaven."

CHAPTER THIRTEEN

"You're more nervous than she was. Babe, sit down. Have a mug of tea. She's going to be home soon." Dean yawned and rubbed at his eyes. Normally he wouldn't be up for another few hours, but he'd asked Marian to wake him so he could be there when Briella got home from her first day at Parkhaven.

"I can't sit." Marian wrung her hands before she realized what she was doing and dropped them to her sides. "God, Dean. I've been waiting all day long for the school to call and say there was a problem. That they changed their minds, and they're going to kick her out of there, too."

"Nobody called, because there aren't any problems," he told her gently. "Southside didn't kick her out. They offered her an opportunity, a terrific chance for Briella to really excel. Parkhaven's going to be the perfect fit for her. She's going to have access to her own lab for experiments. They're going to start her with a foreign language. That's three years before she'd start at public school. And she was so jazzed about going. It's all going to be great, Marian. I promise you."

Marian cupped her elbow in her palm and chewed on her thumbnail. "It's *not* a mutant school."

"Tommy was just being a douche. You know how he is." Dean shook his head. "Even if the school building had a weird past, that has nothing to do with the school itself."

"We should have gone with her the first day."

"You know they said it would be better if she started as normally as possible," Dean said gently. "She's not a baby, Marian. She's ten. She can handle it."

"You've heard the same stories I have. We all did. The big school up on the hill, the weirdo kids that go there. There was that kid who made the news when he built that nuclear weapon. I mean, they came out later and said it was never, you know, usable. But still." Marian gestured with both hands. "There's a reason why Parkhaven has the reputation it does, and it's not just because it used to be a psych hospital."

"My cousin's husband is the nicest guy you could ever want to meet." Dean paused to give her an encouraging smile. "Parkhaven's a good place, even if there are a few weirdos here and there. It has a waiting list for kids to get in, from all over the country. The world, even. We hear the stories because we live close to it, and schools like that always have rumors spread about them. But we got really lucky that they've made a place for Briella, so she can do the day school program."

"Maybe I ought to buy a lottery ticket, if our luck's so good." Marian tried to say the words lightly, but they fell, solid as stones, without humor.

Dean sighed and took her in his arms. Together they danced in a slow circle. She finally gave in and relaxed, resting her head on his shoulder and pressing her face to his neck. She breathed him in, the good warm scents of skin and sweat and his shampoo. She closed her eyes and let him hold her. It didn't make her any less nervous, but she was grateful for the comfort anyway.

"She should've been home by now," she fretted.

"The paperwork said to expect her at three forty-five. That's later than normal. The van will be bringing her right to the driveway. It's all going to be fine. She's not even late yet."

A quick glance at the clock showed her he was right, as usual. It would've been irritating if it wasn't also such a reassurance, a reminder of how fully she could always count on Dean. He'd never let her down.

"I just want everything to be okay," she said. "I'm worried that she won't like the new school. And then what would we do?"

"We'd figure it out, together, because that's what we do. We can go wait out front if you want. Then you can see the van coming up the street."

"Would that make me a...what do they call them? Airport mom?"

"Helicopter parent," Dean said. "Maybe. A little. But not too much."

They both started laughing, and the chuckles turned to guffaws, until Marian had to wipe away tears. Barely able to catch her breath, she straightened, turning to see Briella in the doorway. The kid's backpack looked almost as big as her entire body. Briella hung back, not coming into the kitchen.

"What are you laughing about?"

"Oh, something Dean said struck me funny. Hey, how was your first day of school, big girl?" Marian's voice sounded too bright and fake, even to herself. She tempered it with a smile and went to help Briella shrug off the straps of the oversized pack. "Are you hungry? Do you want a snack?"

"No. They give us snacks at school. Anytime we want," Briella said offhandedly. "There's not a lunch. We eat or drink when we're hungry. We don't have recess either, but that's okay, because the whole day is like recess!"

"Sounds like you had a great first day," Dean said.

Briella nodded, but spoke to her mother instead of him. "I got to pick out my locker and put my stuff in there, and I got to meet Principal Stewart too. He was super nice. My homeroom teacher is Mrs. Addison. She also teaches science and computer programming. And there's a girl in my class, her name is Aubrey, and she's got the same birthday as me, but a year older! Because the classes don't just have the same kinds of kids in them. Which means I don't have to be in a dumb class just because I'm younger."

"Wow." Marian exchanged a look with Dean over the kid's head. "It really does sound like you had a terrific first day. C'mon and sit here and tell us all about it."

"Well, Mom, I'd really like to go out back and get some fresh air. I've been working hard all day long. Parkhaven isn't like Southside. I got to do some real stuff there. I'm going to do some really great experiments." Briella said this so seriously that Marian did not dare laugh.

"Remember when you used to call them 'spearmints'?"

Briella rolled her eyes. "Yeah, well, I was little then."

"Right. Of course. Sure, you go on outside. I'll call you when it's time for dinner. Okay?" Marian shared another look with Dean as Briella let herself out the back door and into the yard. Marian made sure the door had closed behind her before she burst into another flurry of giggles. "What the hell?"

Dean looked past her, out the window. "She's running."

"What? What's she running from?"

"She's just…running," Dean said. "With her arms out. Like she's trying to fly."

CHAPTER FOURTEEN

Lunch with her father was simple, a couple of sandwiches and a glass of milk. They ate at the same kitchen table where she'd had breakfast for her entire childhood, and Marian cleaned up after so that her dad could settle himself in his recliner and watch early afternoon television. She sat on the couch in her old place. Neither of them mentioned her mother's empty chair, but it was clear that both of them noticed it.

She'd told him all about the new school and Tommy showing up. "Acting like he was Mr. Something Special. It makes me so mad at him."

"He's her father. He might not be the best at it, but the boy does try."

"Never thought I'd hear you take his side." Marian frowned.

Her father smiled. "Maybe I'm getting soft in my old age. But tell me about Briella. How's my dolly doing in the new school?"

"She loves it. In the past two weeks, she's talked more about school with more enthusiasm and excitement than she ever has."

"Good, good." Her father hesitated. "She's a good girl. In her heart."

"Yes. She is." Marian eyed him. "Dad, are you okay?"

"Fine, I'm fine. I meant to ask you to stop at the pharmacy for me," he said with a small shrug.

Marian reached to tap the buttons on the remote he kept on the arm of his chair, turning down the volume. "I just got your refills last week, Dad. Are you taking something new?"

He didn't answer her right away, and when he did, she sensed reluctance. "No, no, nothing new. But I misplaced my pills and had to order a refill earlier than I expected. Nothing to fret over," he added hastily.

She knew her dad took a prescription-strength painkiller for injuries in his hip and back. She also knew he'd been on an antidepressant since a few years after her mom's death. Those, along with more standard blood pressure and other, what he called 'old people', meds were always lined up meticulously in their bottles in the lower kitchen cabinet. He never forgot to take them on time, nor had he ever taken too many because he'd forgotten he'd previously taken some.

"What happened to the pills, Dad?" When he didn't answer, Marian shook her head, worried. "Did Antoinette's son come help her with the cleaning again?"

"It wasn't Javier," Dad said. "I know he's given me a bit of trouble in the past, but he's turned over a new leaf. We prayed on his former troubles."

The cleaning lady's son, at sixteen, had been caught lifting Dad's pain meds to sell on the street. Now, two years later, Marian still did not trust him, but she was not the one who got to decide who her father allowed into his house. She sighed, unconvinced.

"It wasn't Javier. I'm sure of it. I think…" Her dad only shook his head. "Never mind."

"I can run out right now and get them," Marian offered, and although her dad insisted it could wait, she felt better about making sure he had his medicines.

By the time she got back, he'd fallen asleep in the recliner with his mouth gaping in a way that made her uncomfortable. *He'd gotten old*, she thought with a pang. Somehow, the strands of silver she'd found in her own dark hair, the wrinkles at the corners of her eyes, those had made sense. It was life, and yet she wasn't ready to face her father growing frail.

In the kitchen, she lined the pill bottles up in their usual spots, but only after searching for the other ones, in case maybe they'd simply fallen down behind the microwave or been pushed to the back of the counter. She came up with nothing but dust and a faded photo of her parents, herself and her brother, Desmond. It had been taken on a family vacation, long ago, when Des was in high school.

Marian pinned it to the fridge with a magnet. In the living room, Dad had woken. He struggled a bit to get out of the recliner but refused her help. He hugged her hard at the front door, longer than Marian was expecting.

She hugged him back.

"You'll always be my little girl, you know that?" her father said against her cheek. "I love you, and I'm so very proud of you, Marian."

The tears came then. "I love you too, Dad."

"I'm here for you. Whatever you need. You know that too, right?"

She nodded against him, still hugging. "I know."

Her dad patted her back. "Sometimes, when we love someone, we don't always love what they do. But that doesn't mean we don't love that person. And when someone does us wrong, sometimes it can be hard to forgive them, especially when we can't understand why they might have done something to hurt us in the first place."

"Dad?" She pulled away from him. "What's going on? Did I do something?"

"No, no…" Her father waved a hand. "You haven't done anything. I just got full of my own thoughts, that's all."

"If this is about Tommy, Dad, I'm never going to think he's Father of the Year. Even if he majorly steps up his game, which I don't think he is capable of—" Marian cut herself off and shrugged, watching her father's expression. "But I guess I could try to be more charitable about him."

Her father nodded after a moment. "Sure. That sounds like a good idea."

"Dad. Are you sure you're all right?"

"Fine." He hugged her again. "I'll be just fine. We'll all be just fine."

CHAPTER FIFTEEN

The rap at the front door was a surprise. Marian hadn't been expecting any visitors or any packages. She opened the door to find Amy from across the street, holding tight to Toby's hand. In his other, he had his familiar toy train.

"Hi, Marian. Toby and I thought you and Briella might want to take a walk with us to the frog pond." Amy's bright grin was sincere.

"Come in for a second while I see what she's up to." At Amy's confused and sort of concerned look, Marian felt the urge to explain apologetically, "Briella's been working in her room all morning on some research for a school project."

"Oh, that's right, how is the new school? Toby and I have been working on his alphabet. Haven't we, big boy?" Amy bent to kiss her son's cheek and squeeze him in a display of affection so sweet Marian felt bad for considering it cloying.

"She's enjoying it a lot." Marian went to the bottom of the steps and shouted Briella's name.

"Your husband isn't sleeping?"

"He has the weekend off but went fishing with a buddy of his." At Amy's second confused and concerned look, Marian explained, "He goes once or twice a year."

Amy nodded, but her lips pursed. "I'm not sure how I'd feel about Jeff going off on his own for the whole weekend."

"I'm sure you and Toby would have a great time on your own." Marian didn't point out that Jeff, an affable man she'd met only a few times, didn't have to go fishing to be utterly, entirely and frequently absent even when he was at home. Briella had not yet come down the stairs or even replied, so she called again.

Toby held up his toy train. Marian admired it. The little boy gave her a broad grin that she returned. He was a sweetie, even if his mother did seem dead set on the path to never letting him get more than a few inches from her side.

"Hi there, Briella," Amy said brightly when Briella finally appeared. "I was just talking to your mom about taking a walk with me and Toby to the frog pond. Want to come along?"

Briella had been fighting Marian about taking care of her hair again, and it looked as though it had not been combed in weeks. Marian gave an inward, beleaguered sigh. The girl looked tired, too. Faint dark circles below her eyes and a pallor beneath her tawny cheeks.

"A walk in the fresh air would do you some good. You've been shut up inside all day," Marian said.

Briella shrugged. "Okay. That's fine."

"Let me pack a few snacks." Marian had already caught sight of Amy's kicky little pack. She was sure there'd be granola bars and juice boxes galore.

"Sure. We'll wait outside for you. It's such a gorgeous day."

"Go on outside and wait with Mrs. Patterson and Toby, Briella."

It took Marian about eight minutes to toss a few small packages of nuts and some fruit snacks into a plastic grocery bag, adding a couple bottles of water she dug out from the back of the fridge. She got out onto the front porch to find Amy watching Briella and Toby running back and forth along the small strip of front yard between the house and the sidewalk. Above them, the raven circled, cawing.

"Beautiful, isn't it? Briella said she fixed its wing after Hank Simpson hit it with his truck." Amy pointed at the bird.

Marian's mouth twisted. "Yeah. Just clipped it, really. It was fine in a couple days."

"He really shouldn't drive so fast through here. I never did talk to him about it after what happened with Briella. But he's never been very receptive."

"No, I can't imagine he would be. He's been that way as long as Dean's known him," Marian said with a small chuckle. "Generally, we leave him alone, and he leaves us alone."

They started off along the sidewalk, Briella and Toby leading the way. Toby had to take a couple running steps for every one of Briella's. Marian couldn't hear everything the girl was saying, but Briella was keeping up an entire conversation all by herself.

"They're cute together," Amy said. "Haven't you ever thought about having another one?"

Marian shrugged, uncomfortable with the question. They'd been neighbors for about a year, but this woman was essentially still a stranger. Too many people felt like it was okay to ask women about their plans for their uteruses, she thought, trying to come up with an answer that wouldn't sound rude, even if she thought Amy's question had been a little intrusive.

She was saved from answering when Amy noticed Briella and Toby had reached the end of the cul-de-sac, passing Hank's house and starting down the small path that cut between his yard and the house between his and Amy's. That house had been empty for the past six months, and the yard was overgrown, providing a border of grass and weeds to the left of the path. On the right side, Hank's electric dog fence was marked about two feet back with small white flags.

"Toby, wait for Mommy!" Amy's voice had risen high enough that Briella and Toby both turned around to look with surprised expressions.

It was because of the dog. Rufus, Hank's ill-tempered hound, wasn't always out in the yard, but today he trotted toward the boundary of the electric fence. The dog kept his distance from the flags, trained by the shock collar, but the moment Briella put a foot to the path, the dog barked and ran back and forth along the invisible barrier.

Toby, startled, began to cry until Amy got to him and picked him up. Briella didn't look frightened, but she hung back to wait for Marian to take her hand. Her little fingers squeezed.

"It's okay, Mama, he won't come beyond the fence."

The girl was trying to comfort her, Marian realized with a pang of emotion, a surge of love so deep and strong she wondered how any mother could endure it without dying a little from the force of it.

"I don't like those shock fences," Amy said in a low voice as they managed to get beyond Hank's yard and into the forest proper. "They don't seem safe. And they feel cruel."

Marian had let go of Briella's hand so the girl could run ahead to the small pond a bit farther down the path. After a moment, Amy hesitantly let Toby down to join her. She gave Marian a sideways glance.

"I admire you," she said.

Marian let out a surprised laugh. "What? Why?"

"You just seem so confident as a mother." Amy shrugged and looked awkward. "I hover. I fret. Jeff says I baby Toby too much, but you know what, he's still a baby to me. Jeff says that soon enough he won't be, and

I guess that's true, so why not let me…you know. Let him be a baby for as long as I can? Toby! Not so far ahead! See? I just…"

Marian shook her head at Amy's self-conscious laugh, and both of them stepped up the pace to get around the bend in the path so they could see the kids. "You don't have to apologize to me. I get it. I'm glad you see me as being so confident, because I can tell you, Amy, I am so, so not."

"Not so close, wait for Mommy!" Amy shouted.

Briella was the one to wait, looking over her shoulder, and she grabbed the back of Toby's overalls to haul him a step back from the pond's edge. The pond itself was little more than a drainage ditch, not deep enough to sustain fish. But it was home to a chorus of peeping frogs all summer long, even into the late fall.

The path continued toward a stream that ran along the power lines, but Marian had never hiked beyond the pond. Dean had told her that as a teen, he and his buddies had hung out by the stream, skinny-dipping and smoking weed, drinking beer. The path ended at the junkyard, where the coyotes were rumored to linger.

"Were you close with your mom?" Marian asked as they drew closer to the pond.

Amy smiled. "Yeah. She's an inspiration to me. She always had time for us, no matter what. Dinner on the table at six. Came to every school event. The whole thing. Even now, she's always there for me when I need her. How about you?"

"My mom passed away about nine years ago. But yes, we were close. We were different in a lot of ways. I know I disappointed her sometimes, mostly about religion. But I always felt like she understood me."

Amy smiled. "Oh, that must be nice for you. To have been so close to your mom, and to have such a great relationship with your daughter. I'm sure that has a lot to do with why you're such a good mom to Briella."

I don't understand Briella, Marian wanted to say. *And I don't know if I could ever have explained that to my mom.*

"Gogs!" Toby pointed at the pond, his face alight.

It was the first time Marian had heard the kid speak, and the toddler way he shouted the word made her laugh…. And it felt good to laugh, she thought, realizing it had been too long since she had. Standing on the edge of the tiny pond, watching her daughter and the neighbor boy hunting all around for 'gogs', Marian breathed in the warm fall air and let herself simply enjoy the moment.

"We're working with him on his language skills. He's a bit developmentally delayed," Amy said, sounding embarrassed. Her chin went up, her mouth giving a little wobble, but she didn't cut her gaze from Marian's. "I'm sure you've noticed."

"I hadn't," Marian assured her. Amy's admission made Marian somehow like her more.

Amy stared past her, toward the kids. "It's harder than I thought it would be. You know when they're born, you have all these big plans. I think I hold on to him so hard because I'm worried he's never going to… that he's going to have trouble. Now he's still little, you know, people give him a break. But the older he gets, the less kind people will be."

"I do know," Marian said a little too fervently.

"I got one!" Briella's breathy scream of excitement brought Marian back to herself.

"Gross," Amy said with a wrinkled nose.

Briella was squeezing the frog in one fist, its legs dangling from between her fingers. Yeah, the critter was supposed to have pop eyes, but Marian was pretty sure they were bulging from the kid's grip. She waved a hand.

"Not so tight, Bean."

"I have to hold him tight, or he'll get away!"

"You're going to squish it," Marian said, but Briella was too busy squealing at the feeling of the frog in her palm to pay attention. She sighed. "Let Toby look."

Annoyance flashed across Briella's face, but she bent to let the little boy see the frog in her hand. When he tried to grab it, though, she held it up too high from him to reach.

"No, no," she scolded. "You'll squish it."

Toby didn't cry, but giggled as Briella bent again to show him the frog, which took that moment to struggle its way free. With a shout, Briella grabbed at it as the frog tried to hop away. She caught it by one leg and lifted it, swinging, while Marian cried out for her to be careful. The weight of the frog's body was too much for it, and as Briella swung, she was left holding only the leg as the rest of it tore free.

Toby was screaming, Amy was shouting, Marian was trying to catch the falling frog. Briella held on to the single leg with a stunned look. The rest of the frog hit the dirt by the pond and lay there without moving before feebly trying to hop with one leg toward the water.

"Don't touch it," Amy told Toby, who was trying to pick it up. She gave Marian a wild-eyed look of panic.

Marian's stomach twisted at the sight of the mangled frog, and she bent to try and nudge it along to the water, even though the thought of touching it grossed her out. "Bean…"

"I didn't mean to!"

"I know you didn't. It was an accident."

From the woods on the other side of the pond, a black shape flew. It circled them, rasping out its rough greeting, before diving toward the maimed frog and stabbing it with its beak. Amy screamed again, this time lifting Toby to shield him from the sight. Marian fell back, still feeling the wind from the raven's wings on her face.

The damned thing had nearly clipped her. For a second she considered trying to wrest the now limp frog from its mouth, out of spite, but she didn't want to touch the dead thing, nor did she want to get close to that sharp beak. It was Onyx, she thought. It had to be.

"Briella, just step back. Let the bird do its thing," Marian said.

Briella didn't listen. She bent to stroke the raven's glossy feathers as it stabbed again into the frog and began gulping it down. She was murmuring to it.

"Aren't you afraid it's going to peck her?" Amy asked.

Marian pulled at Briella's shirt. The bird flew up, shrieking, slapping its feathers in Marian's face before it flew off. The smell of it, somehow dusty, feral, earthy, made her cough. It hadn't hurt her, but her skin crawled.

"Awww, Mama, you scared him away."

"You can get diseases from wild animals," Amy said.

Marian hated the raven, but she thought she might dislike Amy's constant worrying just a little bit more. "It's fine, Amy."

"Here. I have some hand sanitizer—"

"I said it was fine." Marian's words came out clipped, irritated, and she tried to soften them with a smile, but she could tell by the way Amy flinched she hadn't done a very good job.

Toby had stopped crying and now struggled to get down. He ran to Briella, who was bent back to the pond, babbling about 'gogs'. They didn't catch any more, and Marian was glad. The raven didn't return, and she was also glad about that.

"Well. Maybe we should get back," Amy said. "C'mon, Toby. We're going home now."

Briella didn't argue when Marian called her over. She scuffed the dirt with her shoe and gave Amy a solemn look. "Sorry about the frog."

"It's all right. You didn't mean to. Would you like a granola square?" Amy had dug into her pack.

Relieved the other woman didn't seem to be holding a grudge, Marian offered a package of nuts. "Would Toby like some?"

"Oh, he's allergic to peanuts," Amy said hastily. "No, thank you."

Marian put the nuts away quickly. "Sorry."

She and Amy didn't talk much as they walked back along the small path toward the cul-de-sac. Rufus the dog didn't come out barking this time, another thing for Marian to be grateful about. Briella and Toby had gone far enough ahead that it was hard to hear what Briella was telling him, though she was clearly talking a mile a minute to the littler kid.

"She's really good with him," Amy said finally as they hit the sidewalk.

It was an obvious attempt at mending a fence that hadn't really been knocked over, but Marian took it. "She doesn't spend much time with younger kids. My brother has two about Toby's age, but we don't see much of him. He and his wife live in California."

"Well, she's welcome to come over any time. It's good for Toby to interact with an older child. I think it'll help him." Amy gave Marian a sideways look and said like a confession, "Jeff and I are trying for another."

"Oh? Wow. That's…good luck. That's exciting," Marian said.

Amy grinned and nodded. "Yes. Of course, we have no idea when we'll get pregnant. We're just…you know. Trying."

"That's the fun part." Marian chuckled.

Amy's eyes widened, and she covered her mouth with her hand. "Oh!"

But they both laughed together after that, and it was nice. A moment. Marian and Amy had not been friends before this, but wouldn't it be nice if they could be? How long had it been since Marian had made a new friend? Hell, how long had it been since she'd connected with an old friend? Too long to both.

"Let's do this more often," Amy said, as though she were reading Marian's mind.

A shadow passed over them. They both looked up. It was the bird, circling. It cawed or squawked or whatever the hell sound that ravens made. It dipped lower around the children but flew off before either Amy or Marian could take more than a half step toward them.

"Onyx," Toby said clearly with a wide grin on his chubby face. "Onyx!"

CHAPTER SIXTEEN

Marian had expected the bird to be lingering at the back door when they got home, but the yard was empty. Nor did Briella mention a word about the raven. Marian made her the usual snack of apples and peanut butter, grateful beyond anything that the kid wasn't allergic. She served the snack at the kitchen table while Briella scribbled furiously in her notebook, her tongue poking between her teeth in concentration. Marian cleaned the kitchen and started dinner. She pretended not to be looking at Briella's work, but the girl caught her staring and shielded what she was writing with an arm.

Marian kept her voice neutral, trying not to seem too interested. It was obvious the girl was trying to hide what she was doing. "What are you working on, Bean?"

"Just some theories. About frogs."

Marian nodded like that made sense. She'd seen a hint of a drawing. Briella was no artist, but it had clearly been a frog.

"What do you think they taste like?" Briella asked.

"Frogs?"

Briella nodded, still keeping her arm in front of the workbook as she wrote.

Marian shrugged. "Well, in France they eat frogs' legs, so I guess they can't be that bad. But I haven't ever eaten one, and I don't think I want to. Do you?"

"I was just wondering. Why do you think it's okay for Onyx to eat the same stuff we do, but I wouldn't eat what he eats? Like, bugs and stuff. Why do you think it tastes good to him, but not us?"

"I'm not sure. That's just how we're made, I guess." Marian checked the oven temperature and, satisfied there was nothing else to do but wait for the meal to finish cooking, she poured herself a glass of iced tea and took a seat at the table.

"Who made us that way?" Briella closed the notebook with a snap and gave her mother a fierce look.

Marian took a long sip of her drink, trying to think how best to answer. She wasn't going to get away with nonsense. "Some people think God makes us the way we are."

"Grandpa does. He believes in God a lot."

"Yes." Marian nodded. "Grandpa does."

"But you don't?"

Marian tapped the table with her fingers. "I used to. When I was your age, I did."

"Why?"

"Because that's what my parents taught me to believe. I didn't have a choice."

Briella snorted in disbelief. "They couldn't *make* you believe in God and heaven. If you didn't."

"I don't mean that they forced me," Marian said. "I mean that I didn't know any different than what they told me, so I just believed it. The way you believe me when I tell you things."

Briella looked appalled. "Like what? What do you tell me that isn't true? You said we shouldn't lie! That's bad to tell kids stuff that's not true!"

Ah, shit. Marian had gotten herself caught. "My mom and dad didn't try to make me believe stuff that wasn't true. Just like I don't make you believe stuff that's not true. But sometimes, parents tell their children something when they're younger, and when they get older, the kids don't believe it any more. Like Santa. You just told me a little while ago that you don't believe in Santa anymore. But you used to. And when you were little, you loved Santa. Was it bad for me and Dean to tell you he was real, even if you don't believe in him anymore?"

Briella put her chin in her hands to think about this. "So…God and Jesus are the same as Santa, except sometimes people don't stop believing, even if they aren't real."

"Yes. Maybe. Kind of. But, Bean, don't go around saying that to anyone. It would really hurt Grandpa's feelings to hear you say something like that. Even if it's what you believe."

"Is that what I should believe?" Briella looked confused.

Marian sighed and rubbed the spot between her eyes. Both of them shared the same divot there, from frowning. "I don't know. I'm not sure what I believe, now. A person who doesn't believe in God is called an atheist. A person who's not sure about the existence of God is called an agnostic. So I'm an agnostic, but I'm hopeful that someday I might be convinced there is a God. So I'm an optimistic agnostic."

"What's that mean?"

"Optimistic means hopeful. You hope something is true."

"Optimistic agnostic," Briella repeated under her breath. "I guess that's what I am, too. But why *don't* you believe in God anymore, Mama? If you did when you were my age?"

"When Gramma died, I guess I gave up believing. I couldn't believe that if God was real, that he would have let that car hit my mom. I was really angry and sad." Marian said this bluntly, but not harshly. It was the truth, and even if her instinct was to shield her kid from stuff like this, she knew it was better to tell it.

Briella frowned and got up from her chair to come around the table and hug Marian. She was quiet. Marian pressed her face into Briella's tangled curls and held her tight.

"Grandpa says Gramma's in heaven."

"That's what he believes. Yes."

Briella pushed back a little to look her mother in the face. "But you don't?"

"I don't know. I'm not sure there is a heaven, or a hell. Some people think that you can live many lifetimes, and that after you die, you come back as someone else. But I don't believe that, either," Marian said.

Briella went back to her seat. Her brow furrowed, she pulled the notebook toward her and flipped through a few pages, too fast for Marian to see anything. She shook her head, muttering, then took the pencil and scribbled something before closing the notebook again.

"What about animals? Do they go to heaven? Do they come back as other animals, or people?"

"I don't know, Bean. I wish I had a better answer for you, but I just don't."

"If we don't go to heaven after we die, where do we go, then?" the girl asked seriously, looking to Marian for an answer, the way she had for everything else in her life. Only instead of being able to open the closet door and lift the bedskirt to show her there were no monsters, Marian was not able to just give her the right answer. One that made sense and offered comfort. One that would make her feel better.

"I think we just...don't go anywhere," Marian said.

Briella frowned harder, but then the deep groove between her eyebrows eased. She shook her head. "No. We go somewhere. We can't just end. There has to be something else."

"So, you believe in God—"

"Oh, I don't know about *that*," Briella interrupted with that casual wave of her hand and the condescending tone Marian hated. "God sounds like something people made up to keep each other from doing bad things."

Just like Santa, Marian thought.

Briella continued, "I don't think I believe in God, but I'm sure something happens to us when we die."

"Like what?" Marian asked and held her breath, unsure she wanted an answer.

She didn't have to worry, because Briella didn't have one. The girl shrugged and went back to her notebook, scribbling again. "I don't know yet."

"Briella…" Marian waited for her daughter to look up. "How did Onyx find us today at the pond?"

Briella's scribbling went still. Her eyes narrowed, but only for a second before she smiled. "Oh, he always knows where I am."

"How?"

"He's my friend." Briella scowled. "He'd be a pet if you let me keep him in the house."

"We've gone over this. It's wild. It should be free." Marian paused, remembering an earlier conversation. "You wouldn't like it if someone locked you up and put you away in a cage, would you?"

The girl looked horrified, then sly. "No! But…he wouldn't have to be in a cage. He could just live in my room with me and fly in and out of the window whenever he wants."

Something in the way the girl said this raised Marian's suspicions. "You don't let it in your room, do you? After I specifically told you it has to stay outside?"

"No, Mama."

It was a lie. Briella might be the closest thing to a genius that Marian had ever met, but she hadn't yet learned to hide her tells. The way she shifted her gaze and pursed her lips told Marian everything she needed to know. Wearily, she rubbed the spot between her eyes. "Briella…"

"Am I allergic to anything?"

The abrupt change of topic had Marian pursing her lips, an echo of her daughter's expression. "No. I don't think so. Why?"

"It must suck for kids who are. Like Toby. He's pretty dumb, though, isn't he?" Briella had bent back to the notebook, her tone casual.

"I'm sure it does, and that's not nice to say, Briella."

Briella looked up at her. "Some things that aren't nice are true."

Marian couldn't argue with that. She had also noticed how easily Briella had moved the conversation away from that damned raven. She let it go, making a note to check the locks on Briella's windows.

"Mama, would you bring back Gramma if you could?"

Marian's breath hitched. "Yes, Bean. I would."

Briella nodded as though she'd been expecting Marian's answer. She closed the notebook with a snap. "I'd bring her back if I could, too."

CHAPTER SEVENTEEN

Dean had never been the sort of man to say, "I told you so," but Marian had to admit after only a month and a half of Briella attending Parkhaven, he would've had the right to. All of Marian's fears that Briella wasn't going to fit in, that she wouldn't like the new school, that somehow there would still be problems – all of them were assuaged each day when Briella came home from school nearly incandescent with stories of the day and how much she loved her classes and teachers.

This afternoon she'd brought home a small container of metal chips and a circuit board. For the past hour or so she'd been bent over it, explaining to Dean how she'd taken it apart from a bunch of old computers the school allowed students to cannibalize to create their projects. Marian stayed back to watch, ostensibly making dinner but really just giving the two of them time together without her around. It was the first time she could ever recall Briella actively seeking interaction with Dean. She even leaned against him affectionately while she pointed out all the different plans she had for the circuit board. Dean's eyes met Marian's over the top of Briella's head as the girl pulled out her notebook to show him the scribbles of code she was working on.

"So, you're going to build yourself a new computer system?" Dean asked.

Briella frowned and pushed away from him to put her hands on her hips. "Nooooooo. I just told you, I'm studying computer programs to see how they compare to brains."

"Ah." Dean shrugged and chuckled. "How *do* they compare to brains?"

Marian had braced for a snotty reply from Briella, but she didn't go there. She flipped the pages of her notebook again to explain. The tiniest swell of jealousy swirled through Marian. The girl had been deliberately hiding her notebook from her mother, but now she was more than happy to share it with Dean. And that was a good thing, Marian reminded herself. She wanted them to bond this way.

"Well, brains just work. Unless they don't. You know, if your brain doesn't work right, you're sick. Brains use, like, electricity, but it comes from chemicals and stuff, and computers also run with electricity. The thing is," Briella said matter-of-factly, "you can't just plug electricity into a brain to get it to work again. You can do that a little bit with a heart if it's not beating, but it doesn't work with brains. If you try to fix a broken brain with a computer program, you can't just stick it in there, like with a needle and an electric current. You'll fry the brain."

"Ouch," Marian said.

Briella frowned. "Brains don't feel things, Mom."

"Still, frying it doesn't sound any good. The only thing we should be frying is fries, right?" Marian laughed at her own joke, but uneasily, because Briella looked so darn serious.

"It's called pithing," Briella continued seriously. "You do it on frogs."

Both Marian and Dean were silent, exchanging looks. Marian had dissected a frog in high school, a million years ago, set up in pairs in biology class. She could vaguely remember the smell. All those frogs had already been dead.

"Not the electric part, usually. But with a needle. It doesn't hurt them," Briella assured them.

Marian managed to say, "I'd think that killing something with a needle in its brain would hurt it, Briella."

"But it doesn't," Briella insisted as she closed her notebook and clutched it to her chest. "That's why they do it that way."

Dean gestured at the notebook. "Is that what you've been working on at school?"

"No. They don't allow us to experiment on animals at school. Only plants."

"So…how do you know this?" Marian asked reluctantly, already sure she'd know the answer.

Briella looked surprised and then, absurdly innocent. "Research."

"It sounds like gruesome research."

Briella shrugged. "It's science."

"Well, I don't have much appetite after that, but it's almost time for dinner. Go put your stuff away and get washed up." Marian waited until Briella had gathered her things and skipped out of the kitchen before she said to Dean, "It's science."

"I didn't understand ninety per cent of it," Dean said.

Marian dug into the backpack Briella had left slung over the back of the chair, but there wasn't much in there. She was used to Southside sending home dozens of papers every week. Parkhaven had a parent portal she was supposed to be logging in to. She looked at Dean with a frown.

"I guess I need to check the parent portal to see if there's something in there about the science classes? I know I went to school a long time ago, but I remember needing my parents to sign a form saying it was okay for me to dissect the frog, and that was in tenth grade bio."

"She said they weren't doing animal experiments, babe. You know how she is. She just knows a lot of stuff. I'm sure it's fine." Dean got up to peek into the pot of chili on the stovetop, giving an appreciative sniff. "Mmm."

"I should at least maybe check in with the guidance counselor. Right? She's been there over a month and nobody's even called about her," Marian said.

"They shouldn't have had any reason to. But if you're worried, log in to the parent portal after dinner, if it will make you feel better." Dean hugged her, pressing a kiss to her temple.

Marian looked up at him. "Tell me I'm not turning into Amy Patterson."

"Huh?"

"From across the street," Marian explained. "She's uptight. Super involved with her kid. Umm…that sounded shitty."

Dean laughed. "Helicopter mom."

"Right. That."

"No. It's a new school. It's good to check in. But now, I'm starving. Can we eat?"

★   ★   ★

After dinner, Dean insisted on cleaning the kitchen before he had to leave for work. Briella had gone out back to leave a pan of slightly burned corn bread and her leftover chili for the raven. It, in turn, had left her a few new trinkets of shiny metal that Briella showed off.

"I told him to bring me something I really needed," Briella said with a laugh. "He's a good old bird."

Marian tried to log in using the ancient desktop, but no matter how many times she put in the username and password they'd sent her, the portal refused to load. Frustrated, Marian muttered a curse and went in search of Briella.

"I need you to help me," Marian said in the utterly defeated tone of an adult woman who has to rely on her preteen child to help her with technology. "I can't get into the parent portal."

"Oh, Mama, that's because you need to use a different browser." Briella's fingers danced over the ancient keyboard. She also got an error message and gave her mother a look, then a shrug. "This computer is really old. Maybe you can't log in on it."

By this point, Marian was too frustrated to want to keep trying. She pulled Briella onto her knee, aware for the first time in a while how much she'd grown. Not just in height – the girl was still tiny. But her features had gone leaner, her expressions more mature.

"Never mind. It's getting late." Marian hugged her daughter tight, closing her eyes. "You know, when you were a baby, I would sometimes wish you'd never grow up. I wanted you to stay small and squishy forever."

Briella squirmed out of her mother's grip. "You wouldn't really like that. Anyway, I'm going to grow up, unless I die. So you shouldn't want me to not grow up."

"Of course I want you to grow up. That's not a nice thing to say." Marian circled Briella's wrists with her hands to look at the girl. "I love you, Briella."

"Love you too, Mama."

Dean left for work at nine thirty, and Briella had kept up the habit of putting herself to bed earlier than had been her previous practice. Marian had started finding herself at a bit of a loss. Ten at night still felt a little too early for sleep, even though if she stayed up too much later she was tired in the morning, but having the quiet house to herself at night was different from having that same time in the morning before Dean got home from work.

Tonight, she sat at the kitchen table, leafing through a cookbook that had belonged to Dean's mother. It was the sort that had been printed on thick paper and spiral bound, sold to raise funds for the church. *Recipes from Our Friends*. Marian had a chuckle at the familiar recipes for peanut butter no-bakes and friendship bread.

The idea of a part-time job was still in the back of her mind, but far away. The whirlwind of Briella getting into Parkhaven and all the preparation to get her ready had derailed Marian's urge to look for work. With all the other changes going on, adding one more didn't seem like the best idea.

What would she do instead? Make friendship bread all day? Mop the floors?

The soft tapping at the back door did not, at first, rouse her. It wasn't until the large, sharp rap happened that she twisted in her chair and let out a startled yelp. Of course she saw nothing but darkness through the back door's square four-paned window. She braced herself for another blow to the glass, already getting out of her chair and heading for the door.

It was that damn raven – she knew it, even though it was well past dark and it should have been in its nest by now. Or wherever the hell it spent the night. Marian grabbed a broom to yank open the back door, ready to swat.

All she found was the empty corn bread pan that Briella had forgotten to bring back inside. No raven. Not even the hint of wings in the night's chilly air that sent a shiver up and down her spine so that she clutched her cardigan closer around her.

Something rustled in the leaves clustered around the bottom step of the small back porch. Marian froze, brandishing the broom. The back porch light fixture had four chandelier bulbs in it, two of which she now saw had burned out. This cast the yard into a pattern of shadow. Another shift of motion in the leaves had her straining to see what it was. Not big enough to be a raven, even one being sneaky and trying to hide, and they didn't do that. Did they?

Using the end of the broom, she poked at the spot in the leaves that had been moving. At first, nothing. Then with another slight poke, a slow-moving shadow separated from the shadows. When she saw what it was, she first screamed and recoiled even as her laughter hissed out of her in stutters.

It was just a toad. A fat old toad. They often hung out in the dampness under the porch, but that was in the summer. Didn't they hibernate in the winter? Like the frogs in the pond?

A flash of green in the leaves had Marian poking aside the leaves again. She caught sight of a smooth green back, kicking legs, but then it was gone and she couldn't find it again. Toads were brown. Frogs were green. Marian dragged the broom through the leaves but upturned only a few scuttling beetles. From far across the yard, she thought she caught sight of another set of shadows, maybe heard a faint, rasping caw. But only maybe.

She went upstairs to stand in Briella's doorway. The girl's soft breathing meant she was asleep, one small foot flung out of the covers. Marian crossed to tuck her daughter more firmly into bed.

The ever-present notebook was open next to her on the bed, a pencil stuck between the pages. The end of it was chewed. Marian grimaced. She pulled it gently toward her, trying not to disturb Briella, who muttered and smacked her lips in sleep.

Marian took the notebook, intending to put it in the girl's backpack, but an illustration stopped her. Briella had still been drawing frogs. She'd printed out some diagrams of their brains and nervous systems and taped them inside, as well. Her scribbled code meant nothing to Marian, whose heart nevertheless began thumping as she turned the page. More printouts, more scribbles. Another drawing, this time of a raven, sketched heavily in graphite. She didn't need the written ONYX beneath the drawing to know what it was representing. On the next page, an article about a girl in England who'd befriended a raven that had rewarded her for feeding it by bringing her special treats. Mostly shiny things.

Sometimes, other things it somehow sensed she wanted or needed.

"Mama?"

Marian snapped the notebook closed and turned to see Briella sitting up in bed. "Hey, kiddo."

"What are you doing with my notebook?"

"Putting it in your backpack for school tomorrow so you don't forget it." Marian cleared her throat. "You must've been working hard on something, if you fell asleep with it there."

"Yeah. I had some good ideas for my project." Briella yawned and settled back into her pillow.

"Briella," Marian said before she could stop herself.

The girl sighed sleepily. "Hmmm?"

"You're not…what you said tonight at dinner, about the frogs. You're not experimenting on frogs at school, are you? You wouldn't lie to me about that, would you?"

"No, Mama. Lying is bad. I told you, they don't let us do things like that at Parkhaven. They even want us to be vegetarian…." Briella's voice trailed off. She rolled onto her side, away from Marian, and buried her face in the pillow.

Marian slipped the notebook into the backpack but stood watching from the doorway for another minute. The next question she asked was whispered, not nearly loud enough to wake her daughter. "Are you doing experiments somewhere other than school?"

Of course Briella didn't answer her. Marian shook off the feeling and, downstairs, showered and got into bed with a book. Outside, the wind kicked up with a small howl. Rain spattered the glass with a *tap, tap, tap* that could have been the rapping of a beak, but she didn't get up to check.

CHAPTER EIGHTEEN

Marian had always loved the library. It had changed a lot since she was a kid. New computer desks, a bright decor – hell, you could even check out ebooks right from your phone. When Briella was small, Marian had hauled her all the way across town for story times and the summer reading program, but the kid had quickly outgrown the small-town library's children's section and outpaced the non-fiction reference section, too. Even with interlibrary loan, there were too few of the books Briella wanted to read or claimed she needed for her 'spearmints', and they'd stopped going to the library regularly a few years before.

Stepping inside it now, Marian breathed in. There was nothing quite like the smell of a library. Memory, nostalgia, the anticipation of finding something great to read – it all came back to her, and she wondered why it had been so damned long since she'd treated herself to this place.

It took only a few minutes to renew her library card and get it updated with new privileges. She found a spot in a computer carrel and settled in, first pulling up the parent portal and trying once more to log in with the credentials they'd sent home. Again, she got bumped out with an error. She tried another browser, frustrated. She requested a change of password and answered the security questions to reset it.

Next, Marian pulled up a new browser window and typed in a search for the local *Merchandiser* paper. They often listed part-time and work-from-home jobs. Most of them were scams, but there might be something in there.

"Marian?"

She'd just been closing out of the computer, and at the sound of her name, turned. The blonde woman with a toddler on her hip did not at first look familiar, but after a blink or two, Marian knew her. "Jody! Omigod!"

"I thought that was you! It's been forever! What have you been up to?"

A discreet cough and a glare from the librarian had both women in giggles, a throwback to their middle school days. They moved to the library's foyer. It had been a couple years since they last ran into each other, but they caught up quickly.

"We should get together," Jody said decisively. "I mean, it's ridiculous, we both still live in town, and it's been ages. I've just been so busy being a mother.... I mean, I love my kids but damn, I just want to pee by myself once in a while. Angie and I have been trying to get a girls' night out going regularly for the past year or so, but it's so hard to schedule. Everyone's got stuff going on."

"Right," Marian agreed, although the truth was that she rarely had any stuff going on. Dean working nights was part of the reason for that, but what other excuse did she have, beyond having a basically solitary nature? "I was just thinking the other day about how I should try to get in touch with some people I haven't seen in a long time."

Jody nodded firmly and shifted her small daughter to her other hip. "It's done."

*　　*　　*

"Are you sure you're going to be all right?" Marian set Briella's backpack on the floor by the front door. The girl had insisted on bringing it so she could share her projects with her grandfather.

Marian's father nodded and smiled, an arm around Briella's shoulders. "Of course we will. Won't we, dolly?"

Briella grinned, leaning into him. "Yep."

"Okay. Bean, don't wear him out. Dad, I'm only going to be out for a few hours. But text me right away if you need me to come home earlier."

Tomorrow, Parkhaven had something called a planned V day. The V was for virtual, a day when the kids stayed home and worked on their assignments via their school-provided laptops so the teachers could meet about grades. This had worked out great, because it meant that Marian wouldn't have to get up early to make sure Briella got the van on time. This didn't mean she planned to be out late enough for it to matter.

"Was a time when you'd argue with me about staying out as late as you could." Her father laughed and looked down at Briella fondly. "We'll all be just fine."

Marian hesitated, something familiar in her dad's words that she couldn't put her finger on. "Bean, be good."

"Oh, she'll be good," Marian's father said. "She's a good girl in her heart."

Marian was still pondering this conversation when she pulled into the parking lot of the Blue Hen, a local pub that had been around forever. She and Dean used to hang out there when they first started dating. The place had changed a lot since then. New menu, craft beers, a big deck out back, that sort of thing.

She spotted Jody and Angie right away and waved. They'd grabbed a table for six toward the back. Both already had drinks as Marian slid into a chair.

"Hey!" Marian said and laughed as the server appeared at once with a drinks menu. "Wow. Okay."

"Dive right in," Angie offered.

Jody nodded. "God, I need this."

Three other friends from high school showed up in another few minutes. Marian had bumped into Rasheda, Denise and Jenn a few times over the years, and as with Jody and Angie, they all fell into laughter and reminiscing.

"I haven't been out like this in forever. My husband works nights and most weekends," Marian said, three-quarters of her cocktail finished. It had warmed her inside. Buzzed in her head.

"Wish mine did," Jenn said with a sour grimace.

The conversation turned to husbands, children. Good-natured complaining, for the most part, although Marian sensed a deeper dissatisfaction in Jenn. They ordered appetizers. Another round of drinks. Marian hadn't felt this light-hearted in a long, long time.

She lifted her glass. "I'm so glad we did this!"

The sentiment was echoed around the table. Marian checked the time and for any messages from her father, but her phone remained silent. When she made to leave, the protests from the other women convinced her to stay just a little longer.

"I'm not ready to go home yet," said Jenn. "Is it terrible for me to admit that I love my kids, but they're making me crazy?"

Silence for a moment or so as they all looked at each other.

"If it makes you terrible then I'm even worse. I actually found myself thinking last week that I was sorry I'd ever had my third." Jody hiccuped and tossed back the rest of her drink, then gave the rest of the table a guilty look.

Marian sat up straight. "I've been avoiding friends and getting a job and basically keeping myself alienated from everyone but my husband because I don't want to have to tell anyone that I am afraid of my kid. Not afraid of my kid. Afraid for her. No, no, that's not right. I'm…afraid that I'm messing her up. That the reason she struggles is because of something I did wrong."

She was buzzed, she realized as everyone at the table stared at her with wide eyes. She would have to drink some water. It was a good thing she'd told Dad she was going to be a little later – she'd need to let this fade before she could drive back to his house.

"Sorry," Marian said. "Liquor loosens lips, I guess."

"I think we all worry about that. Being the reason our kids are fucked up. I mean, my mom's the reason I'm fucked up," Angie said, but with a laugh and a shake of her head that made it clear she wasn't completely serious.

Relieved, Marian let the conversation turn away from her own internal mess. More drinks arrived. She was glad she'd come out tonight. Glad she'd said what she did, not only for the support but because admitting it aloud had been like ripping off a bandage covering an old wound that wouldn't heal.

"I can't," she said when the server arrived to ask if they wanted another round. "I really have to be able to drive home soon."

"Take a Ryde," Angie urged her when she said this. "I had my hubs drop me off, but I plan on calling for a car to get home. You can leave your car here and pick it up in the morning."

"I'm a little old to be getting too hammered to drive on a Thursday night," Marian protested with the suspicion it was already too late.

Rasheda shook her head. "Bite your tongue!"

"I'm ordering you another drink if the waitress comes back before you do," Jenn said.

Marian made it to the bathroom, laughing to herself and weaving only a little. It wasn't until she was heading back to the table that she spotted Tommy leaning on the bar. He'd shaved and had a haircut. He cleaned up nice, she thought begrudgingly, hoping he didn't see her.

Of course, he did. "Fancy meeting you here."

"I'm having a girls' night out," Marian said with as much dignity as she could, considering she was having trouble not giggling.

"You're drunk."

"I'm buzzed," she said, lifting a finger to admonish him.

"Buzzed and out with the girls. What does Dean think about it?" Tommy smirked.

Marian had not thought to text Dean any updates. He was at work and likely wouldn't check his phone anyway. She gave Tommy an arched eyebrow. "What's it to you?"

"Just curious." Tommy raised his hands. "Don't bite my head off."

"I'm going to get back to my friends."

"Mare," he called after her before she got more than a couple steps away. "Hey. How's the kid?"

"She's fine. Doing great, actually."

He nodded. "We should get together. Talk about her."

"Sure." She felt agreeable right now. Warm and fuzzy and buzzy and muzzy-headed. Not in the mood to argue with her ex.

Back at the table, they had indeed ordered her another drink. Her phone hummed with a voicemail from her father's missed call. He assured her that all was well, she didn't need to rush home. Encouraged her, in fact, to stay out later. Marian checked the time again. It was only ten o'clock.

The final drink did her in. Even with the water and cheese sticks, she was way too buzzed to drive. The gathering was breaking up, everyone whipping out their phones to call for rides – the problem nobody had anticipated was that there weren't enough cars for all of them. Marian, who'd had to download the app before she could try to get a Ryde, was looking at a forty-minute wait before anyone could get to her.

But, there was Tommy.

He'd been chatting up a slim redhead in a too-tight T-shirt, but when Marian walked up to him, he turned. "What's up?"

"Could you give me a ride to my dad's house?"

Tommy laughed. "The hell? Mare?"

"I drank too much." She leaned around him to wave a hand toward the younger woman. "Don't mind me. I just need a ride. I'm the baby mama. No drama."

The other woman's expression creased into dismay, but Tommy turned on the charm. "I'll call you later."

When she'd gone, Marian burst into laughter. She had to hold on to the bar to keep herself from swaying. "Sorry. Did I cockblock you?"

"I wasn't going to take her home." Tommy put a hand on her shoulder. "Steady, there."

"I tried to call for a Ryde, you know, that car app thing. But there weren't any. I need to get home. I mean back to my dad's. He's watching Briella. But I told him I'd be home, not too late. It's not too late, right?" She tried to shake off the pervasive, lingering, boozy feeling, but it had been so long since she'd had more than a glass or two of wine that she was having a hard time.

"I can drive you. No worries. I'm not a total asshole."

"No," Marian said after a second. "No, you're not."

CHAPTER NINETEEN

"Reminds me of all those times I snuck you home after curfew," Tommy said as they pulled into the driveway.

Marian laughed. Inside the house, the flickering blue light of the TV shone through the front windows. She had not yet sobered up, although her head was aching a little and her stomach wasn't too happy with her, either.

"That was a long time ago," she said.

"Don't go in just yet." At the sight of her narrowed eyes, Tommy added, "I want to hear about Briella."

Marian looked again toward the house. "I should get in there."

"You're not driving home tonight, right?"

"Of course not."

"So you have a few minutes," Tommy said. "It's not even midnight, Mare. Talk to me."

He'd always been so charming. Certain of getting his way. Marian stifled a yawn and assessed her need to pee. She gave Tommy a glance.

"Ten minutes," she told him.

"I want to know what's going on at Parkhaven," he said.

She gave him a steady look. "You said you were going to come around more often. Briella doesn't notice, Tommy, but I do."

"Been busy. I do mean to. Hey. I'm here now, right? Asking you about her? Trying to stay informed?"

"It's not the same," she told him, "but then I'm not surprised."

"You always were more honest when you'd been drinking."

Marian laughed. "You want to know about your daughter and the new school? Well, Tommy, surprise, surprise. She loves it. She's thriving there. She's always been a learner, you know? She's smart."

"Fucking genius." Tommy sounded proud, but for once this didn't annoy her.

She yawned again and looked at him. "You need to be consistent. She needs that from you."

He had the grace to look guilty. "You never seemed that happy to have me around. Makes it awkward."

"Because I couldn't count on you. You're not reliable. You don't stick around when things get hard, Tommy." She twisted in her seat to look at him as she unbuckled her seat belt.

"I know that."

Marian sighed. "Thanks for the ride. I'm really tired, and I'm really, really wishing I hadn't had that last drink. Come around more often. Get to know your kid better. Just…call first, okay?"

He laughed. "Yeah. Okay. Hey, Mare?"

"Hmmm?"

"Remember when you told me 'If you kissed me right now, I would stick my finger down my throat to puke the taste of you off my tongue'?"

She laughed at the memory, then winced. "Yeah. I remember."

"Would you still?"

"Tommy," Marian said warningly, moving toward the car door and putting up a hand. "Don't you dare."

"Sorry. I just want you to know that I do realize how bad I fucked up. I know you think I don't, or that I didn't care. But I did then, and I still do. I know you've got a good life going on, and I guess part of the reason why I don't come around as much as I should is because I envy your life." Tommy said all of this matter-of-factly, without drama, but more sincerely than Marian could ever recall him being.

"Wow." For a moment she could say no more than that. Then she shook her head. "Thank you for saying that."

Her dad had been right, she thought as she got out of the car and headed for the front door. About giving Tommy some slack. Her dad had always been right about a lot of things.

She found her father in the recliner, the television turned low to some game show she didn't recognize. Briella was asleep on the couch. Marian got her up as quietly as she could, walking her first to the bathroom to go before she took the girl upstairs and tucked her into the double bed in Marian's old room.

Downstairs, Marian drank a glass of water and took some aspirin against the coming-on hangover. The swell of applause from the living room blocked out most of another noise, a hacking kind of squawk that raised the fine hairs at the back of her neck. She froze, listening for it.

There. Again. A cackle, almost. And then a low warble, tuneless but familiar. Disgustingly familiar. More singing from that fucking raven. Her throat closed as her stomach lurched, threatening to spill a hot mess of bile out of her mouth.

"Dad?"

When the noise came one more time, Marian ran for the living room. She expected to find him convulsing, a hand on his heart. Or worse, that fucking bird hovering over him, pecking at his eyes.

As she watched, her father's mouth dropped open. He let out that noise, that horrible, terrifying noise. A caw, muttered and whispery, the sounds Briella's damned raven made when it had been caged in the den.

"Dad!"

Her father snorted, struggling upward from the chair. "Wha'? Marian? What's happening? Are you okay?"

She grabbed for his hand. "Are you okay? You were making funny noises."

"I'm fine. I was dreaming...." Her father waved his other hand, trailing off.

Marian sank onto the couch, swallowing hard, over and over, against the sour taste in her throat. She was shaking. Her fingers linked through his.

"What were you dreaming about? Was it a bird? A big black bird?"

Her father looked startled. "No, dolly girl. I was dreaming about the angels tapping on the windows. Oh, and singing. They were singing to me. But I can't remember the song now. I'm sorry I scared you."

"I had a little too much to drink, Dad. My head's fuzzy. I'm going to stay the night here, okay?"

"Of course, of course." He craned his neck to catch a glimpse of the clock. "What time is it?"

"Late. Let's get you to bed too, okay?"

"Ah...no, no. I'm going to sit here for a bit. I like to watch the late programs."

"It's not good for you to sleep in your chair, Dad. You should get to bed."

"Marian," her father said gently, "I've been sleeping in this chair for the past nine years. I think one more night won't hurt."

Guilt flooded her. How could she not have known this? Still, she wasn't going to argue with him, not now. She didn't have the fortitude for it.

"Go to sleep. When you wake up, I'll make you and Briella pancakes. Okay? Just like when you were a little girl." Her father squeezed her hand.

It had been quite a night. Marian brushed her teeth and pulled her hair into a soft pineapple puff on top of her head. She didn't have the time or energy for more than that tonight. She changed into a T-shirt and shorts from her old dresser and climbed into bed next to Briella. She texted Dean to let him know she was staying over. After a moment's hesitation, she texted Tommy to thank him for the ride.

She was asleep shortly after her head hit the pillow, but slept restlessly, with lots of bad dreams.

★   ★   ★

She woke later than she'd planned, with a dry mouth and headache, though thankfully that was the worst of it. Briella was not in the bed beside her. The rise and fall of voices through the heating vent told Marian her daughter and Dad were in the kitchen. The smell of pancakes wafted up too.

Downstairs, Marian watched him expertly flip the pancakes, making Briella giggle. Dad looked better than he had in a long time. Chipper, lively, moving about the kitchen without any hint that he might be in pain. He made no mention of the dreams or angels tapping at the windows or anything else.

"You come back and stay with me again," he told Briella. To Marian, he added, "You too."

It took a short trip in a Ryde to the bar parking lot to get her car. Briella buckled herself into the backseat of Marian's car without a word. Marian looked in the rearview mirror, trying to catch her gaze, but Briella was staring out the back window.

"Are you tired, Bean? Did you and Grandpa have a good time? Did you stay up too late?"

"Yeah. We did." Briella yawned. "I love Grandpa."

"Me too." They drove a little farther before Marian added, casually, "Did he talk to you about anything you want to talk about with me?"

Briella looked up and met her mother's eyes in the mirror. "Like what?"

"Like anything."

They drove a little longer, turning onto their street. Briella said nothing. Marian didn't ask again until they'd pulled into the driveway. She shut off the car and twisted in her seat to look back.

"Did he talk about…angels? Tapping at the windows? Or singing?"

Briella laughed. "There's no such thing as angels."

"Bean…did Onyx come to Grampa's house last night?" Ice crystallized in Marian's chest as she waited for Briella to answer her.

"No, Mama. Onyx didn't come to Grandpa's house."

Marian looked hard, but if Briella was lying, she'd at least learned to do it better.

CHAPTER TWENTY

Marian was suspicious about a school like Parkhaven having 'show and tell'. She was still having trouble logging in to the parent portal – no matter how many times she changed her password, it never seemed to stick – but there'd been an email reminder about the upcoming event, so she guessed it was legitimate. She'd suggested Briella take in one of her music boxes from the collection Marian had started before the girl was born, but that idea had been met with a rolling of eyes and a huffed breath.

"I'm going to take Onyx."

The kid still fed the damn bird dinner scraps and spent time every evening talking to it. As far as Marian could tell, it still brought her trinkets, but as November got colder, Briella spent less time outside with it. Marian had started hoping it was the end of what had been an odd obsession, replaced with whatever it was Briella was working on at school, whatever she was filling notebook after notebook figuring out.

Marian sighed and shook her head. "Briella, you know you can't."

Briella put her hands on her hips, looking startlingly like Marian's mother. The kid was a chameleon. "Why not? Onyx's really awesome, and Braxton D. brought in his baby sister last week. Alicia brought her new puppy."

"It's not a pet. Or a baby. It's a wild animal. How would you even get it there?"

"I'll just tell him to meet me at school and wait until it's time for show and tell. Then I'll open the window, and he can fly in," Briella said.

Marian's eyebrows lifted, but she thought of the day at the frog pond. "That would be a good trick, wouldn't it?"

"I haven't been teaching him *tricks*." The girl had tomato sauce from their ravioli dinner, eaten an hour ago, clustered in the corners of her mouth. Her hair had been done up in a couple of cute ponies for school that morning, but they'd come half-loose now. Her pale pink shirt was filthy with smudges. One nostril was rimmed with dried snot that turned Marian's stomach.

She grabbed a paper towel and dampened it. "Wipe your face, please."

"Tricks are behaviors learned to gain rewards."

"So what are you teaching it, then?" Marian turned back to the counter to finish wiping it down. The worn pattern on the Formica reminded her of a fifties sitcom, but here in this kitchen, there was no laugh track to remind her that this argument could seriously be a comedy.

Briella snorted under her breath. "I'm not teaching him anything. He already knows how to do everything."

"And you really think you can just tell him to show up at school tomorrow?"

"I can tell him to do anything," Briella said. "He'll do it, because he's my friend. But I won't tell him to do something *bad*, Mama."

Marian turned to look at Briella's wide-eyed and forcefully innocent expression. "Why would you?"

"I won't," Briella insisted.

"What bad thing have you told it to do, Briella?"

A silence fell between them, tense and twisting. Marian had spoken too sharply. Too accusing. In the face of Briella's blankly cheerful expression, she felt ridiculous.

"Nothing," Briella said. "I'm just going to go tell him to come to school for show and tell. That's all. Can I give him this piece of garlic bread?"

"You know I don't like you wasting food on the bird," Marian said, but relented because although Briella wasn't going to eat it, she'd already put her dirty fingers all over it and it was only going into the trash, anyway. "Fine. But you have five minutes, that's it. It's dark outside."

Cold, too. Autumn had been unusually warm, but winter was coming on hard this year, and Marian shivered as she pulled her oversized cardigan closer around her. The wind from the open back door tickled her under the chin.

On the back porch, Briella whistled. "Onyx! C'mere! I have a treat for you!"

Briella held up the piece of garlic bread. She called again for the bird. Marian stepped closer, getting in range in case something happened.

"Close the door," Marian said sternly, but too late. The bird was in the house, flapping its enormous wings and landing neatly on Briella's shoulder.

"Briella," it said. "Hello, Briella. Give a treat, please. Give a treat."

The look her daughter gave her was purely smug and somehow adult. It pushed Marian back a step. Where had her little girl gone?

Briella stepped out onto the back porch and put the garlic bread on the railing. The raven hopped from her shoulder onto it and pecked at the food. It paused to tilt its head, one bright and unblinking eye studying Marian before it went back to eating.

"You've been teaching it more words?"

Briella shrugged. "Ravens are really smart. I told you that before. Like as smart as chimps, and chimps are as smart as little kids. I mean, Onyx's probably smarter than Toby Patterson."

The bird had finished the garlic bread. Now it ruffled its feathers while burbling something incomprehensible. There were words, but Marian couldn't make them out.

"Onyx, you should come to school with me tomorrow. I'll go in the white van. Okay? You follow the van, and you come to school with me. Good night now, Onyx. Good night."

"Good night, good night." The bird's beak only barely opened with the words, but its throat worked before it flew away.

"Ravens don't talk like people do," Briella said as though Marian had made a comment about it. "They don't have lips like ours. Their vocal cords are different. But that doesn't mean they don't understand what they're saying."

"It's just mimicking."

Briella shook her head and allowed her mother to draw her back inside. "Nope. He understood me. He'll go to school with me tomorrow. You wait and see."

Marian had a hard time believing that, but there was no point in arguing about it. "You know, there are other birds that can learn to talk."

"Yeah. I know."

"If you want, we could get you a parakeet or something. A pet you could keep in the house. Wouldn't you like that better?"

"Right," Briella said in a voice dripping with scorn. "Onyx would probably peck it right in the face!"

Marian flinched, then frowned. "What does that mean? It would peck it in the face? Is Onyx nasty like that?"

"Everyone's nasty like that," Briella said under her breath.

Marian put a hand on the girl's shoulder to turn her. "What does that mean?"

"Just that people are horrible." Briella shrugged off her mother's grip.

"Is someone being mean to you at school?"

Briella looked surprised. "At Parkhaven? No."

Marian took another damp paper towel and gripped Briella tighter to keep her still while she wiped her face clean. When she'd finished, she put both hands on Briella's shoulders. Looked into her eyes. Looked hard.

"You know you can talk to me about anything. Right?"

Briella nodded. "Yes. I know."

"If you have something bothering you. If something is upsetting you. If…" Marian cleared her throat, uncomfortable. "If you're still having trouble with feelings, or like your brains are too full…."

"No, Mama. Not anymore."

"Good." Marian hissed out a sigh of relief. "That's good. I love you, Bean."

"Love you, too, Mama." The kid hugged Marian hard enough to cause a little *oof* of breath to come out of her.

Marian closed her eyes and held her daughter tight. Tighter. She thought of what her father had said, twice now. "We're all going to be fine."

We're all going to be fine.

CHAPTER TWENTY-ONE

It had been a while since Marian had run the vacuum upstairs. Hauling the heavy machine up the narrow staircase was a pain in the ass, and with Dean sleeping during the day, Marian usually tried not to make too much noise. Today, though, it was time. With Briella putting herself to bed, it had been weeks since Marian had been upstairs, but last night she'd taken up some laundry and noticed the rugs were gritty with dirt. The hardwood floor wasn't much better.

Briella was supposed to keep her room at least tidy – toys and books put where they belonged, clothes in the dresser or the closet and not on the floor, the bed made. Marian had low expectations of how competently any of these tasks were completed, but she did expect some kind of effort.

What she'd walked into this morning was a disaster. It hadn't been such a mess even the night before, but now Marian had to actually pause in the doorway to make sure she was seeing things right. The entire room had been trashed.

"Damn it," she muttered.

Briella had been late coming down for breakfast. Marian had needed to call her several times before she did. What the hell had she been doing up here this morning? Or, Marian thought with a slow spiral of unease uncoiling inside her, all night long?

Had the girl looked tired at breakfast? Marian had been too concerned with the tangled mess of her hair, the fact she was refusing to wash her face or brush her teeth, that she was trying to get away with wearing a dirty uniform instead of the clean one Marian had directed her to. All of that had taken Marian's attention, but if she thought hard, hadn't it seemed like Briella was more than just reluctant to obey, but working against exhaustion?

She looked around the room again. It was easy to imagine Briella roaming the room all night long, destroying it. What Marian could not imagine was why.

She didn't want to imagine why. Instead, she focused on cleaning up the mess. One thing at a time. Dirty clothes into the hamper. Books lined up neatly on the shelf.

Under the bed, Marian found a cardboard box that she recognized as one she'd tossed in the garbage a week or so before. With a mutter, she pulled it toward herself. It clattered as she did. She found the earbuds she'd been missing for a few months, the rubber coating stripped off to expose the wires beneath. Also a few rectangles of metal and plastic that said 'USB flash drive' on them, but which she'd never seen before. Small screws, tiny enough to be used in eyeglasses, along with a screwdriver small enough to fit them. Other bits of metal and wire she didn't recognize, all of it jumbled together as messily and without care as the rest of Briella's belongings.

Also, an inky black feather.

She stared at it for a half a minute, not wanting to touch it even to push it aside to see what else the box contained. When she did, the stiffness of it scratched the back of her hand. Distaste curled her lip. Beneath it hid more assorted bits and pieces of what looked like garbage to her. A tangle of wire caught her attention. The ends of it were a different color than the rest, dark and coppery. When she scraped at them with her fingernail, the darkness flaked off. Rust, she told herself and let the tangle of metal fall back into the box. Or dirt.

Finally, the small notebook caught her eye. She still saw Briella using the big notebook the girl had been scribbling in for years, but this smaller one was unfamiliar. It was about the size of her palm, with a flip-top cover. At least half the notebook was filled with tight lines of writing. Some of the pages had been crossed out, others torn jaggedly, leaving behind only scraps. Equations, numbers, an indecipherable mess of code. Marian couldn't understand any of it, except for several notations of numbered experiments. So far, only two of them.

Over the years, she'd found plenty of Briella's 'spearmints.' This was more of the same. A box of junk that Briella would insist was important, and to her, it would be – at least until the next idea hit her, and she moved on to something new. Marian was tempted to toss the entire box, but she didn't. Her own mother had once gone through her room and thrown away all the 'junk' Marian, for whatever reason at the time, had wanted to save. She'd never forgotten the sense of betrayal and grief, even if now as an adult she couldn't recall why those broken bits and pieces of things had meant so much. Instead, she pushed the box back beneath Briella's bed and resolved to ask her about it.

When Marian's phone hummed from her pocket, she pulled it out to look at the screen. "Hey, Tommy. What's up?"

"Checking your Thanksgiving weekend plans."

Marian paused and sat on the edge of Briella's bed. "I'll be cooking at my dad's the way we always do for Thanksgiving. Not much going on the weekend after. Why?"

"I was hoping to take the kid," he said. "To my parents' house."

Marian thought about this for a minute, reluctant to agree but knowing if she didn't, she'd be the hypocrite. "The whole weekend?"

"Or only Friday to Saturday, if that's better." His voice lowered. "I'm trying, like I said I wanted to."

"I'll have to check with her, but yes. I think that will be fine."

He sounded happy when he answered. "Great. Terrific. Thanks, Mare."

"Sure." She looked around the room at the mess and nudged the box with her foot. "Tommy, remember that time you tried to build a time machine?"

"Yeah." He laughed.

"What made you think you could get it to work?"

"Umm...a fuckton of weed and Coors Light."

Marian smiled. "You worked on it for a couple weeks straight."

"Never got it to work, though. Maybe I should've been drinking Bud." Tommy laughed again. "Why'd you bring that up?"

"Just thinking about our kid and where she gets stuff from. I just found a box under her bed full of what looks like trash. It reminded me about how you always thought you could build things."

"She's a little young for weed and shitty beer," Tommy said.

"I don't think she's smoking or drinking. I think she's just...smart," Marian said after a moment.

"I guess she'd get that from you, then."

Awkward silence descended.

"Just let me know about next week," Tommy said, breaking it.

"I will. I think it'll be fine."

They disconnected. Marian finished vacuuming the room. She didn't look again in the box under the bed. In fact, she put it out of her mind. They'd all be fine, she reminded herself. All of them.

CHAPTER TWENTY-TWO

"Don't worry about her," Dean said as he kissed Marian's temple and laced his fingers together at the small of her back. Keeping her solid and steady. He'd met her at the front door and hadn't let go of her since. "He'll take care of her."

Marian sighed. Her agreement to let Tommy take Briella for the weekend felt too hasty now that she'd dropped the kid off at his parents' house. "He's not reliable, Dean. No matter what he says about wanting to be different, I know he's not."

"First of all, you know exactly where she is. His mom and dad are both there, so it's not like he's got to do the whole parenting thing all on his own," Dean said.

"That makes it worse," Marian said. "His parents…ugh. Just because his mother has cancer, that doesn't make her a good person."

Dean didn't reply at first, although she could see him chewing on his words. He'd heard stories about her former mother-in-law, but he hadn't really had occasion to see the woman in action. His own mother had been as close to a saint as a woman could be, much like Marian's own. She knew that Dean believed her when she told him Tommy's mom was a bitch and a half, but Dean was…Dean was good, Marian thought as she watched him struggle with what he wanted to say. He was good, and therefore it was hard for him to imagine that not everybody was.

Instead of speaking, Dean kissed her mouth. She melted a little bit under that embrace. When he made as though to pull away, she grabbed him. Held him close. She breathed him in. Cologne, soap, laundry detergent, an organic, earthy scent from him raking leaves, machine oil. Under everything else was Dean's own particular smell, the one that had driven her crazy from their very first date. Their chemistry had always been out of control and had never faded. Even now, she loved to press her face to the furriness of his armpit and breathe him in, over and over. Yes, she knew that was sort of weird and a little gross. Still, she couldn't get enough.

"If you're worried—" he began, but she shushed him with another kiss.

"It's not that," Marian admitted and tucked her head into the curve of his neck. "I'm jealous."

Dean pushed her away to look at her face. He frowned before a slow, teasing smile tipped one corner of his lips. "Of that jackass?"

"She was so excited to go with her dad. And she's been acting so different lately...." Marian swatted him. "Stop looking at me like that."

Dean gathered her close again to nuzzle her mouth, then the line of her jaw. The sensitive places on her neck. When he nibbled her there, Marian shivered, her body responding the way it always had – and, if they were lucky, the way it always would.

"Briella loves you, baby. If she's excited about going with her dad, it's because she doesn't get to see him a lot. And he's usually taking her to fun places and doing fun things. He gets to be the good guy, and that's automatically going to make him more popular."

"He's *not* the good guy," Marian said with a frown, biting out the words before she could stop herself.

She'd promised herself she wouldn't keep holding Tommy to account for his mistakes for the rest of his life. She'd vowed to give him the chance to prove he could... Well, if he couldn't make up for the shit he'd pulled in the past, at the very least she could give him the chance to prove he wasn't going to keep making the same mistakes. He'd asked her for that much, and even if she didn't believe she owed him anything, what did it cost her to be kind?

"*You're* the good guy," she said anyway, because that was the damned truth. "You're the one who's been there for her. Not him. I guess it makes me mad and jealous that he gets to swing in here with a handful of balloons and make her life a party."

Dean didn't answer that. Not with words. He rested his forehead against hers, his breath softly puffing over her face, until Marian closed her eyes and breathed him in again. This time with long, slow breaths, until she felt like he'd filled her up.

"She deserves a little bit of a party, though. Doesn't she?" Dean kissed her temple again. "The kid's had a bunch of shit going on lately. Big changes. The new school, new kids, all of that. She's been working herself hard. Let her have the party. She's going to have to buckle down and deal with reality soon enough."

Marian wanted to be the one to give Briella that freedom. She wanted it to be Dean, not Tommy, who made the girl's eyes light up. She frowned, trying hard to be a better person.

"You're my everything, Dean. You know that? I love you so much."

Dean's hands slipped down her back to her ass, nudging her closer to him. "I love you, too. You okay?"

She wasn't, but she didn't want to waste their first night alone in so long by dwelling on stuff she couldn't change. Marian nodded. She kissed him again, pressing closer to him. Heat grew in her lower belly as the kisses deepened. Her breath caught, rasping in her throat.

"Yeah. I'm fine."

"I know something that will make you feel better." Taking her hand, Dean led her from the living room into the kitchen.

Marian gasped. He'd set the table with a real cloth and those disposable plastic plates that looked like real china, with matching plasticware that looked like silver. He'd even added wineglasses. Candles flickered, and on the stove a pot of something smelled good.

She faced him. "What...? How did you...? Oh my God, Dean, what did you do?"

"Made you dinner," he said as though it were the most natural thing in the world for her to come home to something fancier than pizza or reheated turkey leftovers. "I figured you deserved it. You spent all day cooking yesterday. And I don't get to do nice things for you too often."

"You do nice things for me every day," Marian protested. Instead of arguing further, she kissed him again. "But thank you, this looks awesome."

"Sit." He pulled out the chair for her, then poured them each a glass of wine as he took the seat across from her. "Toast."

"You go first," she said, feeling shy. Not sure what to say that would be meaningful enough to compete with this effort he'd made.

Dean lifted his glass. "To me and you."

"To us." Marian laughed, relieved he hadn't come out with some kind of fancy toast. Cloth napkins were a big enough change. But Dean was looking at her expectantly, and she had to say something. "Umm...let's hope we're always as happy as we are right now."

"Amen."

They clinked glasses, and Marian sipped. He'd picked an earthy red. The first sip went down hard. Thick, almost. She wasn't sure she liked it, but she wasn't about to complain, not when Dean got up to bring plates of steaming pasta with a hearty meat sauce to the table.

"Wow, you made your mom's sauce," she said.

Dean grinned. "Just like our first date."

Marian didn't mean to cry, but something about Dean's smile had the tears coming. She swiped at them quickly, not wanting to worry him. "Our first date was at the bowling alley."

"Okay, so the first time I cooked for you," Dean said with a shrug and another lift of his glass. He sipped, then frowned. "I guess one of the only times I ever cooked for you. I wanted to impress you."

"You did. You do." It was not likely that the wine was already going to her head, but Marian felt a little wobbly. She took another sip. It went down better this time. She lifted the glass again. "To my awesome husband. You're a better man than I ever thought I'd deserve."

It was Dean's turn to blink rapidly. "Ah, baby. That's…"

"It's the truth," Marian repeated. "You have been nothing but good to me and Briella since the first time you took me out. I couldn't ask for a better husband than you. I love you, Dean Blake."

Dean's chair clattered on the worn linoleum as he pushed back from the table. She was in his arms in the next second, wine sloshing as the glass tipped over. Marian didn't care. Their mouths were hungrier than her belly in that moment. The heat that had begun with his earlier kisses flared, roaring the way a campfire does with the push of wind against it.

"Bedroom," she said. "Now."

They were naked before they got through the door. The bedroom was so small it took only a few steps to get them to the bed, where they tumbled in a tangle of arms and legs. Mouths open, tongues stroking, Dean rolled them both so Marian was on top, straddling his thighs.

She reached between them to tease him fully erect, her breath catching at the feeling of him in her fist. "God, you feel so good."

Marian slowed, leaning forward to kiss him. Her hair fell down around them, tickling and shadowing his face. She let her mouth brush over his mouth, cheeks, forehead. She nuzzled his ear. Maybe Tommy wanting to spend more time with Briella wasn't going to be so bad, after all.

Marian wanted to slow down, but she hadn't been this turned on in…well, she couldn't remember how long ago it had been. She stroked him a few more times until she lifted up to fit him inside her. They both groaned as she took his length all the way, her knees gripping his hips.

"Yeah, that's it." Dean moved beneath her, a hand sliding between them so he could give her the sweet pressure of his knuckles right where she needed it.

She was going to get there fast. Hard. Marian rode him, oblivious to anything but how good it felt. She closed her eyes. Her mind, heart, body, all focused on this. Being with the man she loved. This pleasure.

This life.

Marian threw back her head as her breath came in short, panting gasps. A flicker of motion from the hallway caught the corner of her gaze. Shadows.

Too caught up in what was going on, she couldn't pay attention at first. She was tipping over, over the edge into mindlessness, more than ready to give up to it. Another flicker of movement, the shadows stretching.

Briella, in the doorway.

"Oh, shit." Marian clipped her tongue with the tips of her teeth. The pain didn't stop the pleasure coursing through her. If anything, it forced her climax to its peak. She shook with it, keeping her cry locked behind her teeth, even as she desperately tried without success to pull up the sheet to cover them.

Dean couldn't see the doorway unless he twisted, and her writhing had sent him over, too. He finished inside her with a grunt. His fingers gripped, too hard.

Right behind Briella, Tommy.

Marian didn't care as much about her ex seeing her with Dean – she wasn't much of an exhibitionist, but Tommy was an adult. And she hadn't given birth to him. And now, bless him, he was shuffling Briella away down the hall toward the kitchen while Marian finally managed to wrestle a sheet over at least her hips.

"What?" Dean asked, confused.

"It's Briella," Marian said. "She's back."

CHAPTER TWENTY-THREE

It had taken Marian about forty minutes to get Briella into bed and asleep. By the time she got downstairs, every nerve felt raw. Her hands were shaking. She went into the kitchen, ready to tear Tommy apart, but stopped at the sight of him and Dean tipping back bottles of beer. When they both turned to look at her with almost identical expressions, all the fight went out of her.

"Give me one of those," she said, pointing at the cluster of beer bottles in the Styrofoam cooler, and grabbed a jumbo bag of chips from the cupboard.

They were seconds-quality in a plain white bag. Dean brought them home from work by the case. Marian had lost her taste for them years ago, but right now she was dying for something greasy. She tore open the bag and dumped half the contents into a mixing bowl and put it on the table. She took a seat between them.

Tommy plucked a dewy, glistening bottle from the cooler at his feet and twisted off the top for her. "Is she okay?"

Marian looked at the cooler. "Where did that come from?"

"I ran out and got it," Tommy said.

"And you came back here with it? Not what I expected, to be honest. I thought you'd be long gone." She didn't know if she should be pissed off or impressed. She tipped her head back to let some cool, golden liquid bite its way down the back of her throat.

"I figured you might need backup," Tommy said. "The kid was out of control."

Marian set the bottle on the table hard enough to make beer splash out of the narrow top. "What the hell, Tommy? What happened? I give you permission to take her for the first time in, like, forever, and you're not even gone three hours before you bring her home without so much as a phone call to warn us? What the hell?"

Dean put a comforting hand on her shoulder, squeezing it, but Marian pulled away. There'd been too much of a conspiratorial expression on both their faces when she'd come into the kitchen, and she didn't like it. Dean and Tommy weren't friends, but they sure as hell looked like they were both up to something.

"It was my mom," Tommy said, but stopped to drink some beer.

The slow rotation of the world seemed to stop right then, abruptly. Marian scowled, already furious. Already guilty. She never ought to have let him take Briella to his parents' house. "What about your mother?"

Tommy didn't answer at first. He shook his head as though in defeat. He drank more beer. Shook his head again, mouth opening and closing as he fought for words that wouldn't release themselves.

Marian had plenty of words for him, but she too was having a hard time giving them a voice. To give herself time, she dug into the bowl of chips and settled a handful in her palm. She plucked out the darkest, burned ones and pushed them toward Dean. He loved them. She nibbled at a chip, savoring the salt and crunch, but couldn't force herself to eat the entire handful. Her stomach still churned. She thought she heard a thump from upstairs and froze, listening hard, but it didn't happen again.

"You'd better come out with it, Tommy. No matter what it was. Did she call Briella a retard?" Marian asked flatly when it became clear that Tommy wasn't going to answer her. "Because she has in the past."

Dean looked sick and wiped a hand over his mouth. "Jesus. She didn't."

"She never said that to Briella," Tommy protested.

"She didn't have to. She said it about her," Marian said.

"She never said it to me," Tommy shot back.

Marian guessed it was hard not to defend your own mother, even if she was a total bitch, but that didn't make it okay. "She said it to me. I should never have let you take Briella. I knew what kind of person your mother is. What she thinks about Briella, what she's always thought about her. My God, Tommy. That's your daughter!"

Tommy's guilt-stricken face told her enough. Marian got up and dumped her handful of crushed chips into the garbage, then dusted her hands into the sink and washed them. She focused on that so she didn't turn around and punch the shit out of Tommy's face.

"This was the last time. The very last. You hear me?" she said without turning.

"My mom is sick."

"Yeah. She's sick. And I don't mean the cancer," Marian said bitterly.

Tommy's chair scraped back. "She wants a chance to get to know her grandchild. She didn't say anything like that to Briella, and if she did, that was a long time ago. And honestly, didn't she have reason to? I mean—"

"Fuck you, Tommy. Get out of my house." Marian's voice was colder than the beer had been.

Dean held up a hand. "Babe, wait. Just listen to him. You need to hear."

"I don't need to hear shit," Marian spat. "I don't care if his mother decided that all of a sudden she's interested in getting to know my daughter. She used a toddler's misbehavior to label my child and refuse to have any kind of relationship with her until now when it suits her? As far as I'm concerned, she can fuck right off."

"She's dying," Tommy said in a low voice. "She'd told me the cancer was only stage one, but it turns out it's much farther along."

"Oh, your mother lied to you? Imagine that. It's not like she's ever had a mouth full of bullshit before." The words tasted like poison. Dean and Tommy exchanged another look that infuriated her.

Tommy scratched at his head. "Look, I know my mom's been mean in the past—"

"I should never have let you take Briella there," Marian said again, her voice shaking and rough. "I should never have let you take her anywhere even close to someone who would say such a thing. I tried to tell myself I'd heard her wrong, because who the hell says something like that about a child, one of their own blood? About anyone?"

"I'm sorry!" Tommy shouted. "Jesus Christ, Marian, I didn't know. Okay? She never said anything like that to me, and if she had, I wouldn't have allowed her to get away with it. You have to know that."

"She knows better than to say anything to you," Marian said after a moment.

Tommy ran a hand through his thinning hair. His shoulders slumped. "You don't have to like my mom. You don't even have to forgive her, okay? But this isn't about anything she did to the kid. It's about what Briella did to my mother."

Marian wished she hadn't poured her beer away. Something told her she was going to want a drink after she heard what Tommy had to say. She crossed her arms over her chest and stared him down without saying anything. Waiting.

"We got to the house, it was fine. We had something to eat. She asked me if she could take the leftovers to the bird." Tommy paused. "How the hell did that fucking thing know she was at my parents' house?"

Marian just shook her head.

"So we put out some leftover stuffing and rolls, and sure enough, it flew right onto the deck and ate it. And it talked. Did you know it could talk, really talk?"

"What did it say?" Dean interjected when Marian didn't answer.

Tommy looked incredulous. "It said, 'We'll be fine. We'll all be just fine.'"

Marian sat at the table again and plucked a fresh beer from the cooler. She took a long, slow swig, giving herself time to think about what she wanted to say before she answered. Her father's words, she thought. Echoed now by that goddamned raven.

"That hardly sounds like a reason to bring her home," Marian said.

Tommy didn't speak. His mouth worked, but only silence escaped. He gulped the last of his beer and cracked open another before finally managing to get the words out.

"After we finished feeding the bird, the kid went up to my mother and sniffed her, and then she said, 'How does it feel to know you're dying?'"

"Jesus," Dean muttered.

Marian felt her mouth twist. "She must have overheard you talking about it. Or something."

"Even if she did, that's pretty fucking rude to say," Tommy said.

Marian frowned. "Kids are more honest than adults. Anyway, that still doesn't explain why you brought her home."

Tommy shifted, looking at Dean, who didn't dare raise his gaze to Marian's. Tommy finished the rest of his beer and set the empty bottle on the table. He wiped his mouth with the back of his hand.

"She asked my mom if it hurt, and my mom said yes. She said, 'Dying hurts like a bitch and a half.' And then Briella said…" Tommy trailed off. He gave Dean a pleading look, but Dean was studying his beer bottle like it held the secrets of the universe.

Marian looked back and forth between the two men. "What? She said what? Fucks' sakes, Tommy. Spit it out."

"She asked my mom if she wanted help to go faster, or if she'd like to suffer a long time. My mom said she didn't want to suffer, that nobody would want that. So then Briella said my mom should just kill herself and get it over with, because at least that way, nobody else would have to do it for her." Tommy shook his head.

It sounded practical to Marian. Then again, she wasn't going to shed a single tear when her former mother-in-law kicked the bucket, whether she went fast or lingered on. "And then what?"

"I told her she needed to apologize, and she wouldn't. And then I said…" Tommy struggled again to speak.

Marian leaned forward. "What did you say, Tommy? Jesus, stop dragging this out."

"I told her that kids who talked like that got sent away to a place where they locked you up until you could behave like a normal person. That's when she started to flip out. She wouldn't stop screaming until I got her back here." He hung his head, looking ashamed, but Marian had seen that look on him too many times to feel even the tiniest scrap of forgiveness.

A white-hot rage swept over her. Shaking, she lifted the beer bottle but couldn't drink from it because the glass chattered against her teeth hard enough to hurt. She set it down and gripped her hands together. Dean put a hand on her shoulder, and she didn't shrug it off. The look she gave him made him take it away, though.

"You told my daughter that you were going to lock her up in a psych ward?" The words came out calmer than she thought they would.

She knew Tommy, and he still knew her. At her calm tone, he blanched and looked even more miserable. "She can't talk to people like that, Mare. It's not…right. *She's* not right."

"Are you saying there's something *wrong* with her?" Marian demanded through gritted teeth. "You waltz in and out of her life and you think you can figure her out? She's smart. She's…Briella's just smart. Sometimes really smart people have a hard time relating or dealing with other people. It doesn't mean there's something wrong with her!"

Dean reached for her hand. "Babe, you know that what she said isn't okay."

"Being rude," Marian replied with a sneer directed toward Tommy, "doesn't mean she's crazy. Seems to me that your mother was rude as hell to me more than once. Does that mean she's not right in the head?"

"Look, I just thought it was a better idea if I brought her home," Tommy began.

Marian cut him off. "You said you wanted to do more. You wanted to try to be a real father to her. Well, guess what, that means dealing with her even when you don't want to."

He looked caught and awkward, his gaze shifting from hers to the empty bottle and then to Dean, who shrugged. "Yeah, well, I guess I'm not cut out for it."

"I let you take my kid to see your dying mother, who's been nothing but an asshole to me for as long as I've known you. She decided years ago to write off my kid and has never asked to see her when you weren't around. Once," Marian began and stopped herself so she could get her voice to stop trembling, "once we passed her in the grocery store aisle and she pretended she didn't see me, Tommy. I agreed to let you take Briella against my better judgment, because I felt like, yeah, maybe it was time for you to get to spend some time with your kid. Maybe it would be a good idea for your mother to have a chance to realize what she's been missing out on. I *trusted* you to take care of my kid!"

"Our kid," he put in.

Marian waved a dismissive hand at him and leaned forward, her jaw clenched. "Mine. My kid. You don't get to claim her, not when you can't put in the fucking effort."

"Maybe you should tell that to the judge next time you try to come after me for support," Tommy said, but looked instantly embarrassed.

She did not point out that the minuscule amount of support he did provide was not something to brag about. "I trusted you to take care of her. Not tell her you were going to send her away and lock her up."

Tommy stood. "I shouldn't have said that. I'm sorry."

"It must run in the family," she said coldly. "Saying things you should know better than to say."

Marian fought tears of fury and guilt because she'd been complicit in allowing him to put her daughter in a bad place. She clenched her fists until her fingernails dug into the skin. Tommy couldn't meet her gaze, but she kept hers steady and staring on him, waiting for him to speak.

"I'm sorry," he finally repeated, at last looking at her. "But seriously, Marian, the kid has changed. There's something going on with her, and you should get someone to talk to her. Hell, even someone at that freaking school should be able to tell you that she might be smart, but she's not... normal."

Dean stood at that. "You should go."

"I *am* sorry, man. I know that doesn't mean much—"

"It means shit," Marian said flatly. "Get out."

When he'd gone, she gathered the empty bottles and put them in the recycling bin. She rinsed her hands at the sink, blinking away tears and the bitterness of fury. Behind her, in silence, Dean went about cleaning up the dinner they'd left on the table in their haste to get to the bedroom. At the sound of a fork scraping the uneaten spaghetti into the trash, Marian turned.

"It's my fault. I knew better. I let him talk me into it, I knew better but I still let him…."

Dean set the dirty dishes in the sink. "Baby, he's her father. His mother is dying. You were trying to do the right thing. Sometimes, when we try to do the right thing, we make mistakes. Why don't you go up and check on her? I'll finish cleaning up."

Marian nodded and hugged him hard, pressing her face to his chest while she took in his comforting scent. "I love you."

"Love you too, babe. We're going to make sure this all works out. Okay?" He squeezed her. "We'll get Briella help, if she needs it…."

Marian froze, then looked up at him. "You think she needs help?"

For a long moment, Dean said nothing. Then he shook his head. "I'm just saying that if she does, we'll make sure she gets it. Okay?"

"She's so smart. She's so scary smart," Marian whispered, not wanting there to be even the slightest chance Briella overheard her. "But she's my child, Dean. I have to protect her."

"I know you do."

You don't understand, Marian wanted to say, but stopped herself just short of that cruelty. Dean didn't understand, because although he'd been a parent to Briella, she was still not 'his' no matter how hard Marian had tried to make that be true. He loved her. He loved Briella. She knew that. But it was not the same.

CHAPTER TWENTY-FOUR

Briella was not asleep when Marian went upstairs. The girl turned a tear-streaked face toward her mother and sat up in bed when Marian came in. She clutched an old stuffed toy Marian hadn't seen her play with in ages.

"Hey, Bean." Marian sat on the edge of the bed to cuddle her close. "How are you doing?"

"I'm sorry I made Daddy mad."

For the first time in a long time, the girl sounded sincerely apologetic. Another pang of jealousy pricked at Marian's heart, that Briella could show remorse about Tommy and not her or Dean. She couldn't shake it off, but she wasn't going to let it affect her.

"You didn't do anything wrong, kiddo."

"He was really mad because I made Gramma cry. I didn't mean to. I was trying to make her feel better about dying. I told her I could help her fly up to heaven." Briella sniffled loudly.

Marian stopped looking in the nightstand for a tissue. Tommy had told her that Briella had asked his mother if she wanted someone to help her die faster. Hearing that Briella had offered to be the one to do it was even worse. She tried to tell herself she'd heard the girl wrong. "What?"

"I told her, if she didn't want to take a long time and hurt the whole time, that I could help her get to heaven sooner."

"Briella, why would you say that?"

"He's a…" She mumbled something that sounded like "psycho."

Marian took the girl's face in her hands and looked at her steadily. "Who's a psycho? Your dad?"

Briella shook her head, bursting into another round of hysterical sobs. "No, no, no! He could help her. But please, Mama, please, promise me that you won't send me away and lock me up in a cage! Please!"

"Nobody will lock you up in a cage, I promise you, Briella. I promise, I will never, never let anyone do that to you." Marian gathered her close.

"I don't want to go over there again," Briella said.

"You never have to."

Briella sniffled and burrowed closer. "Daddy doesn't love me."

"Of course he does, Bean."

"Not like you do." Briella's voice was muffled against her mother's chest.

Marian pressed her face into the kid's mess of hair. "Nobody will ever love you like I do."

By the time Briella's sobs had faded and she slept, an exhausted, snotty lump in her mother's arms, Marian's back and arms ached. She eased herself free of the sleeping child and went downstairs. Dean had cleaned the kitchen and left a glass of wine on the counter for her, the last of the bottle. From down the hall, she heard the faintest sound of his snoring.

She wanted nothing more than to crawl into bed with him, but sleep would be a long time coming. Instead, Marian sipped the wine and shot off a text to Tommy. It was probably a mistake, but she'd run out of fucks at this point.

Did you really call my daughter a psycho?

His answer came within the minute. *I didn't say she was a psycho. She told me he was a psycho-something.*

Marian typed quickly. *Who? A what?*

I don't remember, came Tommy's reply. *But she said the psycho would help my mother when she died. Get the kid some help.*

Marian didn't answer him. She didn't finish her wine, either. Angry again, she paced in the kitchen until she went outside with her cigarettes to sit on the back porch. She smoked fiercely until her head rushed, but too fast, because her stomach curdled too. Phone in hand, she scrolled through her limited social media and found nothing to hold her interest or to get her mind off the night's shitshow.

Crushing out the cigarette, she idly typed 'psycho' into the phone's search browser, not sure what the hell she thought she was hoping to see. A photo of a young and handsome Anthony Perkins, maybe, or a link to a local shrink. In the long list of suggested search results, one stood out.

She dialed Tommy's number with a shaking hand, and when he answered, she spoke without even a greeting. "Psychopomp? Is that what she said?"

"Shit, Marian." Tommy sounded like he'd been asleep.

She didn't care. "Is that what she said, Tommy?"

"Psychopomp. Yeah. That's it, I couldn't remember. How did you know?"

She hung up without answering him and used her fingers to enlarge the photo on the screen. There was a single word, along with a brief definition.

PSYCHOPOMP
A guide of souls to the place of the dead

Below it, there was a line drawing of a raven.

CHAPTER TWENTY-FIVE

Because Briella caught the van earlier than she had the school bus, this gave Marian more time in the morning before Dean came home. She could have spent it exercising or menu planning or maybe doing some sort of self-improvement. Or a craft. Or hell, looking for that job she kept telling herself she wanted but never got around to finding. Today, all she wanted to do was go back to bed. She'd been sleeping like shit lately. Tossing and turning, waking with stiff and aching muscles.

With a jaw-cracking yawn she took her mug of coffee and her single smoke out to the back porch. One puff turned her stomach, so she stubbed it out and settled for the caffeine. The leaves had all fallen off the trees along the street out front, but here in the back most of the forest she could see was pine and evergreen. The chill in the air promised snow, if not today, then soon. They'd probably have a white Christmas this year.

Marian had never loved this rural setting. She'd grown up in town, close enough to walk at least to the small local market, or with a little more effort, to catch a bus to the mall or other stores. This house had come along with marrying Dean, and she supposed it hadn't been an awful trade. Her father had always said it was better to be heart-rich than house-poor, and while she agreed, there were still times when she longed to be able to stroll to grab a muffin or coffee, or to even have a pizza delivered.

It *was* pretty out here, she had to admit that. And quiet, with little noise beyond the soft sigh of the wind through the forest. In the fall, deer often wandered into the backyard, along with squirrels and rabbits and plenty of birds that enjoyed the feeders Dean made sure to keep filled. Coyotes yipped sometimes from a few miles off in the woods, but they never came close enough to be a worry. Marian might never love the forest, but she could appreciate the beauty of it.

Now a few squirrels chittered at each other from out in the grass. The low hooting of what she thought was a dove curled from the trees. She couldn't see any birds, but the edge of the forest just below the tree line was dark with shadow. She would have no idea what lurked there. Watching.

"Onyx," Marian called, startling herself. She waited for the bird to fly out of the trees, but it didn't. She laughed, self-conscious, aware of how her voice had rung out into the early morning stillness. Of course it wouldn't come when she called it.

She hadn't seen the bird since the day Briella had gone with Tommy to his parents' house, but today was the first time she'd actively noticed its absence. Now, Marian stood to shade her eyes and stare toward the tree line. She didn't call out the bird's name again. Names, she thought, had power, and she didn't want to give the bird any.

Idly, Marian sat again on the porch steps and pulled out her phone to scroll through the search results for *psychopomp*. Ravens, as it turned out, were far from the only creatures that had been listed in the role of death assistant. Other birds, too, as well as wolves and even deer and dogs had been thought of as able to lead the dying to the afterlife.

She closed her eyes for a moment, listening to the whispering shuffle of the evergreen trees. Was that a far-off caw? Marian leaned forward, intent, but at last had to open her eyes to find no big black bird. Maybe it was gone for good. She could hope, right?

Briella had not said a word about Onyx's absence. That meant something, although Marian could not decide what. She took a long, slow breath of the cool autumn air, relishing it and the silence and the solitude. This was her life, in this moment, and it was a good one. A simple life. Nothing fancy. But it was hers, and the thought of it pushed her lips into a smile.

She'd make slow-cooker lasagna for dinner, Marian thought as she got to her feet. A small flutter of dizziness had her reaching for the railing to steady herself, but it passed so quickly that she could hardly be sure it had happened at all. Again, she thought she might have heard a distant squawk, something that might or might not have been the voice of a raven from the trees, but when she swung around to look, again there was nothing.

Dinner took only a few minutes to put together, and the clock told her she still had twenty minutes before Dean would be home. When another yawn threatened to take the top off her head, Marian decided to stop fighting her exhaustion. She snuggled down beneath the comforter and dozed until she heard Dean come in.

She smiled without opening her eyes and wiggled under the covers. "Hey, handsome, come on in."

The sound of an embarrassed cough had her startling to full awareness. She sat up in bed, clutching the blankets. "Tommy, what the hell?"

"Oh shit, Mare. Sorry." He covered his eyes and turned away dramatically. "I'm not looking. The front door was unlocked. I knocked but you weren't answering."

"So you just let yourself in? Again? What the hell is the matter with you? God, Tommy, you scared the shit out of me!" Marian flipped the covers back, glad she wore a T-shirt and leggings instead of something more revealing. "I'm not naked this time, so you can look."

"I'm sorry," he said again, still not looking.

Marian pulled on a hoodie and zipped it up. "Kitchen."

There she tested the coffee carafe and found it cold, so she poured them each a mug and put them in the microwave. Tommy took a seat at the table, tapping his fingers rapidly while a sudden hunger had Marian rummaging for some bread to make toast.

"You want some?" When he shook his head she gave him a mug of warmed coffee instead, then popped the bread in the toaster. She leaned on the counter with her own mug. "What's going on?"

"I just felt like shit after what happened with Briella," Tommy said. "I wanted to come talk to you about it."

"It's been three weeks."

"Yeah, well, I felt like shit for three weeks, okay?"

"You could have texted me," she said.

"This is the sort of thing that's better said in person."

Marian's brows lifted. "It's not even eight in the morning."

"Yeah, I know. You look like shit, by the way."

"Well, you *should* feel like shit. That kid, for whatever reason, worships you." She scowled.

"You know I'm an asshole, Marian. If the kid thinks I'm a good father, where'd she get that idea from? Not me." Tommy shrugged and swigged coffee. "Your toast is burning."

"Shit." She pulled it out and tossed it on a plate with a sigh, then grabbed a butter knife from the drawer to scrape off the burned bits. She added butter and some cinnamon sugar while she said, "I have no idea where she got that idea. From TV, for all I know, where the kid's supposed to hate their step-parent. Or maybe it's because you've swept in and out of her life since she was born, always the guy taking her to the fun places, never the one making her eat her lima beans."

"Lima beans are fucking noxious."

Marian cut back her smile, not wanting to give him the satisfaction. "That is not the point."

Tommy sighed and ran a hand through his hair. She shouldn't take such glee in how much older he looked with the start of the bald spot, but she did.

"Look." He hesitated. "Let's put things in perspective. My mom is going to die. Soon."

Marian contemplated her toast quietly, before saying gently but without much sympathy, "If you want people to say nice things about you when you're dead, you shouldn't be an asshole when you're alive."

"Exactly. I'm trying hard not to be an asshole. It's not about my mom, Mare. It's about me and you being okay," Tommy said. "I want to be okay with Briella."

Marian didn't have an answer for that, but she fortunately didn't need one, because Dean's booming voice echoed through the house.

"Baby! I'm hoooome! And I see we have company." Dean came into the kitchen with a broad grin that didn't falter even when he saw who sat at the kitchen table. "Yep. I thought I smelled bullshit all the way out at the street. You parked in my spot, douche."

Tommy rolled his eyes. "Whatever."

Dean gave Marian a kiss, long and lingering and deliberate, she thought, but allowed it to go on as long as he wanted. "Hey, baby. You look scrumptious."

"Gross," Tommy said.

Marian looked over Dean's shoulder. "*You* can go home any time."

Tommy didn't get up from the table. He looked uncomfortable, but his discomfort didn't seem to be about Dean. He scratched his fingers through his hair again. "Look. About the kid...."

"I'm not okay with you taking her to your parents again," Marian cut in. "I know your mom's sick and everything, but—"

"Yeah, about that. It's about that," he said and stopped himself again without finishing.

"Coffee?" Dean asked.

"I'll make you fresh." Marian kissed him again and started toward the cupboard. She put in fresh grounds and water, expecting that Tommy would have said what he had to by the time she was done. He still hadn't, and, irritated, she gestured at him. "You know, for the guy who used to run his mouth nonstop, you sure ended up without a lot to say. What is it?"

"That bird. The black one, the raven."

Marian's insides twisted. "Onyx?"

"Yeah. He was at my parents' house again the other night."

Dean frowned. "How can you be sure it was the same one?"

"Because when I called it by name, it said 'Briella'."

CHAPTER TWENTY-SIX

The story Tommy told was brief but took a long time to get out of him, because he kept stopping to shake his head, as though he couldn't believe his own words. When he got to the part where he talked about the bird tapping on the house windows, whichever one it could see his mother through, he went silent and shuddered, over and over.

"Did you let it in the house?" It was the only thing Marian could think of to ask.

"Of course I didn't let it in the fucking house," Tommy retorted. "God only knows what it was intending to do!"

Dean laughed, and if Tommy's glare bothered him, he didn't show it. "It was probably intending to get something to eat. You fed it the last time, right?"

"Yeah," Tommy answered reluctantly.

"Ravens are smart, and they'll remember where they got food before." Dean caught Marian's glance and shrugged. "I listen to the kid when she talks about it."

"If it was just begging for food, why was it there at night? Tapping the windows? Fucking singing?" Tommy got up and went to the fridge to help himself to the jug of orange juice. "Ugh. Pulp."

"Forgive me, the next time I shop I'll remember to buy the kind of orange juice *you* like." Marian refilled Dean's mug with coffee, stopping to look down at him when he touched her wrist. The smile he gave her made everything seem okay.

We'll all be just fine, she thought, and the taste of something sour coated her tongue and closed her throat.

Tommy took the juice to the table. Marian gave him a glass, and he filled it, gulping half the contents before swiping a hand over his mouth and setting the glass back on the table with a *thump*. He looked up at both of them.

"I just thought you should know about it, that's all. I mean…it said her name."

His tone prickled the hairs on the back of Marian's neck. "You come in here, talking about how you want things to be okay, but you still think there's something wrong with her. You couldn't stand the idea of her going to that 'weirdo' school, but you want to lock her up in some psych ward, is that it? It will never happen, Tommy, not over my dead body!"

"Babe. He's not saying that." Dean shook his head.

Marian whirled on him. "Don't you dare hush me."

"I wasn't hushing you. Just saying. I'm sure he only wants the best for her. That's all. He's worried."

"Do you think he has reason to be?" she retorted. "Do you think he's got reason to think we aren't going to keep Briella safe and take care of her?"

"I don't think that." Tommy got up from the table. "But it's that bird, okay? I think you need to be careful with it. Don't let it get too close to her. It's not healthy."

Marian crossed her arms over her chest. She wouldn't agree with Tommy if he said the Pope was Catholic. "There's nothing wrong with Briella having a pet."

"That thing's not a pet, and you know it. If it comes around my house again, I'll shoot it," Tommy said.

"Big man," Marian replied.

After that, Tommy got the hint he might not be totally welcome there, and he left. Dean followed him out to his car so he could move his into his normal spot. Marian watched them both from the front window, standing behind the curtains so they couldn't see her.

"What were you talking about?" she asked when Dean came back in the house.

He looked surprised. "He was apologizing for coming over so early and taking my spot. I assume he meant the parking spot."

"That's not funny," she snapped.

"I'm sorry. He was just apologizing, baby. That's all."

"That doesn't sound like Tommy."

"Maybe he's changed a little, Marian. People do."

She frowned. "So what, you're taking his side?"

"I'm not taking any sides," Dean said. "Wow. What's going on with you?"

"Nothing's going on with me."

Truth was, Marian did feel unsettled. Irritable. She didn't usually blame PMS for bad moods, but that seemed a likely cause now. Forcing the crankiness aside, she hugged him.

"Sorry," Marian said. "I didn't get a good night's sleep."

Dean yawned. "Come back to bed with me for a little while."

She looked at the clock. "I'm supposed to go to my dad's for lunch."

"Come back to bed with me," Dean said with a grin.

★　　★　　★

Her father seemed surprised to see her when he answered the door, but let her in with a smile and a hug. He'd forgotten she was supposed to come for lunch, Marian realized, but didn't point it out to him. She didn't want to embarrass him. Maybe she didn't want to have to face it, either, the fact that he was slowly but clearly declining. She hadn't spoken to her brother in a few months, but she would have to call him, Marian thought. She would have to tell him to visit from California, soon. They would have to talk about what to do about their father.

But not right now. Now, she made them both macaroni and cheese, with tuna fish sandwiches on white bread, pickle spears and chips on the side. It was a comfort meal from her childhood, her mother's specialty, and usually Marian loved it. Today it left her stomach rumbling and unsettled.

Dad fell asleep in his recliner after lunch, the way he usually did. Marian left him there while she went upstairs to her old bedroom to sort through some boxes of stuff she'd left behind almost a decade ago. If she hadn't needed it in all that time, she doubted she'd need it now, but she did find some childhood books that she packed up for Briella. She took the rest down to her car and put it in the trunk to be donated. The entire house would have to be cleaned out, eventually. She didn't let herself think about the reasons for that.

Halfway down the stairs again with a heavy box in her hands, a rise of nausea hit her so hard she almost dropped everything. By the time she got to the bottom, Marian had to let the box fall. With a hand over her mouth, she ran for the small bathroom off the hallway. She barely made it before her lunch came up, bitter, sour, burning.

"Marian?" Her father's voice in the doorway was concerned, but Marian didn't dare turn to face him. She could only concentrate on heaving into the toilet.

When she'd finished, her dad handed her a damp washcloth and a paper cup from the dispenser so she could rinse her mouth, then gave her privacy. Marian pushed her hair off her sweaty forehead and waited to see if she was going to have another round. Her stomach had settled enough for her to risk going out to the kitchen, where she found him with the kettle on.

"Peppermint tea," he said. "Good for your belly. Was it something you ate?"

"I don't know. I hope not." Marian pressed on her stomach but the sickness had passed.

"Lots of good memories in this house," her dad said abruptly.

Marian sipped her tea. "Yes. Lots."

"Me and your mother, this is the only house we ever lived in together."

"I know that, Dad," she said.

"I miss her."

"I miss her too." Marian reached across the table to squeeze his hand.

"It'll be yours and Desmond's. When I pass." Her father squeezed back.

"Dad, that won't be for a long time," she began, but he waved her quiet.

"I knew when your mama left us too soon that I was going to have too many years without her. It wasn't supposed to be like that. But that's what God gave us." Her father smiled. "It won't be long now, though. The angels tap every night now."

Marian blinked, sighed. Frowned. "Do they sing?"

"Sometimes." Her father patted her hand with his gnarled fingers. "Sometimes they just call my name. That's how I know it'll be my time soon. I dream about flying every night. Sometimes, when I wake up, I still feel as though I have wings."

"That's a little scary, Dad." Marian shook her head.

"It's not scary at all. It's a comfort. It feels like a freedom, Marian. And it's been a long time since your old dad felt free that way." He patted her hand again, then got up to take their mugs to the sink.

Marian got up and pushed him gently aside. "I'll wash these. I'm just worried about you, that's all. I'm worried about you being here all by yourself."

"You don't need to worry about me." He put a hand on her shoulder.

She turned, fighting tears. "I love you, Dad."

"Love you too, baby girl. You bring that dolly of yours around to see me soon, you hear?"

"Yes, of course."

"And don't you worry about me," her father said. "We'll all be just fine."

CHAPTER TWENTY-SEVEN

She got home barely ahead of the Parkhaven van. The entire drive, Marian had been thinking about Tommy's story of the raven at his parents' house, and how it connected with the idea her father had about 'angels' tapping on the windows. Then there'd been the day when her dad had woken up making those awful noises – those, she had to admit, bird noises. And if she really wanted to dig deep, scrape away the layers of determined ignorance and piece the puzzle together even more, there'd been the time he'd needed her to pick up new meds because his had gone missing. The combination of his pain and blood pressure meds could cause seizures. She knew that because she'd gone to the doctor with him for his last appointment.

Seizures.

She threw up again just before Briella burst through the front door. There'd been nothing to bring up but sour strings of bile and air. Marian had stopped at the drugstore on the way home to pick up something she hadn't thought she'd ever need again. The instructions said to wait for first morning urine, but Marian couldn't wait that long. She'd bought the twin pack, anyway, so she had a spare if she needed one.

She peed on the stick and set it on the counter on top of a scrap of toilet paper.

She washed her hands, studying her face in the mirror again for any signs that something had changed inside her. There weren't any, of course. Some faint circles beneath her eyes that came from the lack of sleep she'd been having over the past few weeks. Some new silver threads in her dark curls, more prominent now that she'd pulled her hair back.

It was too soon to check for a result, so she went out to find that Briella had already helped herself to some cubed cheese and grapes. "Hey."

"Hi, Mama. See, you didn't have to help me. At school they let us fix our own snacks, because we should learn to be self…self…efficient." Briella stumbled over the term and grinned, showing the gaps between her teeth.

"Self-*sufficient*. How was school?" The correction and the question both came out automatically, but Marian, suddenly starving, was too distracted by her hunger and the anticipation of what the stick in the bathroom would tell her. She nodded and murmured as Briella told her all about what had gone on that day, but she wasn't really listening.

"...so they gave me my own lab room," Briella said.

This caught Marian's attention. "They did? All to yourself?"

"Yep. Because I've got a project that nobody else wants to work on." Briella shrugged and ate more cheese.

"That sounds..." Marian shrugged, uncertain what she meant to say. It sounded suspicious, but she wasn't going to tell Briella that.

Briella paused, her glossy dark brows furrowing. "It sounds what, Mama?"

"Sounds like I need to call and talk to your teacher. To make sure everything's okay." Marian plucked a couple of cheese cubes from the plate and tossed them in her mouth.

"You don't need to do that," Briella said.

Marian was anxious. Stressing. Yet beneath it all, a certain unanticipated hope had begun to rise. She didn't want to think too hard about it, convinced she was psyching herself out, but...

A baby?

She and Dean were going to have a baby. The past month or so made so much sense now. The achiness and mood swings, the trouble sleeping. The puking.

Briella was still talking about school, the lab and her experiments, but Marian had zoned out. Standing in front of the sink, staring at the backyard, she roused herself with a shake of her head at her daughter's impatient tone. She turned.

"What?"

"I said," Briella replied with a frown, "you can just check the parent portal."

Oh, that thing. The tech that so annoyed her, because every time she tried, the system booted her out. "Right. Finish your snack. I'm going to go to the bathroom again."

"You just went," Briella said.

Marian ignored her. She went to the bathroom and checked the stick. Two lines.

Oh my God.

"Mama, I'm done with my snack— What's that?" Briella flung the door open hard enough to bounce the handle off the wall.

"Be careful," Marian scolded and tucked the pregnancy test into her pocket. "It's nothing. You don't need to worry about it. Let's go see if you can help me get logged in. If the desktop is too old and slow, we'll have to use your school laptop."

"Why'd you put it in your pocket?"

Marian turned the girl and nudged her forward. "Go. Out of the bathroom."

The portal, as it turned out, had to be reset again. For some reason, the email listed under Marian's contact profile was wrong again – just another typo, but a guarantee that she wouldn't actually get any of the emails from the school. With Briella hovering over her shoulder, waiting anxiously to get her laptop back, Marian changed it and checked the site's inbox for messages.

Along with the usual updates about the daily menu and extracurricular activities, there was a message from Briella's homeroom teacher, Mrs. Addison. She explained that although Briella was new to the school, she'd adapted wonderfully and they'd decided to shift the focus of her curriculum to something she called a 'student-led learning module'. There wasn't anything in there about Briella having her own lab to work in, and the student-led learning bit sounded a little more hippy-dippy than Marian was used to. The note went on to praise Briella for being 'focused', 'determined' and 'creative'.

The last part suggested that she might benefit from some sessions with the school psychologist.

Marian's fingers twitched on the keyboard. Giving up on bugging her mother to finish, Briella had finished her snack and gone into the den to watch TV. She hadn't asked permission, but Marian didn't scold. She read the message again.

Focused, determined, creative.

Reluctance to participate in classroom activities, trouble relating to other students, an occasional less-than-respectful attitude toward authority.

"It's candy sprinkles on a shit cake," she said to Dean an hour or so later when he'd woken to amble into the kitchen, where Marian was fixing dinner. She showed him her phone, where the email had finally arrived.

He scanned the message quickly and shrugged. "Sounds like she's doing well in school, but they have some concerns. That can't be a total shocker."

"First of all, that message is from two weeks ago. If there are issues," Marian said, "they should be following up with a phone call or a paper sent home, since I didn't reply to it. They also need to get their stupid parent portal fixed. And they need to just come out and say what those issues are, so we can be prepared to address them. I don't want to sign off on her going to some shrink without making sure it's really what she needs. I mean, trouble relating to other students? Briella's *always* been friendly to other kids."

Almost always, she thought guiltily. *Unless she wasn't.*

"It didn't say she wasn't friendly. Said she was having trouble relating. She's new. Maybe she's having a bit of a hard time fitting in. That couldn't be such a surprise, could it?" Dean lifted the lid on the pot of chili she'd defrosted and had simmering.

Marian felt the narrow plastic stick in her pocket. She'd almost forgotten about her news. The message from school had left her mind churning. She seemed to be royally screwing up with the kid she already had. What made her think she could possibly have another one without screwing that one up, too? And forget about getting a job, even one part-time. She could hardly go back to work now. And nights out with the girls? She'd had only one and could kiss those goodbye too, at least for a while.

She was pregnant, and everything was going to change.

"Babe?" Dean was looking at her with concern.

"She's my kid. I worry about her."

Dean hugged her from behind. "I know. There's been a lot of change recently. We're all a little stressed out. It'll get better. This is the best thing for her. You'll see."

She opened her mouth to tell him about the double lines that meant *yes*, but Briella came into the kitchen. "Hey, there. Dinner's almost ready."

Marian could have sent her back to watch more crappy television. She could have told Dean right then about the positive test and shared the news with both of them at the same time. Instead, she waved at the table for them to sit.

Briella kept up the chatter about school nonstop throughout dinner as she devoured two bowls of chili along with rice, corn bread slathered with peanut butter, and a couple glasses of milk. She answered Dean's questions without even a hint of attitude, and while Marian might have tried to correct the girl's table manners, she was more than happy to deal with a spray of crumbs if it meant Briella and Dean were bonding. Marian herself stayed a little quiet, her stomach not queasy but the promise that it might become so enough to keep her nibbling lightly.

"So hold on," Dean interrupted. "Back up, Bean. What exactly are you trying to do with the computer program?"

"Make copies."

Dean glanced at Marian. "Of what?"

For the first time, Briella looked cautious. "Whatever I need to."

"Aren't there programs that copy things already?" Dean asked.

Briella nodded slowly, her cautious expression turning to reluctance. "Yes."

Dean was smart enough to see that he'd pushed for too much. He backed off. "Cool."

"It's all Greek to me," Marian said with a laugh.

Briella scowled. "It's not *Greek*. It's Blackangel."

Dean and Marian shared a look, and she said carefully, her every sense tingly, "What's that, Bean?"

"It's my computer code." The girl had gone from bubbly to sullen. Her gaze shifted from Marian to Dean and then to her plate. "I'm done eating. Can I be excused?"

"Sure." Marian watched as Briella carried her bowl to the garbage and scraped it clean to put it in the sink. Before the kid could escape the kitchen, Marian said, "You're not going to go out and feed Onyx? He's going to miss his dinner."

Briella turned in the doorway. "Oh. I guess I could take him some rice. He might eat that."

"We haven't seen him in a while," Marian said, watching her daughter carefully. Using the word *he*, not *it*, on purpose to make it sound like she cared.

Briella didn't answer at first. She chewed her lower lip, then shrugged. She went to the back door and opened it to step onto the porch. "Onyx! Come on, rice!"

She was back inside half a minute after that, barely enough time to have waited for the bird at all. "He didn't come."

"Oh." Marian went to the back door herself to look out. "You're sure? Maybe you should call him again. He might need a few minutes."

"I'm sure. He's not coming. Can I go up to my room and read?"

"Of course. Sure. Wait. Briella?" Marian said. The kid turned. "Did he end up going with you to show and tell? You never told me."

"No, Mama, you were right. He didn't know how to go to school with me. I was silly to think so. Just because I taught him a few tricks, that doesn't mean he would know enough to go to school with me."

Marian studied her. Briella didn't look broken up about it, not about the school absence or the bird's refusal to come when she'd called it just now. "When's the last time you saw him? Was it at your other grandparents house?"

"I guess so."

"Since then?"

"No…."

"You don't seem very upset or worried."

"He's a wild animal, Mama. He'll be fine." With that Briella left the kitchen.

Like all of us, Marian thought and swallowed another rush of bile.

Dean started running the water in the sink, scrubbing at the plates while Marian put away the leftovers. She'd told him often enough that he didn't need to wash up, not when he could use some downtime before he had to leave for work. He generally insisted on helping her anyway.

"I hadn't thought about it until you mentioned it, but yeah, the bird hasn't been around for a bit." Dean lowered his voice. "Do you think… you know. Tommy?"

Marian shivered and tried to think when exactly they'd last seen the bird. It had been before Tommy's story, but how long ago? She thought about telling Dean what her father had said about the angels, how it related to Tommy's crazy, stupid story, but it hurt her brain to think about it, much less try to explain. Of the other matter, the one she could not bear to think about, she wasn't going to say a word. Anyway, that had nothing to do with the raven.

"If he killed it? I wouldn't put it past him. Maybe. It's been a while since it's been around, but I can't remember how long."

"Briella didn't seem to notice," Dean said. "I have an excuse because it wasn't my pet, but that seems weird, doesn't it? Considering how attached she was."

"Let's hope that's because she's over it. She's focused on her new experiments and stuff." Marian thought about the plastic stick in her pocket. "I have something to tell you."

After all the trouble she'd had with miscarriages, Marian became convinced she wasn't going to get pregnant again. Not without help anyway. Maybe the kind that came from angels, although not the sort that tapped at the windows of the dying.

Marian took a deep breath. Dean was frowning, brow furrowed. She took another breath, determined to keep her voice from shaking but not sure she was going to be able to. Instead, she pulled the pregnancy test from her pocket and held it up.

"We're going to have a baby."

"Oh, shit. Oh, my God. Oh, wow." Dean blinked rapidly.

"Is it going to be okay?" Her voice wavered, despite her best efforts.

"Baby, it's going to be perfect. Wow. I didn't think…wow." Dean let out a small burst of laughter and swiped at his eyes.

His happy tears made Marian cry, too. In a second they were both laughing and crying and kissing. Her sobs ratcheted up and out of her, too hard, too fierce.

"Baby?" Dean asked with a frown.

"It's just…I was going to talk to you about going back to work. Doing something out of the house. We were on the downward slide to having more time with each other." Marian drew in a ragged breath and tried to swipe at her eyes. "I was looking forward to when Briella could be off and on her own a little more, you know? And now we'll be right back to the start."

"Aren't you happy about it, though?"

"I am happy," she told him with a watery smile, and it wasn't a lie. "I am confusedly happy. This time around, maybe I can do a better job. Second chance."

"You're an amazing mother, Marian. Don't talk like that." He squeezed her too hard, then let go with an apology, putting a big hand on her belly. "Oops. Gotta be careful."

"With what?" Briella asked.

Marian's laughter faded. She still held the pregnancy test in her fist. She gently disengaged from Dean's embrace. How long had the kid been standing there?

"We have some good news for you, Bean. You're going to have a baby brother or sister soon."

Briella's eyes went wide, then narrow. She looked at the test stick. "What's that thing?"

"It's a special test that tells you if you're going to have a baby. See the two lines? That means I'm pregnant."

"You said that was nothing."

"Ah, well, I wasn't ready to share the news yet." Marian put the test on the counter and moved toward her daughter.

Briella took a step back. "Lying is supposed to be bad. You said that was nothing, but you *lied*. A baby is a big something."

"You're right. I'm sorry I didn't tell you the truth right away. But Bean, this is a good thing." Marian hesitated, thinking of the days when her daughter had been pliable and not this bundle of prickliness. "A baby brother or sister is going to be so much fun."

"Not for me," Briella said.

CHAPTER TWENTY-EIGHT

Briella took herself off to bed. Marian waited until Dean had left for work before climbing the stairs. The girl's door was closed, but the light was on, a thin strip of gold showing at the bottom and sifting into the hall.

Marian held her breath, listening for the sounds of Briella talking to the raven, but she heard nothing. She knocked lightly and heard a faint response. She pushed open the door.

"Hey," she said.

Briella had been sitting up in bed, scribbling in a notebook, but she put it aside. "Why do you have to have a baby?"

"That's a good question." Marian crossed to sit on the edge of the bed. She reached for Briella's hand, squeezing her warm and slightly sweaty fingers. "The short answer is, because I got pregnant."

"Were you trying to get pregnant?" Briella demanded.

Marian shook her head, so not ready for this conversation but knowing it had to happen. "No. I didn't think I could have another baby. I had a lot of problems before I had you. And a few times after, too."

"I know. The babies died before they were born."

"Yes. I thought that would always happen."

"So why would you take a chance that it could? Can't you take a pill to stop it?" Briella asked.

Marian had never had 'the talk' with Briella, but she wasn't surprised the kid knew about reproduction and birth control. "Sometimes, accidents happen. But this baby is a good thing, Bean. It means a brother or sister for you."

Briella pulled her hand from her mother's grip and turned on her side, facing away. Her shoulders rose and fell with a long, deep sigh. Marian put her hand on the girl's hip but said nothing. Briella muttered something Marian couldn't hear.

"What's that, Bean?"

Briella didn't roll over, but her voice rose. "I said, you're going to love this baby more than me."

"Oh, no." Marian tried to gently nudge the girl toward her, but Briella resisted and Marian stopped. "Briella. No. I can promise you that I have more than enough love for you and the new baby."

"You can't promise that. You don't even have the baby yet."

Marian sighed. Desmond was older than her; she'd never had a younger sibling, had no idea what it felt like to know your parents were welcoming in another child. All of this still felt so surreal. Truth was, she didn't know what it would be like to have more than one child. When she'd had Briella, the love had been brutally all-encompassing. She had thought more than once, though never admitting it to anyone, that once she'd had her baby, there had been no room for anyone else, not until Dean. She and Tommy might have stayed together if she hadn't had Briella.

"I believe that love is infinite," Marian said finally. "That means I have room in my heart for you, Dean, for Grandpa. And the new baby."

Briella said nothing. Marian squeezed her hip again. Briella made a low, irritated noise, and Marian let her go.

"I understand you're upset, Bean. But it's all going to be okay. I promise."

Briella didn't turn. Marian waited a moment or so longer, trying to think of something to say, but finding no words. Sometimes silence was a better reply.

Downstairs, she made herself a mug of sleep-enhancing tea and sat at the kitchen table with her phone. She logged into Connex. She wasn't looking now to get caught up on her high school friends or national news or pictures of funny cats. She searched her friends list. She couldn't remember Pamela Morgan's mother's name, but she thought they'd Connexed sometime back when the girls were younger.

Social media could be magic. There was Pamela's mother, her profile picture of a smiling family at Disney World, all in matching mouse ears. Marian navigated to the woman's profile page. She hadn't updated recently, but there were plenty of posts to her feed.

No funny cat pictures.

No news.

Post after post of sympathy to a mother who'd lost a child.

Marian covered her mouth, expecting the tea to rise. She scrolled, horrified. Pamela had died the day after she'd started having seizures in the Southside Elementary parking lot.

Dead. The girl was dead, and Marian hadn't heard about it because she hadn't logged on to stupid social media, and Briella no longer went to Southside. The girl was dead because...

The girl was dead because accidents happen, Marian thought firmly.

She swiped away the app to close it and put her phone on the table. She wrapped her hands around her mug, cool now. She closed her eyes. She counted, first to ten, then to twenty, and finally, after some long minutes, she made it all the way to one hundred.

She finished her tea.

She went out back to stand on the tiny porch. No gifts had been left on the railings. No sign of the bird. Nothing but air cold enough to bite, nothing but the clear winter night sky and the points of brightness overhead.

CHAPTER TWENTY-NINE

Christmas came and went with gifts and a tree and a ham. They spent the day with her father. Tommy sent a box of presents, but when Marian asked if Briella wanted to go with him, she said no. Tommy didn't argue about it. His mother had not yet passed away, but a few terse texts from him told Marian they expected it to be any day.

Now that she knew why she was so tired and half-sick all the time, Marian felt better. Still a little queasy, not just in the mornings but all day. Still sleeping like crap. But the idea of a new baby lifted her heart every single day.

So far, she hadn't told anyone else: not her brother or his wife, not her father, even though the news about Tommy's mother had her wondering if she ought to tell him before it was too late. It was still a little too early for that. She wanted to. She wanted to start shopping for little clothes and stocking up on diapers and wipes and all the things she knew they'd need. She kept herself from it because she could not forget the losses she'd suffered before, and even though her doctor had assured her there was no reason to think she could not expect to carry this baby to term, superstition was keeping Marian quiet.

The only thing she had started to do was clean out the small second bedroom upstairs. Dean's parents had used it for storage, and she and Dean had never cleaned it out, which meant more boxes to sort through and donate. Marian liked the tasks. They gave her something to do every day after Briella got into the white Parkhaven van and went off to school.

A call to speak with Mrs. Addison had convinced Marian that allowing Briella to have weekly sessions with Dr. Garrett, the school psychologist, was not a bad thing. The weeks passed without any updates from him, and Briella rarely mentioned it, so could anyone have blamed Marian for thinking that meant everything was fine? Briella hadn't even brought home a note.

The message that had shown up in Marian's email account that morning hadn't come through the parent portal, which, Marian realized, she'd once again been locked out of. That meant the message was important enough that Garrett had made sure it got to her. He wanted to see her and Dean as soon as possible.

What was wrong with these people, Marian fretted, that they couldn't be bothered to state up front what the issues were? She was so tired of the schools contacting her about Briella without just coming out and giving a full explanation, so that she had to worry. For a moment, Marian's thumb hovered over the phone screen. A quick swipe could delete it. She could pretend she hadn't received it.

But that wouldn't make the problems, whatever they were, go away. And there had to be problems, didn't there? Everything had been going along too easily. With a mental shake, she dialed the number the psychologist had listed. It took only a short conversation. She agreed to go in that afternoon.

Dean had been putting in overtime, banking the extra paychecks and also the hours toward paid time off to give them some breathing room when the baby came. He wasn't home yet. Marian drove herself to the school, her fingers tapping nervously on the steering wheel. By the time she got there, she'd begun to fear she was going to embarrass herself by getting sick all over the place. It would be from nerves more than morning sickness, but it didn't matter. A stick of ginger gum helped. Her palms still sweated.

Storm clouds had gathered in the early January sky by the time she pulled into Parkhaven's parking lot. When Marian got out of the car, a brisk wind whipped up. It tangled her hair and battered the hem of her coat against her calves, but it also pushed the clouds of pending snow away from the sun. She told herself it was a good omen and went inside.

Dr. Garrett greeted her in the school office. Today his funny tie was emblazoned with snowflakes. His grip was firm and his smile reassuring as he ushered her into his private office and offered her a seat in front of his desk.

"Something to drink? Coffee? Cola?"

Marian shook her head. She was off that for the next seven months. "No, thanks."

She did accept a bottle of water he pulled from a small fridge by the window, though. Sipping it helped settled her stomach. Dr. Garrett opened a file folder and glanced at the contents, then closed it. He folded his hands on top of the desk.

"You have an exceptional daughter," he said.

"Thank you."

"It's not the first time you've heard that, I'm sure."

Marian shook her head. "No. But it's always nice to hear, isn't it?"

Something in his tone reminded her of what she'd said to Dean about the first message from Mrs. Addison. *Sprinkles on a shit cake.* Marian shifted, getting ready to tell him to please just get to the point.

"Is she happy, Mrs. Blake?"

This was not the question she'd expected, and it took her a couple seconds to answer. "I…what do you mean? She's ten years old. Why wouldn't she be happy?"

"At home, does she seem content and engaged with you? Does she spend a lot of time by herself?"

"She's always been independent," Marian said defensively. "I've always encouraged her to occupy herself and not need to be constantly entertained."

"I understand. Of course." Garrett tapped the files. "What I mean is, have you noticed any changes in Briella's behavior lately?"

Sunny smiles had been replaced with frowns and temper tantrums, but Marian couldn't say that had happened 'lately'. "She's had some growing pains."

"Has she seemed…" Garrett cleared his throat. "Obsessive?"

You know how she gets about things.

Marian hesitated. "Briella's always been really focused. Mrs. Addison even sent home a note saying what a great quality it was."

"I'm not saying it's a bad thing at all. Briella is definitely a focused and determined young girl. But I've been a little bit worried about her."

"Has she been having problems with her classmates? Has she been… unkind?" Marian bit hard on the inside of her cheek, waiting for a revelation that her kid was a bully. *Worse than a bully*, her mind whispered, and she shoved the thought away again.

"No, nothing like that."

Frustrated and irritated but also relieved, Marian said bluntly, "Be up front with me, please. If there's something wrong with her, just say so. Her last school didn't know what to do with her, so she came here. If you're going to tell me you don't know how to deal with her, either—"

Garrett held up his hands and spoke in a soothing tone Marian hated for making her feel like a hysterical airport parent. *Helicopter mom*, she reminded herself. Which she was not. Maybe she ought to be.

"I'm not saying that at all. We've been really pleased to have Briella here at Parkhaven. But while we do love it when our students succeed academically, Mrs. Blake, we also try to make sure we don't lose sight of them as human beings. Young human beings who sometimes experience a lot of pressure to succeed."

"I've never pressured Briella about school. I've never had to," Marian conceded, "but even if she wasn't bringing home straight As, I wouldn't have pressured her about it."

"I'm not suggesting you are. The pressure with these kids comes from themselves a lot of times. Sometimes from their peers, though we monitor that and make sure, if we notice anything going on among the kids, that we have them work it out. But children of Briella's intelligence, especially ones who are driven and focused and determined – well, they can end up driving themselves too hard."

"Is that what she's doing? I ask her every day when she comes home from school to tell me about what happened that day. She's enthusiastic about it. I don't usually understand half of what she's talking about, to be honest. But yes, she seems happy enough. It's not like I ask her specifically if she's happy. But she's not moping around the house or crying or anything like that." Marian sipped more water.

Garrett nodded. "It's my understanding that you're expecting a baby?"

Marian put a hand on her stomach automatically. Her grin was equally as instinctive. "Yes."

"Congratulations, that's terrific news. How do you feel Briella's handled the news? Research has shown that siblings with more than five years' age difference often interact more like cousins than brothers and sisters. Ten years of having you all to herself means a big change is on the way for her."

"For all of us," Marian said.

"Yes. Of course. Have you spoken with Briella about how she feels about it?"

"Of course I did. We told her as soon as I found out. She understands what a baby brother or sister means. And I've talked to her about it. Of course."

"She hasn't expressed any concerns about being...replaced? That you might be looking at this baby as a...well, a fresh start of some kind?"

Marian's bottle of water splashed at the sudden shaking of her hands. Tears welled but she fought them down. Damn her hormones, making every emotion rise so fiercely to the surface.

"Absolutely not," she lied. "And we would never let her think that, so if she did say something, we'd be talking to her about how that can't possibly be true. She's my daughter, Dr. Garrett. I love her. Her step-father loves her. That's not going to change just because we're having another kid."

"My partner and I have four biological children between us, plus a fifth we adopted together. I have no doubts that there's plenty of room in a parent's heart for multiple children. Or for those not related by DNA."

"Early on, she did express some concerns, yes. Of course." Marian frowned, hating how guilty she now felt. "But we talked about it and she's seemed...fine. Has she been complaining about it here at school?"

"Yes, although it was in relation to the work she's been doing in her private study project. She told me that she had to work harder to get her program to work before the new baby came, because it would be too late, after."

"What does her project have to do with the new baby?"

Garrett hesitated, his brow furrowing. "I don't think the project itself has anything to do with the new sibling. It's my perception that Briella has it set in her mind that you'll fall in love with the baby and forget all about her, so if she wants any accolades from you for this project, she needs to get it finished before that happens."

"Oh, God." Marian rubbed the spot between her eyes where an anxious headache had been brewing and was about to burst open. "That's awful. I feel terrible that she could even think that."

"We know it's not true, obviously. But because kids can be so perceptive, especially really bright ones like Briella, it can be easy to forget how much we assume they're able to understand. You might not have felt the need to continue to reassure her that she won't be replaced because to you it seems so obvious, but to Briella it can feel enormous and terrifying to learn that a new little person is going to come into your lives. It's very common for older kids to feel pushed out by new siblings, and let's face it, there will be some of that just by necessity. Babies take up a lot of time."

"I'll talk to her again." Marian had finished the bottle of water, which meant that she was going to have to use the bathroom soon.

"That would be great." Garrett smiled, then looked serious. "There's something else we need to talk about. Briella has been working harder and harder, pushing herself with her independent study project, and we're wondering if perhaps it might be a good idea for her to step back from it. Kids at this level can come up with some amazing projects, but it's also likely that, despite her advanced intelligence and her determination, she really won't be able to make it a success. It's such an ambitious idea that I don't think there's any way she *can* get it working. I don't think anyone could, to be honest."

Marian had only the vaguest idea of what Briella was working on. Only that it involved a computer program, something about memories, some sort of personality thing, like a robot or an artificial intelligence. "You don't? Why is that?"

"Well." Garrett looked briefly uncomfortable. "It's just that…well, the idea is like something out of a science fiction novel. Which is not to say that it's not viable," he added hastily. "Who knew even a couple of decades ago that the personal handheld communicators from all those Saturday-matinee B movies would become reality?"

It took her a moment to realize he was talking about cell phones. Marian laughed lightly. "I've never been a big science fiction fan. I get *Star Trek* and *Star Wars* confused all the time. Makes my husband crazy."

Garrett flipped through the folder again, pausing on a stapled packet of papers and pulling them out to hand to her. "For independent study projects, we require the kids to fill out a set of forms. Supply requests, estimated budget, their theories and what they think the outcome will be. A timeline. The idea is to make them fully aware of every aspect of a project."

"That's really…that's a lot. When I was her age, we were doing times tables and story problems," Marian said. "To be honest, I could never figure out what time the trains would pass."

"A lot has changed," Garrett agreed with a laugh. "And beyond that, Parkhaven is not a regular school. Because students work so closely with the teachers on their study projects, none of them are expected to meet all the requirements on their own. Eventually, by the time they graduate, they're able to do it, but the younger students get a lot of help. Part of the packet is an essay about what they think the project will accomplish, what they will do if it doesn't work, that sort of thing. Briella's essay was short, although adequate. I think you ought to read it for yourself."

"All right." Marian took the packet and scanned it.

Briella's chicken-scratch handwriting, familiar, was not her best asset, for sure. In a few places, someone had made notes in the margins to clarify what Briella had written. Marian got through the entire sheaf of papers in a few minutes, skipping most of the number stuff about equipment and costs. By the end of it, she was still uncertain what the kid was trying to do or make or build.

She looked up at Garrett, who'd been typing on his computer while she read. "Briella has talked about her computer coding and making copies of things. Umm, recording memories. I have to admit, I don't get much of it at all, if any."

"I understand. That's part of the reason I asked you to come in. I wanted you to be aware of what Briella's been working on. She's been adamant that she doesn't share things with you and your husband at home, because, according to her, you don't care. That you only care about the baby."

"That's not true. I ask her every day what she's been doing in school," Marian said again, miserably, because if you picked it apart to the very baseline of things, it was at least a little true. She and Dean couldn't follow what Briella was working on, and they didn't care about it other than that they cared about her, but it was absolutely not true about the baby. Why, then, did she feel so guilty?

"Again, I'm sure that's her perception," Garrett said in a tone that did not convince Marian that he did, in fact, believe it.

Marian sat up straighter. Her bladder was twinging now. She squeezed her thighs together and took slow, deep breaths. "So. What do we do?"

"Talk to her at home. Ask to see her progress. Spend time with her. All things I'm sure you're doing already," he added hastily when Marian opened her mouth to reply. "Mostly, Mrs. Blake, just *listen* to her. Briella is a little girl with lots to say."

"Yes. I know that." Marian chuckled and looked again at the papers in her hand. "But all of this stuff is talking about neural pathways and computer programs…and the existence of angels? I didn't know Parkhaven was a religious school."

"It's not. We're a privately funded institution, so the rules about religion in the classroom are different for us than for public schools, but we're not religiously affiliated. That bit about angels is all Briella's."

Marian thought about this for a moment with a frown, remembering what Briella had called her computer program or code or whatever it was.

"She's been talking about something called Blackangel."

"That's the name of the coding program Briella wrote and has been using for her projects. Extraordinary, really. I'm like you, I can't write code or even understand it at all. I can use a computer, but programming it is way out of my scope. The kids here in Parkhaven are truly gifted, in so many ways...." Garrett shook his head, seeming to run out of words. "I am constantly amazed. And honored, too, that I have the opportunity to help them along when they find themselves in difficulty, whether it's learning how to interact socially, dealing with depression—"

"Are you saying my kid is depressed?"

"No. I am saying that Briella is sometimes so focused on her goals" – Marian noted he did not say *obsessed* – "that she finds it difficult to interact socially with her peers, as well as her teachers. That's not uncommon here."

With the weird kids, Marian thought, but did not say aloud. "Yet you're concerned enough to call me in."

"Just to make sure you're up to date with what's happening. It's good for the parents to connect with me, so that nothing gets out of control."

She couldn't argue with that. She looked again at the paper, going quiet as she made some connections. She didn't have to understand the complicated computer parts of it to be able to link the bits about angels and Tommy and her father and the bird that had gone missing. The psychopomp.

"Am I reading this correctly? Briella is working on a way to prove the existence of an afterlife by copying memories that can be...downloaded and saved?"

Garrett looked uncomfortable. "That's my understanding. Yes."

"We don't even go to church."

"It's possible she picked it up from mainstream media. I myself am not a Christian, but the truth is that we do live in a Christian-dominated society, particularly in this area. You don't have to be practicing at home for her to pick up a certain pervasive world view," Garrett said, almost apologetically. "But it's clear that whatever you might talk about with her at home, Briella has formed some strong opinions about the afterlife and the existence of angels."

"What about this other stuff? This science-fiction stuff, like you said? That's what you're talking about, right?" Marian waved the packet of papers and then folded them to tuck inside her purse.

"Yes. That. The use of computer programming and technology and the brain's neural network and pathways to copy not only memories but…personality." Garrett coughed. "The soul, if you will."

"Briella's trying to copy people's souls?" Marian laughed aloud at the absurdity of it.

Garrett did not laugh. "Yes."

"That's not…of course she can't do that."

"We don't think it's possible, no."

"If you don't think she can make it work, then why would you be encouraging her to spend so much time on it?" Marian uncrossed and recrossed her legs against the twinge in her bladder.

"Because here at Parkhaven we think the process of trial and error and failure is more important than ultimate success. These kids are learning how to use their brains and talents, but if we only let them work on things we *know* they can do, they're going to have a very skewed view of the world. Like giving everyone a gold star for participation, not accomplishment." Garrett smiled.

"Briella used to get so angry if her grade wasn't perfect," Marian said quietly after a moment. "It could be something as simple as poor penmanship or a lower score in gym class because she didn't do enough sit-ups. She'd get really furious and blame herself. She'd be upset about it for hours."

"That's exactly what I'm talking about. That drive and focus can become disruptive or detrimental. When a student becomes too tied up in their project and it begins to affect their well-being, we have to redirect them toward something a little more beneficial to them, long-term. Sometimes, taking a break is all they need. Other times, we have to terminate the project permanently."

"Which are you going to ask Briella to do?" Marian shifted in her chair, regretting drinking that entire bottle of water so fast. It was becoming clear, now, why the doctor had called her in here, and once again, she wished they'd just freaking get to the point already. She'd been here almost an hour.

Garrett hesitated, looking serious. "In the beginning she was working on something that was less focused on the concept of an entire personality or soul, more on simply recording or copying memories. Something like that could have real, practical applications. Of course we understand that no matter how gifted our students are, the truth is that most of them are still too young and without enough experience to really do everything they think they can. But even if she didn't manage to get it to work, it was something she could work *toward*. Possibly a project she might have continued to pursue after she's finished here at Parkhaven and has gone on to higher education. She might have ended up making a huge contribution to the world."

"But you don't think so anymore?"

"The moral implications of what Briella wants to do are more of a concern at this point than whether or not she can actually accomplish it. The question about if the soul exists is not for us to answer. That's a matter of personal revelation or family upbringing. Not our business or responsibility, frankly. But we do feel as though this concept has become the focus of Briella's work for her personally. Her teacher, Mrs. Addison, and the rest of the staff all feel uncomfortable allowing her to continue. And I agree with them."

"So, you want to take it away from her." Another shift, another twinge. Marian squeezed her thighs tighter.

"Yes."

"I need to use the restroom," she said. "Can we finish this after I do that?"

"Of course, of course. You're welcome to use the staff restroom rather than the one the kids use. It's out the door, down the hall to the right. Next to the library. I can walk you, if you want." Garrett stood.

"No, I can manage. I'll be fast." She wouldn't have a choice to be anything else, not unless she wanted to embarrass herself by leaving a puddle beneath her seat.

Marian found the bathroom without a problem. The relief of releasing her bladder was so deep that she had to bite back a groan that would have echoed in the tiled room. She went, then waited a minute without getting up, then went again in another short burst.

Welcome to pregnancy.

By the time she got back to Garrett's office, she knew she was going to have to go again, and soon. She didn't take a seat once inside, even though he clearly was expecting her to. She picked up her purse, instead.

"Dr. Garrett, you've given me a lot to think about and a lot to talk about with my husband, for sure. I'll make sure we discuss this religious stuff with Briella. But as for the project, I don't really know what to say. If you think it's best she be redirected to something else, I'm not going to argue with it."

Marian drew in a breath. "I want what's best for my daughter."

"Of course you do, Mrs. Blake. Nobody here doubts that. I'm sure that despite some recent insecurities, Briella knows it, too."

"She's so smart." Her voice trembled. "Scary smart. I have to tell you, I really don't know what to do with her. She used to be this happy little girl who could also just…you know, recite the alphabet backwards and give you a ten-minute lecture on facts about the states. She was figuring out the tip on restaurant bills when she was four. It was like…" Marian fought to keep her voice from trembling. "It was like she could do tricks. That's all. Fun tricks, things we could be proud of her for."

Tricks are behaviors learned to gain rewards.

Briella had told her that.

"You can still be proud of her, Mrs. Blake. I don't want you to think anything less of her. When I said Briella was an exceptional child, I meant it."

Marian wanted to tell him then, about the weirdness. The bad moods, the secretiveness. Her daughter had gone from being exactly as she'd just described to something else. Something much darker, and if Marian had not known why or how or what had prompted the change before today, everything Garrett had told her was shining a light into those shadows.

But what would he do if Marian revealed to him that she was starting to believe she'd lost all control of her own child? That it had nothing to do with there being another one on the way and Marian's exhaustion or the hormones or her preoccupation with being pregnant and what it was doing to her body? What would he do – what could he possibly do – if Marian told him the truth she had not dared to say to anyone else, not even Dean?

Briella was becoming someone different, and if she'd started an obsession with angels and the afterlife and the existence of the soul, it might be, Marian thought reluctantly, because the kid herself did not seem to have what anyone might consider to be one.

Marian couldn't tell him that. She could never admit aloud that although she'd given up her faith a long time ago, she still remembered what it was like when she had believed. She couldn't tell anyone that she feared something had sneaked inside her daughter and started to take over. Marian would sound insane, and what would happen then?

They'd take Briella away, first of all. They might take Marian's baby away from her after that. They might even try to put Marian herself away.

"Mrs. Blake?" Garrett looked curious and concerned.

"Nothing. I'm sorry. Just…pregnancy vapors, as my mom would have said." Marian made a show of fanning her face and putting on a smile that hurt her cheeks to make. She lifted her chin, meeting Garrett's gaze. Giving away nothing.

"Do you need to sit down? Some more water?"

"No, thanks. I should get going, if that's okay." Marian held her smile with the emotional equivalent of hanging on to a ledge by her fingernails.

Garrett nodded. "Of course. Thanks for coming in. I'll walk you to the front."

Marian didn't protest, although all she could think about was getting out of the office and behind the wheel of her car. She needed another bathroom stop. She needed a drink. She needed a nap. She needed to be anywhere but here.

At the school's massive front doors, she gave him a nod and a handshake, already halfway down the concrete steps before his voice called her back.

"Oh, Mrs. Blake! I forgot, there's one more thing we need to talk about!"

She turned, wishing she could pretend she hadn't heard him. "Yes?"

"It's about the bird," Dr. Garrett said. "Onyx."

CHAPTER THIRTY

"You lied to me, Briella. What have we talked about with lying?" Marian's voice sounded tight and controlled, although she felt anything but.

Briella had just gotten out of the van and had made as though to go right to her room, a habit she'd been in for the past couple weeks. Marian had stopped her at the foot of the stairs and ordered her into the kitchen to sit at the table. The girl had admitted immediately that the bird had been spending time at the school, caged in the lab they'd given her to use. She'd also admitted to telling her teachers that the bird had been a pet for years and that she'd had full permission from her parents to bring it in. Not for experiments. Just as a pet.

"*You* lied to me," Briella answered, sounding sullen. "You told me that stick was nothing, but it meant you were going to have a baby. I asked you in the bathroom what it was, Mother, and you lied right to my face."

Mother. Briella had never called her that. Marian's chest constricted. She hadn't started calling her mom "Mother" until her teen years, but she'd done it with the same level of scorn.

Marian's fingers tightened, but she made sure to let them fall open, loose. Not making fists. Trying hard not to be confrontational. She remembered how it had been to battle with her mom over things that now, looking back, had been so stupid. But she remembered how important they'd felt at the time. "That was different."

Briella's lip curled. "It's not okay when grown-ups don't tell the truth, not if it's not okay for kids to do it. But grown-ups lie all the time, and they're allowed. So why isn't it okay for kids to do it?"

"Because it's not. Because there are things adults can do that children cannot, and that's just the way the world works!" Marian gave in to the shout, hating the way the kid recoiled but finding a certain grim satisfaction in it, too. It felt good to yell. To be angry.

It was better than being terrified.

"Like swears," Briella said.

"Yes. Like that. And other things. You're right. Lying isn't okay. But sometimes not telling the whole truth is necessary for...reasons." She'd started to run out of steam. "But you flat-out lied to my face about that bird."

"I didn't," Briella said after a moment. "You asked me if Onyx came to school with me for show and tell. And he didn't. He came to school with me to help me with my project. That's totally different. You never asked me again."

"You know I would have wanted to know about it. You knew that's why it wasn't coming around after dinner anymore, because you had it locked up in a cage at school."

"Not always. He's not always locked up. I let him out sometimes."

"You should have...damn it, Briella. Why lie? What's so special about this goddamned bird?"

Briella was silent for a long time, so long that Marian thought she wasn't going to answer. Marian was too tired to fight now. Dean had left already for work, picking up extra hours to support this little family, which was starting to fall apart. And whose fault would that be? Marian's, of course.

She was the mother. She should have paid more attention. She ought to have known something was up with the kid, her *child*....

"He's smart. Like me," Briella said finally.

Marian turned. "What?"

"Onyx. He's really smart. Ravens are smart, but Onyx is extra smart. Like me. That's why I like him. He's different. Like I am. I love him!"

All of Marian's anger and frustration fizzled away, leaving her bone-tired and aching with her own emotions. She could blame it on hormones, of course, but if she couldn't control her own feelings, how could she expect her daughter to?

"Being different isn't a bad thing, you know," she said.

"I know."

"Tell me about your project, Bean." Marian sat down across from her at the table.

"You won't understand it."

"I want to know about it. I want to listen to you. Even if I can't understand everything about it, I want to try," Marian said.

Briella's face twisted. "Mrs. Addison said there's no way to prove the existence of souls. It's just something you have to believe, or not."

"What do you believe? I know you told me you think there's something else, after we die."

Briella hung her head and shrugged. "I don't know."

"Talk to me, Briella. Please," Marian pleaded. She reached across the table to put her hand over her daughter's. It was still so small. *She* was still so small, even with the inches she'd sprouted since the beginning of the school year. She would be eleven just after the baby was born. Her body was changing. She wasn't going to be Marian's little girl much longer.

"You must believe in your project, right?" Marian asked.

The girl looked up. Her eyes were alight. Her mouth wet and slightly slack. She hadn't pulled away from Marian's grasp, but now she turned her hands over to take her mother's. Squeezing.

"What is a soul?" Briella asked. "It's something nobody can see, right? But people have believed in it since…well, since forever. Nobody can see it or feel it, but we know it's in there, because it's what makes us people. Duncan MacDougall was a doctor in 1907, and he weighed people who were dying. He discovered that at the moment of death, people got lighter. They lost twenty-one grams of weight. That's the weight of the soul."

"Okay," Marian replied, because what else was there to say?

Briella went on, her expression becoming animated. "But what is it? What makes us who we are? It's our personalities. Our experiences. It's everything we see and hear and smell and taste and do, it's everything that happens to us. It's why nobody is the same, not in our heads and hearts. We're all different. Because nobody has all the same experiences, and that's what makes us who we are."

"And you want to record memories so they can be downloaded." Marian thought about the papers Garrett had shared with her. "Like on a disc?"

"In a chip," Briella said. "You'd connect it to your brain, through your spine."

Marian pondered this for a moment. "And then what?"

"Then you could be inside anyone you wanted," the girl said. "You would never, ever have to die."

"What would happen to the person you went into?" Marian's voice scratched but stayed steady, her throat so dry she had to swallow over and over just to get the words out.

The girl did not answer. The light in her gaze did not vanish, but her demeanor changed. Became secretive.

"I don't know," she said.

A rushing buzz threatened to overwhelm Marian, filling her head until she sipped a few breaths of air while struggling to keep her expression completely neutral. "How were you planning to figure that out?"

"By testing it, of course."

Marian let her dry tongue scrape along the roof of her mouth. "How would you test it?"

No answer but a shrug. She was only ten, Marian thought frantically. Only ten years old.

"Did you test it on frogs?"

A flash of something like guilt or fear lit in Briella's eyes, gone in an instant. She gave a derisive snort. "Frogs aren't smart enough."

"Did you test it on Onyx?"

"Parkhaven doesn't allow us to experiment on animals," Briella said at once. "They even want us to be vegetarian."

Marian sat very still. "You said that exact thing before. Those exact words."

"Well," Briella said, "they do."

"Would you test it on yourself?" Marian asked. "Promise me you wouldn't test it on yourself. It sounds very dangerous, Briella, and to be honest, I'm not surprised they don't want you to keep working on it at school."

"What?" Briella jerked her hands from Marian's grasp. "They're going to make me stop?"

"Bean...."

"Why are they going to make me stop? Mrs. Addison said that even if projects don't work, it's important that we learn from our mistakes! They're going to make me stop it?" Briella's voice pitched high and higher, strident enough that Marian wished she could cover her ears against the stab of it into her eardrums.

She couldn't do that, of course. She could not cover her ears to stop herself from hearing. She could not cover her eyes to stop herself from seeing.

"Was it Mrs. Addison?" Briella demanded.

"I spoke with Dr. Garrett today. But yes, Mrs. Addison suggested you find a new project."

Briella's fury did not fade. It went…invisible. Her shoulders squared. Her chin lifted.

"Oh," she said. Then, her tone frostbitten and rimed, she added, "They're going to make me send Onyx away too, aren't they?"

"You're going to have to let him go back to the wild. Yes."

Briella drew in a hitching, sobbing breath.

"You shouldn't have lied," Marian told her, even though it wasn't really the lies that had brought them to this point. "This is the consequence of your actions. You need to take responsibility for that, Briella."

The girl looked up into her mother's eyes, her smile bright and sunny. Sharp and brutal as a serrated knife. "It's okay, Mama. I'll find another project to do. There are lots of things they like us to do at Parkhaven. I'll be able to get something else started. It was a dumb project, anyway."

"It wasn't a dumb project," Marian began, but stopped herself. *Gold stars for showing up*, she thought. Keep their self-esteem, no matter what. Shield them from the world, turn them into people who had no idea of what it felt like to fail. Create a generation of monsters.

Briella shook her head, keeping that same cheerful tone, the fake, plastic brightness. The voice of a much younger child, fitting to her small stature, perhaps even her maturity, but not her intellect. "Yes, it was. I'll find something better. I love Parkhaven, Mama. There are lots and lots of really neat things I can do. I can grow soybeans or figure out how to filter dirty water and make it clean. Something good for the environment."

"Those all sound like terrific projects." Marian was ashamed at the relief in her voice. Shamed by her own desire to put this all away from them.

"I know. I'm sorry I lied to you. I knew you'd be upset about Onyx. I shouldn't have kept it a secret." Briella got out of her chair to come around the table and give Marian a hug. She felt bony and lean beneath the white polo shirt of her Parkhaven uniform. The knobs of her spine ridged under Marian's palms, but in the front, small breast nubs had started to form.

Marian found this more alarming than the girl's skinniness. Marian had started her period in sixth grade. It would happen soon for Briella, she knew that. But she wasn't ready for it. She wasn't ready for any of this.

She held Briella tighter again for a moment or so before letting her go. She put on her 'mom' voice, the no-nonsense and matter-of-fact tone that was supposed to make them both think she had all this shit under control. "There are going to have to be consequences, Bean. No tablet for a week."

Briella took that news with a nod, as though she'd expected it. It was the first time Marian had ever really needed to discipline her that way, and she'd expected more of a fuss. Briella hugged her again.

"Can I go upstairs and read?" the girl asked.

"Yes. Wait, Bean...." Marian called after her as the kid headed for the stairs. Briella looked at her, expression neutral. "I'm sorry I lied to you, too. You're right. If it's not okay for kids to do it, it's not okay for grown-ups, either. I don't want the bird in the house, but if you want to play with it outside...that's okay."

"I forgive you, Mama," Briella said, turned away then looked back over her shoulder. "And please don't call me 'Bean' anymore. I'm too old for that."

CHAPTER THIRTY-ONE

Tommy's mother passed away at the beginning of March, weeks and weeks beyond how long they'd believed she would last. He called Marian in the early afternoon on a Wednesday. She'd been checking out her reflection in the bathroom mirror, monitoring her bump, but at the sound of his rasping, grief-laden voice, she let the hem of her shirt fall down.

"The funeral is tomorrow," he told her. "I thought you might like to know."

She would have liked to know last week and not last minute, she thought, but could not let that irritation show in her voice. "Of course. I'm so sorry."

"You hated my mother," Tommy said.

"I'm sorry for *you*," Marian told him gently.

Silence.

"Thanks."

"I can be there," she said. "Briella has a planned home study day tomorrow, so—"

"No," Tommy cut in.

Marian hesitated. "You don't want her there?"

"No. I don't."

She waited for him to make an excuse or apology about how it wouldn't be good for the kid, which honestly, Marian herself wasn't sure about but would have been willing to concede to for his sake.

"She's old enough to know about death," she said at last.

Tommy's derisive snort sounded very much like his daughter's. "Oh, I'm well aware that she knows all about death. I remember what she said to my mother."

"Tommy...." Marian sighed and pressed her fingertips between her eyes. There wasn't much she could say other than, "I'm sorry."

"You can be there, if you want. But don't bring the kid. It would be... too much."

"All right. And if there's anything I can do to help, please let me know," she said.

Tommy huffed into the phone. "Thanks, Mare."

Dean had been sleeping when she'd gone into the bathroom. She found him sitting on the edge of the bed, blinking sleepily. The grin he gave her was pure light. He gestured for her to come closer.

"Hey, baby. And baby," he added, bending to push her shirt up so he could kiss her bare, slightly bumped-out belly.

"Tommy's mother died." Marian ran her hands through the brush of Dean's hair.

He looked up at her. "We knew that was coming. Still sad."

"Funeral's tomorrow." She paused. "He specifically asked that Briella not come."

Dean yawned so widely she could see his back teeth. Scrubbed at his face. "Damn. That might be for the better, right? A funeral's not the time to be dealing with weird family dynamics. It would be stressful enough, for Tommy and for the kid, too."

"Yes. I know. It just felt…wrong," she said. "It makes me feel bad for her. Her own father. I mean, yeah, for years he's not been around, but this definitely felt…bad."

"She told you herself she didn't want to go around his mother anymore anyway, and she hasn't wanted to spend any time with him, either. I think it'll be fine, babe." He tugged her down to his mouth for a kiss, interrupted by another broad, jaw-cracking yawn. "Damn it, I just can't seem to wake up."

"You're doing too much. Working too many hours," she told him firmly.

Dean shook his head. "Nah. Not doing too much. It's not the amount of hours, baby, it's the schedule. Having a hard time getting enough sleep. That's all. I'll power through. They're still talking about letting me switch to the day shift, if I agree to keep taking the extra hours."

"You haven't told them you're banking the time to take off when the baby's born, have you?"

"Uh…." Dean laughed self-consciously.

Marian knuckled his arm. "Dean."

"I think it's in my best interest not to reveal that as the plan," he told her. "They'll cut my overtime back, they definitely won't switch me to days, and I'd go so far as to say that they might even try to find a way to dock my vacation hours. But if they do that, the money I'm getting now means I can take unpaid leave, if I have to."

Marian had, as Tommy said, hated his mother, but she'd still been fighting sympathetic tears since the phone call. Now, she burst into sobs. Braying, snot-filled sobs that had Dean pulling her down to rock her against him.

"Hey, hey," he soothed, stroking her hair. "What's going on?"

She couldn't find words at first. Just another series of sloppy sobs. Dean let her cry.

"You're working all the time. You're hardly ever here, and when you are, you're asleep," she managed finally. "You're exhausted, and I'm exhausted and I'm pregnant and I just...I miss you. I miss you, baby. I miss you at night, I miss you during the mornings when you used to get home earlier."

"It's temporary," he told her.

Marian nodded, wiping at her face with disgust. "I know. And I know you're doing it for us. I'm being selfish."

"You're allowed." Dean put his palm flat on her belly.

"I love you. God, so much." They leaned together, saying nothing, letting the rhythm of their hearts sync. She rested her head on his shoulder. His breath caressed her face.

"Are you going to the funeral?" he asked her.

Marian sighed. "I don't know. It's no secret that I thought his mother was an awful person. But you don't go to a funeral for the person who died. You go to support and show love for the people left behind."

Dean squeezed her shoulder. "Right."

"But I don't love him any more, Dean. I mean, I did. A long, long time ago. But I haven't in a long time. So...I don't know. Do I go? If I do go, what do I tell Briella?"

"Do you have to tell her anything?"

Marian shifted to look at him. "Yeah. I do. She needs to know that her grandmother died, first of all, and I'm pretty sure Tommy isn't going to tell her. Also, she doesn't have school tomorrow, so if I'm going to the funeral, she can't stay by herself."

"And I'll be at work," Dean said.

"She can go to stay with my dad. I'm not worried about that part. But I do have to tell her." Marian sighed. "What do I say if she asks to go?"

"That's a tough one. I don't know."

As it turned out, Marian didn't need to worry. She broke the news of Tommy's mother's death to Briella, who accepted it calmly and without question. She'd been accepting everything calmly and without question for the past few weeks, ever since her teachers at Parkhaven had forced her to put aside the Blackangel project to focus on something else.

It had made life at home much quieter, although Marian had often found herself watching the girl too closely, waiting for an outburst of temper that hadn't yet come. She searched Briella's room for evidence that she was continuing to work on the project at home, but found nothing. And of Onyx? Marian could find no evidence that Briella was letting the bird in through her window at night. It still did come around the house in the afternoons to be fed, but it no longer left behind any gifts.

CHAPTER THIRTY-TWO

Marian had always been prone to laughter at inappropriate times. Listening to the mourners wax poetic about Tommy's mother was sending her into a fit of giggles, and choking them back was upsetting her stomach. She was barely out of the first trimester, still suffering from occasional morning sickness that could hit at any hour of the day. Somehow, she thought that bursting into guffaws would be worse than puking all over the pew.

At the graveside service she stood toward the back, both in case she had to make a hasty exit and also because although she was there for Tommy's sake, she had no desire to be pushed into the public role of mourner. Stifling laughter in the church had been hard enough. If someone stated to her face how sorry they were for her loss, she wasn't going to be able to hold it together.

The weather was nice, at least. March had come in like a lamb, that was for sure. The grass was still brown beneath her sensible flats, but it was soft and the sun was shining. Marian let herself enjoy the promise of spring. If it felt a little disrespectful to do that, well…it was much better than pissing on the old bitch's grave.

After, Tommy hugged her for a long time. "Thanks for coming."

"No problem." Marian patted his back. Over his shoulder, she spied a flash of dark shadow darting among the tombstones. A flutter of wings.

When she pulled away from him to stare, though, there was nothing. If the bird had come to the funeral, it was gone now. *Or hiding*, Marian thought with a shudder.

"You okay?" Tommy asked.

Marian pulled her attention back to him. She'd been imagining it. Onyx was not stalking her, or Tommy, or God forbid, the corpse of Tommy's mother.

"Yes. Just feeling a little sick to my stomach. I'm pregnant," she added, because of course he couldn't have known before now.

Tommy blinked rapidly. "Congrats."

"Thanks."

"Dean's a good guy," he said next. "He's a lucky fucking guy."

"Yes. I know."

Another flash of shadow, of wings, of fluttering feathers from behind him, this time closer. Her stomach lurched. The sun that had been so welcome now seemed too hot. She needed water and shade. Marian excused herself to head for her car, but although she kept an eye out for the bird, it never showed.

By the time she got to her father's house, her stomach was still unsettled but not threatening to erupt up her throat. The house was dim and quiet. Her father was in his recliner, as usual. Briella was in the kitchen when Marian came in.

The girl spun around at the sound of her mother in the doorway. She'd been reaching into the cupboard by the microwave. A glass shattered. Briella cried out.

"You scared me." Briella sounded breathless. She put a hand over her heart as though to press against its pounding. Her tawny skin had flushed a deep, dark russet.

"Careful," Marian said and waved the kid away from the mess. "No, don't touch it. I'll clean it up."

"I'm sorry!"

Marian looked at her with narrowed eyes. "Accidents happen, Bea… Briella."

"It was the Tweety glass!"

Marian found the dustpan and broom to sweep up the shards of the *Looney Tunes* glass that had been around since her childhood. She pulled another glass from the cupboard, knocking over her father's pill bottles in the process, and handed it to Briella. The girl poured herself some juice from the fridge while Marian cleaned up the glass.

By the time she'd finished, her father had woken up and come into the kitchen. He assured Briella that he wasn't angry about losing the glass. He hugged Marian and kissed her cheek. He reminded her of the doctor's appointment he had the next week, and that she'd promised to drive him.

She hadn't forgotten, but it had slipped her mind. She made sure to add an alert to her phone's calendar so she wouldn't forget next week. They said their goodbyes.

In the car, Marian looked into the rearview mirror to catch Briella's gaze. "If you want to talk to me about Grandmother Gallagher, you know you can. Right?"

"I know."

"It's okay to be sad," Marian said.

Briella shrugged. "I'm not sad."

The rest of the drive was quiet, except for the radio. They pulled into the driveway as Amy and Toby were walking along the sidewalk, probably heading for the frog pond. Briella got out of the car first.

"You want to come for a walk with us?" Amy called.

Briella looked at her mother. "Can I?"

Marian waited until she got closer to Amy before greeting the other woman. "Great day, huh?"

"Spring is definitely on the way." Amy eyed her. "If you don't feel like taking the walk, Marian, Briella is still welcome to come with us. It would be a shame to waste such a pretty afternoon."

"Sure, if you don't mind."

"Not at all," Amy assured her.

Briella and Toby were already heading for the edge of the cul-de-sac. Toby chattered to Briella, his words still unclear, but he was using so many more of them now. Briella had even taken him by the hand.

"He found his voice," Amy said with a small laugh.

"Thanks for taking her. I'm a little tired. I'm..." Marian, thinking of Amy's confession that she and her husband had been trying for another, paused. "Well, I guess it's okay to start letting people know. I'm pregnant."

Amy blanched. A moment after that, she forced a smile. It seemed genuine enough, but Marian still felt guilty.

"Congratulations," Amy said.

CHAPTER THIRTY-THREE

The magazines in the waiting room were battered, the pages bent and some torn, but Marian flipped through them anyway. The obstetrician she saw belonged to the same medical group, and the magazines were mostly the same, but she gleaned them anyway for something she might have missed.

"Mrs. Blake?"

She looked up, confused. "Yes?"

"Dr. Cole was wondering if you had a few minutes to chat about your dad."

Marian's heart lurched. She stood. "Yes. Of course."

She had forgotten to put down the magazine and still clutched it as she took a seat in front of the doctor's desk. Dr. Cole was in her mid-forties, skin the color of dark amber, with a broad smile of white teeth and kind hazel eyes. Marian's father had spoken highly of her as a practitioner, but Marian had never met her before.

"Marian," Dr. Cole greeted her. "Thanks for bringing your dad in. He's having some blood drawn right now, but I wanted to talk to you about a few things. First, did your dad mention any falls or injuries lately? There's a wound on the back of his neck, at the base of his skull, and we can't seem to pinpoint how it might have happened."

"No." Marian shook her head, grateful for the doctor's ability to get right to the point. "Is he all right?"

"Oh, yes. It's healing fine. He couldn't recall how he cut himself, though, and that's troubling, because he also seems to have been forgetting his meds. Or possibly taking the wrong doses. At any rate, he's run out of his prescriptions earlier than he's supposed to a couple times now."

"I know there was once, months ago. There've been more?"

"He asked for refills at this visit, too. Now it wouldn't normally be such an issue – things happen, pills get spilled, whatever. But coupled with the cut on the back of his neck that he can't recall, or honestly didn't seem to know about, that's concerning." Dr. Cole pulled a pad of paper toward her and scribbled something on it before handing it to Marian. "I'm going to give you the name of a specialist in elder care. Specifically dealing with neurological problems."

"You think he's got Alzheimer's or something?" Marian tried but failed to keep her voice calm.

"Your dad might simply be experiencing the normal mental decline of aging," Dr. Cole said kindly.

Marian twisted her hands in her lap. "Does dementia make people do weird things? Like imitate animals? Make...bird noises?"

"It could, I suppose. Why? Is that what happened with your father?" Dr. Cole's smile had faded, replaced with concern.

"Just once. A few months ago. He woke up, said he'd been dreaming. I thought it was nothing at the time." That was mostly the truth.

Dr. Cole nodded. "I'm sure it was nothing. Talking in your sleep or reacting to dreams is very common and has nothing to do with any indications of a declining mental state. But make him an appointment with the specialist and keep an eye on the cut on the back of his neck. Please don't hesitate to call me if you have any other questions."

In the car, Marian waited until they were on the drive to ask her father about what had happened to his neck.

"I cut myself shaving," he told her blithely.

"Why were you shaving the back of your neck?"

He gave her a look. "Because it was scruffy."

"Dad." Marian sighed, clutching the steering wheel as she navigated the lunchtime traffic. "I'm worried about you. That's all."

"I've told you, dolly, you don't have to be."

"That doesn't stop me from worrying," she told him.

★   ★   ★

The visit with Dr. Cole had been so disheartening that the first thing Marian did as soon as she dropped off her dad was to drive herself straight to the local fast-food burger joint, where she ordered a two-patty burger with extra cheese and mayo. Extra pickles, too. A jumbo order of fries and a strawberry milkshake completed the indulgence, but what made it truly disgusting was that she ate it all in the driveway because she couldn't stand to wait until she got it in the house.

Marian stared at her greasy fingers, still glistening although she'd tried to wipe them clean, first with the handful of cheap paper napkins that she'd stuck inside the paper sack along with the food. Then with a couple of baby wipes from her bag. She'd never stopped carrying them with her, even when Briella no longer wore diapers. She was going to have to get used to all of that all over again, Marian thought, staring stupidly at the soft, moist squares of fabric-like paper.

Then suddenly she was weeping, the food as heavy in her gut as if she'd eaten a pile of rocks. She clung to the steering wheel so hard her fingers ached, the knuckles swollen and sore like she'd been punching things all morning long. Her belly was barely bumped, but she was already starting to have a hard time breathing with the baby pushing upward on her lungs all the time. Now her nose clogged and she had to gasp for breath and still felt like she couldn't get enough air.

The Parkhaven van pulled up at the end of the driveway. Marian muttered a string of curses and tore another couple of wipes from the package. She scrubbed at her face, glad she hadn't bothered to put on mascara this morning. Yeah, she looked like a hag, but at least it wouldn't be smeared all over her face now. She blew her nose hastily and shoved the nasty, used wipes into the empty fast-food bag. In the rearview mirror, her eyes looked puffy. Her face, bloated. She looked like shit.

Briella had gotten out of the van and was already on the front porch. She hadn't seen Marian in the car, so at least there was that to be grateful for. Marian stifled a belch with the back of her hand, waiting to see if she was going to gag on the rising taste of grease and onions. Heartburn tickled her behind the ribs, but she was used to that.

The bird flew over the roof and landed on the front porch railing with a squawk. Marian couldn't hear what Briella was saying, but she could see the girl pull a handful of something from her jacket pocket and hold it out. Goldfish crackers, it looked like. The bird pecked a few delicately and flapped its wings before flying off.

Marian opened the car door. "People food can't be good for it."

She wanted to say more than that. She wanted to ban the damn bird, but what was the saying? *Keep your enemies close*, something like that? The bird wasn't an enemy, exactly, but it was definitely not Marian's friend.

Briella had turned with an almost comical look of surprise. She watched as her mother heaved herself out of the front seat, then ran down the front porch steps to greet her.

"Mama, what the heck?"

Marian laughed softly at the kid's expression, even as she gave her own confused look. "What are you doing home so early? Are you sick?"

"No. Everyone got out of school early. There was a message sent out to the parents."

That damn parent portal must have screwed up again. Marian was getting totally frustrated by it. She closed the driver's side door and hitched her bag higher on her shoulder. She tucked a strand of Briella's curly hair behind her ear. "Why was everyone sent home?"

"I don't know." Briella shrugged.

"I didn't get the message, so I guess it's a good thing I got home when I did. How was school?"

"Oh, it was awesome. Today I got to work in the art room, at least until Mrs. Addison got sick. Hey, Onyx!"

The bird had returned. Marian suppressed her distaste as it swooped around them to land on the railing again. Something shone in its beak. Briella held out her hand, and the bird dropped its gift into her palm.

"Briella," it said.

"Thanks! Look, Mama. What is this?" Briella held up a small silver key attached to a tiny scrap of crimson ribbon.

"It looks like the key to a diary. Someone's going to be sad they're missing it," Marian said. "You should tell it to take it back."

Briella snorted laughter and stroked the bird's sleek black head. "You always say you don't believe he's that smart, you know, but then you want him to do stuff like that."

"Fair enough," Marian said as she got the front door open, pushing hard because it tended to stick. She cast a few last warning words over her shoulder. "It doesn't come in the house."

"I know, I know. Onyx, I'll play with you later, in the backyard." Briella followed her mother into the shadowy front hallway. "You smell like burgers. Are we having burgers for dinner?"

Marian pushed away her guilt, glad she'd forgotten the empty wrappers in the car so she didn't have to explain her greedy indulgence. "You have a nose like a bloodhound, you know that?"

"Does that mean you think I look like a dog?" Briella swung her backpack onto the hook by the closet and kicked off her shoes.

"It means you've got a really sensitive sense of smell."

"Yeah, I do. Like when I smelled Daddy's mom, and I knew she was… you know." In the dim lighting it was hard to see Briella's expression, but her tone was casual, even though she cut herself off.

Marian went into the kitchen. "We're having baked chicken and mashed potatoes with green beans for dinner."

"Yuck. Would rather have burgers and fries! Why can't we go get some?"

"Because I already planned for us to have baked chicken and mashed potatoes and green beans." Marian opened the freezer door to pull out the package of chicken to defrost.

Briella kicked at the floor. "Ugh."

"C'mon, Bean. Briella. You like chicken."

Briella shrugged and gave her mother a sideways glance. "Did you go to see Grandpa today?"

"Yes." Marian hesitated, facing the sink as she washed her hands. She kept her question light. "How did you know?"

"I can smell it on you," Briella said in a low voice.

Marian was silent for a moment. She dried her hands. She turned to her daughter. "He's going to die, isn't he?"

Briella looked caught, guilty, although she had no reason to feel that way. "I don't know."

"You can tell me, Briella. If you know something. If…Onyx told you." Marian cleared her throat. On impulse, she moved forward to take her daughter by the shoulders and held her still so she could look deeply into Briella's eyes. "Please. I know you love Grandpa, and you love me."

"I don't *know* anything," Briella insisted. Her eyes were bright, but not with tears. "I'm going to play outside in the yard, okay?"

Marian nodded, then added after a pause, "Don't leave the yard."

"Why can't we have burgers?" Briella cast this last plea over her shoulder.

"I'm making the dinner I planned, and that's what you'll eat."

And there it was: Marian had lost it completely. That tenuous thread of bonding with her child. Marian's biting tone had clearly broadcast her irritation. The scant few moments they'd shared in which she had thought maybe she might be able to connect with her kid had vanished.

She was a shitty mother.

Marian's hands went protectively over her belly. The baby inside probably twisted and squirmed, but it was too early to feel it kicking. The child in front of her gave Marian a steady, unblinking stare.

"Go outside and play," Marian said in a low voice.

It was still a little too early to make dinner, but it took her only a few minutes to defrost the chicken in the microwave and put it in the oven along with the potatoes she would serve baked instead of mashed – less effort that way. Before she'd even had time to finish cleaning up the counter, Briella had returned.

"I thought you were going to play outside."

"It's cold." Briella shrugged. "I'm going upstairs to read."

That was even better, since a sudden wave of exhaustion had washed over Marian. "Dinner's in the oven. You can have a small snack if you want one."

Briella declined a snack. It would be another few hours before Dean woke up and it would be time for dinner. Marian went into the den and powered up the old computer. She fought with the slow browser and changed her password one more time to get into the parent portal. When she was finally able to access it, she checked the email address listed for her. Once again, the same as it had every other time she'd been locked out, her email had been subtly changed by one letter.

"Damn it," she muttered.

She changed it back to the correct address. Along the side of the site, a menu bar listed several options. One of them she'd never paid attention to before was 'Previous History'. She clicked on it. It listed each of her failed log-in attempts and password changes. It also listed several other log-ins with password changes, all of them to that same subtly incorrect email address.

She stared at the list for a long time.

She rarely used the computer, but when she did, it was never at two, three or four in the morning, which was when the previous email addresses and passwords had been changed. Marian clicked on the portal's News tab. She saw the announcement for the early dismissal, and the reason why.

Mrs. Addison, Briella's homeroom teacher and her advisor for the work on the Blackangel project, had suffered a severe grand mal seizure during class. The trauma had been enough that the administration had sent all the kids home early.

Marian closed the browser window and shut the computer down. She went upstairs, feeling very calm. Very measured. She knocked on Briella's door, but didn't wait for a greeting to push it open.

She found the girl sitting on the window seat, the window open. No sign of the bird, but that meant nothing. Briella turned when Marian came in.

"You're supposed to wait for me to say 'come in'," she said.

"Mrs. Addison had a seizure today."

Briella nodded. "I know."

"You told me she got sick," Marian said. "You didn't tell me she had a seizure. Did you think I wouldn't find out?"

Briella's expression didn't change. She did not smile or frown. She made no twist in her expression. She met Marian's gaze without flinching.

"Have you been changing the parent portal log-ins? So I can't get information from the school? Answer me, Briella!" Marian tried to shout, but her throat had closed up tight. The words squeaked out, without force. She swallowed hard. Made another attempt. "Have you been changing my password and my email address?"

"You asked me to help you!" Briella cried.

"I asked you to help me when I couldn't get logged in! But someone's been changing the information so I can't get in there, I don't get any of the messages, I can't check up on your progress...." Frustrated and well aware she sounded like a crazy person, Marian used both hands to scrape her hair away from her face. She drew in breath after breath until she could ask calmly, "Briella. Did you...do something...to Mrs. Addison?"

Briella launched herself against Marian and clutched her around the belly. The girl's shoulders shook as she wept. Maria cradled Briella against her, smoothing the girl's curls. Her own tears flooded down her face, choking her.

"Talk to me, Bean. My God, please, please, talk to me!"

For a moment, Marian thought Briella was going to, that she would spill everything. Disclose all. And what would Marian do then, when her daughter had revealed herself to be the monster her mother had begun to suspect her of being?

But then the girl pushed out of her mother's embrace and wiped at her eyes. Her lower lip trembled, but she drew herself up. She made a visible effort at shoving away her tears.

Her mouth worked before she could speak. "I can't."

"You can't talk to me? Why not?"

Briella shook her head. "I can't tell you what you want to hear."

"What is it that you think I want to hear?" Marian's voice had risen a little too high, squeaking, and she knew at once she'd lost. She'd made it too obvious about how deeply she cared.

Again, Briella shook her head. She pressed against Marian without saying anything. Her sobs had eased, and now she took a few long, deep breaths. Marian held on to her, her own tears still leaking down her cheeks.

This could not be happening. Why was this happening? This could *not* be happening.

Marian closed her eyes tight. She held her girl. She found her voice.

"Did you do something to Mrs. Addison? Did you...did you do something to Pamela Morgan?"

Briella tightened her grip on Marian's back. Her face pressed hard into Marian's breasts, which had gotten bigger along with her belly. The pressure hurt a little. Not too much, but enough.

"What do you think I did, Mama?"

The girl's voice had gone soft. Soothing. Tinged with the edges of tears, but not hysterical.

Marian could not bring herself to say what, exactly, she suspected the girl of doing. She could not force the accusation: that Briella had stolen her grandfather's medications and somehow slipped them to a girl who'd been unkind to her and a woman who'd taken away something she loved.

"I'm just a kid, Mama, what do you think I did?" Briella's voice had risen a bit. Not too much.

But enough.

"Nothing. Of course you didn't do anything. Mama's just...tired," Marian said over the rise of another series of sobs. "The baby is making me very tired, that's all."

"It'll be good when you don't have to deal with it anymore then," Briella said in a hitching voice Marian had trouble making out.

"What?"

Briella's tone changed from tears to fake, plastic, sweet. "After it's born, that's all I meant. You'll be better after it's born."

CHAPTER THIRTY-FOUR

The morning sickness did not go away.

It got worse.

Nothing helped. No peppermint or ginger tea, no acupressure wristbands, no saltine crackers. One day, Marian fainted after heaving nothing but strings of yellow bile into the toilet. It had been lunchtime, last she recalled. She woke with a goose egg on her head from where she'd struck the rim of the toilet when she went down. Briella stood over her, staring without a word. Marian reached for her daughter.

"Run across the street. Tell Mrs. Patterson we need the ambulance."

An overnight stay in the hospital. IV fluids. A diagnosis – hyperemesis gravidarum. Fancy talk for never-ending nausea, frequent violent vomiting and a relentless sense of illness that kept Marian confined to bed.

Dean had been moved to day shift a week or so before; Marian refused to allow him to go back to nights, even though it meant she was by herself during the day. She wanted him beside her at night, when and if she could sleep. She needed him to be there to fix dinner for Briella, to wake her for school in the morning, to fight with her about her clothes and teeth and hair.

Marian had never told Dean about the day she tried to accuse Briella of hurting both her teacher and former schoolmate. She and Briella never spoke of it. Her log-in information to the parent portal never changed again, but they didn't talk about this, either.

Her belly grew as the rest of her body shrank. Getting to her OB appointments was a nightmare of emesis bags and the drugged semiconsciousness that was the only way she could manage a car ride.

The days she was able to keep down the peppermint tea and some crackers were good days, but it was enough for Marian to get through the day without feeling as though she were going to die. Without wishing she could. She was too sick to read or watch television, too sick to sleep. She spent ninety per cent of her time propped in bed, dreaming while still awake. The days spun into weeks. Then months – one, then another – and a few more weeks, until Parkhaven finished its school year and Briella was home full-time.

By the middle of June, though, Marian felt good enough to shuffle to the kitchen for a mug of peppermint or ginger tea every now and then, instead of relying on what Dean or Briella brought her. She'd even been able to get herself to the bathroom without falling down or immediately hurling from the mere motion of walking.

Two more months, she told herself now. The baby would come, maybe even a little early if they felt they could induce her safely. She could make it until August. The agony of unmedicated childbirth would be a relief compared to this.

"Here, Mama," Briella said now. "I made you some tea."

Marian propped herself up on the pillows. She felt grungy, sweaty, gross. She hadn't showered in what felt like forever, and didn't dare try with only Briella in the house. If she fainted, that would be bad. Today, at last, Marian was feeling good enough to take the mug in both hands and let the fragrant steam bathe her face. She couldn't bring herself to drink any of it right then.

"What have you been up to?" she asked, eyeing the girl's stained white shirt. Purple splotched it, along with various older stains. "What's on your shirt?"

Briella sat on the edge of the bed and looked down at her shirt. "Grape Popsicle."

God, that sounded good to her, surprisingly. Much better than the tea. "Can you get me one, please?"

"Does your stomach feel better?" Briella brought back the twin Popsicle, breaking it in half so they could each have one.

"Yes, today it does. A little, anyway."

"You should drink your tea, though. Dean said your doctor said you need to keep your fluids in you."

"Yes, ma'am," Marian joked, but Briella didn't laugh.

"I just want to take care of you," she said.

"I'm sorry I don't feel better," Marian apologized. "I'm sorry all of this has been so gross and kind of scary."

"Don't feel bad, Mama. You're the best mom. The greatest mom. The very best mom." Briella said this all so genuinely, so sincerely, so…brightly… that Marian had to fight tears. "It's not your fault. It's the baby's fault."

"The baby isn't doing it on purpose." Marian could not bear another single sip of peppermint tea. Even the Popsicle that had seemed so appealing now was too sweet, too sticky. She tossed it into the trash can by the bed. "Can you get my pills?"

She took regular doses of antinausea medicine. It didn't always help, but she took it because the doctor prescribed it. To stop taking it had felt like she was giving up hope.

Briella gave her the small foil pill packet from the mess on the nightstand. "I don't ever want to grow a baby inside me and be sick all the time."

"Not everyone gets this sick when they get pregnant." Marian's eyes slipped closed. She yawned. The baby inside her shifted and kicked, and she tensed, waiting to see if it was going to start doing a line dance to keep her up. She rested her hands on the mound of her belly, which seemed much bigger because the rest of her had grown so frail.

"I'd rather just have an egg. Just lay an egg in a nest and sit on it so it hatches. That's much better and easier. I'm going to have an egg instead."

Marian forced herself to open her eyes. The meds made her drowsy and groggy, even if she hardly ever slept and only just...floated. "Huh?"

But Briella was already gone. She'd left the door wide open, but Marian was too tired and too encased in her pillow fortress to get out of bed. Too tired to yell for the girl to come and close it. Normal noises weren't going to keep her awake. Not right now.

For the first time in what felt like an eternity, Marian actually slept.

★   ★   ★

Screaming.

Marian was screaming. Her throat raw with it, tears thick in her nose and on the back of her tongue, salty and bitter and sharp enough to scrape her to the bone. She was screaming and fighting the weight pressing her down, keeping her in bed.

And then she was awake.

Muzzy-headed, her mouth a trash can. No, a slaughterhouse, she thought. In her mouth, she tasted thick, greasy slabs of meat and cheese, the sort of meal she'd been unable to eat for months.

She wasn't screaming, but someone was. "Briella?"

Was the girl watching something on TV that she wasn't supposed to?

The screams sounded breathless, whistling and far away. Shit, was she boiling water? That was a kettle, not a person. What was going on?

Marian couldn't think straight. The blankets had tangled around her feet. She was trapped. The screaming faded. She'd been dreaming, right? She fought to get herself upright. Failed. Fell back against the pillows.

The doorbell rang. Then again. The bell itself had been sounding like a dying cat for the past year or so; Dean had changed the battery and the wiring, but nothing had helped. Now it wailed, urgent and demanding, and Marian couldn't get herself out of bed to reach it.

She made it out of bed. Lumbered, confused and disoriented, toward the source of the noise. She hit the bedroom doorframe with her shoulder, hard enough to send her spinning back into the room before she gathered herself sufficiently to move forward again. She wanted to shout out to the person ringing the bell so incessantly that she was on her way, but she was too out of breath. By the time she got to the front door, the bell had stopped.

She opened it, expecting a delivery person, maybe a door-to-door evangelist, someone she could pointedly dismiss. Instead, it was her neighbor, Hank, and in his arms was a shivering and whining Briella. Marian blinked rapidly, not sure what to do or say. Her stomach lurched and her gorge rose. Her head pounded.

"She ought to have stayed in her own yard," Hank said. "Rufus didn't mean anything by it. But she ought to have stayed in her own yard. I've told you all that, over and over again. All you kids, you never listen."

Marian grabbed her daughter from the man's arms, mindful of the weight and how it made her back ache. "What happened?"

Briella squirmed to get her feet on the ground. She held up her hand. She'd grown a lot over the past few months, sprouting up at least two inches, but in this moment her hand seemed as tiny as a doll's.

It was covered in blood that oozed out between her clenched fingers. Marian gasped and grabbed at the girl's hand. Briella cried out – in pain or fear, Marian didn't know and didn't care. She pulled the girl inside the house and behind her, putting out a hand to keep Hank from coming any closer, even though he hadn't made so much as a move to do so.

"I just wanted to play with the dog." Briella's hitching breaths made it hard to understand the words, and Hank cut her off almost instantly with a shaking, breathless retort.

"She was trying to take him. She had him by the collar, and she was dragging him over the electric fence. That hurts him, you know. Rufus knows he's not to go beyond it. It shocks him if he does. She had him—" Hank broke off and took a few steps back, off the porch. His hands were trembling. "By the collar. He was yelping and trying to get away. He must've bit her then."

"Briella, is this true?" Marian put her hands on the girl's shoulders, her grip tight. She was up and fully out of bed for the first time in months. She could only guess that the adrenaline was keeping her upright. "What were you doing?"

"I just wanted to play," Briella said stubbornly. "My hand hurts!"

"C'mon. Let's go." Marian straightened. "I'm sorry, Hank. Your dog bit my kid though, so I'm not sure what to do about that."

"She ought to have stayed in her own yard," he repeated.

Marian closed the door on him and took Briella into the bathroom, where she washed the wound carefully, taking her time. Breathing in through her nose, out through her mouth. She had to stop once, thinking she would vomit, but she managed not to. There was a lot of blood, but the injury itself turned out to be two small punctures on the back of Briella's hand and palm, as though the dog had nipped, for just a moment.

Stretching to pull a package of adhesive bandages from the medicine cabinet, Marian caught sight of her own face. The scars had faded, but she could still find them if she wanted to. A series of ragged holes along her chin and into her cheek. She'd needed fifty-seven stitches. She remembered hearing her mother once say that if Marian hadn't hit the dog as hard as she had, it would have torn off her jaw. She didn't know if that was true, but the memory of the pain flashed back to her hard enough that she had to grip the sink to keep from falling over.

Compared to what had happened to Marian, Briella's injury looked like almost nothing.

The girl had stopped crying, anyway. She'd watched her mother cleaning the wound carefully, with an avid fascination. She held still while Marian pressed the bandage over the small punctures. They weren't even bleeding anymore.

"Can you curl your fingers for me?" Marian asked.

Briella did, holding up her hand. "Yes."

"It doesn't look too bad." Marian settled herself on the edge of the tub, thinking for a moment that she might lose her balance and flip over backward. She caught herself on the edge and let her head droop, eyes closed. The rush of fear had faded, leaving her shaking internally and ready to collapse. She'd be lucky if she made it back to bed.

Briella, seated on the closed toilet lid, turned to her. "It hurts."

"Want to tell me what happened?" Marian closed her eyes again. Buying time. If she could sit here long enough, she might be able to make it without passing out or throwing up. She'd consider it a win if she managed only one.

"I was just playing with the dog. I wanted him to meet Onyx. I thought maybe they could be friends and have a playdate or something." Briella had slid into that plastic tone of a much younger child, that bright and empty voice. She could be telling the truth or straight-up lying to her mother's face. Marian had stopped being able to tell.

"You know you're not supposed to go out into Mr. Hank's yard." Marian cracked open an eye.

Briella nodded. "I know."

"He said you were trying to take the dog."

"I knew I wasn't supposed to go into his yard, so I thought if the dog could come play in ours, that would be better. But I didn't know he had a bad collar on," Briella said in the babyish voice, too young for her age.

It set Marian's teeth on edge. She could no longer bear to sit on the edge of the tub with her ass aching. She heaved herself to her feet, one hand on the enormous mound of her belly, the other on the edge of the sink to keep herself steady. She desperately had to pee.

"Don't talk like that," she said.

Briella gave her an innocent look. "Like what?"

"Like a baby," Marian snapped.

Briella's smile vanished. Her eyes narrowed. In the months of Marian's sickness, and even for a while before that, the girl had been pleasant and obedient and helpful, but here was the flash of anger and defiance Marian had been expecting.

"You're not a baby," Marian said, trying to soften her tone.

Briella's lip curled. "If I was a baby, would you like me better? You would, wouldn't you? If I was the one making you sick, you'd be angry and hate me, unless I was a damn baby!"

"Move," Marian managed to croak out, gesturing at the toilet. "I'm going to—"

She couldn't finish before she was gagging, bile flooding her mouth. Briella flew off the toilet and out of the bathroom, leaving Marian to flip up the seat and lean over to unleash the hot liquid that scalded her throat. She heaved a couple times, bringing up little more than air. Yet, when she stood to rinse her mouth at the sink, despite her sunken cheeks and shadowed eyes, she felt…better.

Better than she had for a while, anyway. She brushed her teeth, expecting that simple task to start off another round of vomiting, but it didn't. In fact, she felt good enough to go to the kitchen and pull out the bowl of soup Dean had left for her before he went to work. In the two minutes it took for her to heat it in the microwave, Marian went to the back door and looked out at the yard. It was lush, overgrown, a jungle. Dean wouldn't have had much time to mow lately. She searched automatically for signs of the raven. Birds dove in and out of the pokeweed that had grown as tall as her head all along the tree line, feasting on the purple berries that were poison to humans, but she saw no sign of an oversized black bird.

She thought about calling for Briella to come down, but could not make herself do it. She spooned soup slowly into her mouth, savoring it, making sure not to eat too fast. No more than a few bites was plenty, but at least she was keeping it down.

Dean had texted to check in with her, and she took the time to answer him. She was feeling better. She loved him; he loved her. Briella had been bitten by Rufus, but although the bite had bled a lot, it didn't look that bad. They'd keep an eye on it, see if it started to look infected. If so, Dean could take her to the urgent care center. Marian was not to worry about it, not to even think about trying to get in the car and drive.

ILYSM, Marian typed. *I love you so much.*

The sound of footsteps scraped on the ceiling overhead. Marian drank some water drawn from the tap, waiting again for it to revolt, but it stayed settled. She put both hands on her big belly, feeling the baby inside. The press of its foot, what was surely a rump. It – she could not refer to it by a gender, since they'd determined not to find out – was not permanently head down yet, but the OB doc had assured Marian that it would be, soon enough.

If I was a baby, would you like me better?

The truth was, she *had* liked Briella better as a baby. She would never say so, but she didn't have to, did she? The kid had it all figured out.

Halfway up the stairs, Marian heard the distinctive sound of muffled sobs coming from the girl's room. For a moment much longer than it should have been, Marian considered turning around and going back downstairs. Briella hadn't called out for her. She could pretend she hadn't heard.

She *was* a terrible mother.

Marian closed her eyes, one hand gripping the railing hard, as her shoulders slumped. One foot in front of the other. That was all she could manage right now. One step at a time, until she got into the upper hallway.

The sobbing was louder up here, and Marian's heart broke a little at the sound. A few more steps took her down the worn paisley runner to Briella's closed door. Marian put her hand on the knob. She told herself to turn it.

She didn't. She took a step away from the door, her heart squeezing and a fire rising in her throat. She put a hand to her chest, pressing against the pain. If Marian didn't take care of herself, she couldn't take care of her child. Right? It didn't mean she didn't love Briella. It didn't mean she cared more about this unborn baby than she did for the one she already had. Just because she didn't like her kid, that didn't mean she didn't love her.

The sound of the door opening stopped her at the top of the stairs, and Marian tensed, eyes closing again as her jaw clenched. She didn't turn at first. She waited for the small, sad sound of Briella calling out to her.

Then she put on a smile and went to her daughter.

CHAPTER THIRTY-FIVE

There wasn't much room in Marian's lap for anything but her belly, but she managed to get Briella settled in it. The girl's sobs had fallen off, but her face, hot and moist, pressed to the scoop neck of Marian's shirt in a way that made her want to pull away in distaste. She forced herself to hold her daughter as close as she wanted to be held, soothing and rocking. After a minute, her own eyes closed as she fell into the back-and-forth rhythm.

This was how it had been when Briella was young. *Before*, Marian thought, but could not be sure what she meant by that. Before what? Before this pregnancy, before Parkhaven, before Briella had started becoming so… different.

But she had always been different.

"I didn't mean to make Mr. Hank mad," Briella said now. "I was so bored, hanging around the house all day with nothing to do. I just wanted to play with his dog."

"I know, honey. But you can't let yourself into someone else's yard like that. You never know if someone's dog is nice or not. And you know for sure that you were never supposed to pet Rufus without Mr. Hank there."

Briella held up the hand Hank's dog had bitten. The wound, cleaned and bandaged, was hard to see, but Marian knew it was there. Her stomach turned at the thought of it. Guilt sawed at her nerves. She gathered Briella closer, shifting her even though there really wasn't enough room for both of them on this chair.

"Does your hand hurt?"

"A little." Briella squirmed and looked up at her mother.

Snot had crusted in her nostrils and there was more crusty ooze in the corners of her eyes. Her hair smelled sour, unwashed, full of tangles and frizz that broke Marian's heart. Dean had been doing his best, but he didn't know how to take care of Briella's hair while Marian had been too sick to even think about it. Her breath was stale with an undertone of something rotten. God, all the smells. Marian had to swallow hard against them. The truce she seemed to have made with her stomach earlier was in danger of being broken.

"That dog shouldn't have bit me," Briella said.

"No, Bean. It definitely shouldn't have."

They rocked a bit longer. Briella was growing too heavy. Marian was going to have to shift her again, or ask her to get down. Her back ached. Her arms ached. Hell, there weren't many parts of her that didn't.

"The baby's kicking," Briella said against her skin.

Marian tipped her head back to get a little breathing room. The places Briella's face had pressed felt sticky and gross. "Yes. I feel it."

"Did I do that?"

"Yeah. You were a little squirmy worm."

Briella laughed and squirmed, but too hard. Marian couldn't hold on to her. Her strained back complained as she tried, and failed, to keep the girl on her lap. Briella slid off and ended up on the floor with a thump.

"Briella, damn it," Marian said, her patience once again worn to a nub. "Be careful. You're going to hurt me, and hurt yourself, too."

"Sorry." Briella got up, dusting off her bottom with her uninjured hand.

Marian softened. "It's just that you're such a big girl now."

"But I'm not. I'm small. I'm smaller than all the kids at school. Am I going to be the right size? Ever?"

"Of course you are. You're small, but that doesn't mean there's something…wrong…with you." Marian hesitated on the words.

There *wasn't* anything wrong, physically. Hygiene issues aside, Briella was tiny but as perfect as she'd always been. If anything, she was becoming more and more beautiful as time went on. Beneath the boogers and the tangled, dirty hair, it was still possible to see the young woman she was going to be in just a short time. Before Marian would be ready for it.

At sixteen, Marian had clashed with her mother over dates and curfews and the length of her skirts. Normal arguments. Once, Mom had forbidden her to go out with friends, but Marian, furious at what she'd felt then was relentless parental interference, had stormed out of the house without even pretending she was trying to be obedient.

It was the only time she'd done that. Her mom had waited up for her until she got home, and they'd talked it out. They'd made compromises.

"There's a time," her mom had said, "when you realize that you can't actually make your children behave the way you want them to. You have to hope that you've already raised them to make the best choices, and then you have to let them make theirs."

Marian had never forgotten that conversation. She could not get it out of her mind now. She could not make her child behave the way she wanted her to, that was clear, but had she raised her to make the right choices?

"What are they going to do about Rufus?" Briella asked suddenly.

Marian chose her response carefully, gesturing for the girl to come closer and stand by the side of the rocker. She pulled Briella close into a one-armed hug. "I don't know."

"Are you going to put it in the pound?"

"I don't think so, Bean. Rufus made a mistake. He was hurting from his shock collar, and he might have been scared." Briella had called the dog an "it", not a "him", but Marian had deliberately done the opposite.

"What did they do with the dog that bit *you*?"

Marian pressed the small lump of a foot or a bottom that bulged up from her belly. The ache in her joints intensified as she shifted in the chair with a small groan. "That was totally different."

"What did they do to the dog, Mama?" Briella tugged at Marian's arm until she looked at her.

"They put it down," Marian told her reluctantly. "But, Briella, that dog viciously attacked me without warning. It was a bad, bad dog. Rufus was just scared and…he made a mistake."

She never would have dreamed she would defend a dog for biting anyone, particularly her child, but the memory of Hank's face twisted in fear and sorrow as he carried the screaming Briella toward her was still fresh and strong. Rufus was not a bad dog, and Marian knew it. She might never have stopped to pet him, and yes, she'd often warned Briella away from the yard where the dog was kept, but that was from her own fears and not because of anything the mutt itself had ever done.

"Put him down." Briella seemed to muse on this a moment. "You mean they killed him because he bit you."

Marian shuddered, not wanting to flash back to the snarls and slashing pain and smell of blood. The sound of her own screams and of her mother's. The baby inside her kicked harder, maybe sensing her upset.

"Yes," Marian said. "They killed it."

"Rufus bit *me*." Briella sounded sullen. Pouting.

"It wasn't the same."

The moment the words were out of her mouth, Marian wished she'd said something else. It was not the same, that was the truth, but what kind of mother excused an animal that had taken a bite of her daughter's flesh? That the bite was small and the animal had been pushed to it shouldn't matter, should it? Briella was her child. Marian should defend her against whatever harmed her.

Right?

She would not let herself admit that maybe Briella had deserved to be bitten. She couldn't go that far. The best she could do was soothe the pains and try her best to love her child and keep her safer in the future.

Marian wrestled herself up and out of the rocker. "If you're not going to sleep, then you need to go take as shower. Let's go."

"I don't want to."

"You have to. You stink." Marian looked at the clock. There was an hour or so before she could expect Dean to get home from work. She might even be feeling up to making him some dinner. "Go. Now. Don't make me have to talk about consequences, Briella."

After that, Briella got into the shower without too much fuss. Marian stood outside the bathroom door, listening to her daughter sing pop songs off-key and with the wrong lyrics. The water turned off too soon.

"Use soap. And shampoo. If I have to come in there and do it for you, Briella, I will."

"You're supposed to give me privacy!"

Marian nudged the door open to see the girl peering at her from around the shower curtain. Marian's heavy eyes and aching hips told her it was late. She wanted to be in bed, hugging her mountain of pillows and trying to sleep as best she could without her guts turning themselves inside out.

"You stink," Marian repeated flatly, her patience wasted. "Your body stinks, your hair stinks, your breath reeks."

Briella grimaced. "That's mean!"

"I'm your mother. It's my job to help you be the best person you can be, not be your best friend," Marian said. "Turn the water back on and wash your hair and your body. With soap."

"I did."

"God dammit, I have fucking had it with you." Marian snapped and crossed the room to grab the kid's arm with one hand while she whipped back the shower curtain with the other.

She turned on the water, not caring if it sprayed all over. Briella shrieked and struggled, but Marian's fingers gripped her hard. The girl wasn't even slippery, which meant she probably hadn't been in the water at all.

"Shut your mouth. Now. Get under the water. Now," Marian said. "I'm tired and sick and you stink."

She steeled herself to the sound of Briella's sobs and grabbed the shampoo from the shelf. A squirt into the thick mass of the kid's hair, then a dunk under the water. Briella stopped fighting her and suffered the scrubbing, then the conditioner that Marian left to soak while she handed her a washcloth and the soap and ordered her to use it.

Twenty minutes later, she had Briella wrapped in a towel and had taken her into the master bedroom to sit on the edge of the bed while Marian pulled out a pick to get through the tangled curls. Briella's hair, dry, hit just above her shoulders, but soaking wet hung midway down her back. Briella was silent. Exhaustion plucked at her, but Marian made sure to take her time with the knots, using both the pick and her fingers, along with extra conditioner to leave Briella with sleek, untangled curls.

At the sight of the bruises and raw flesh at the base of the girl's neck, Marian's heart leaped into her throat. "What's this? What happened here?"

Briella pulled away. "Nothing."

"Did the dog do that, too? Hold still." Marian gripped her again, aware that she might be causing bruises of her own on her daughter's upper arm, but determined to see what the hell was going on. She touched the wound, which was almost healed. "That's not a bite. That's a cut. What happened?"

"Nothing," Briella insisted and tried to pull away.

Marian turned her. "Tell me what's going on. Did someone do this to you?"

"No." Briella shook her head. "I was…my hair was tangled and I wanted to cut it, so I tried to do it by myself, but I cut myself with the scissors."

"Oh, Briella."

"I'm sorry, Mama." Briella hitched a sob and buried her face in Marian's neck.

At least she smelled better, Marian thought, and felt instantly ashamed for the thought. She hugged her daughter as best she could around the bulge of her belly, then pushed Briella gently back. "Do you know why I want to you to keep it taken care of, then? So it doesn't get so tangled that you have to cut it?"

"Yes. But I was embarrassed to tell you."

Marian sighed. "Let me finish combing it out, and we'll put some more conditioner in it. You can wrap it in a scarf the way I do before bed. Then you won't wake up with it all a mess."

"I want to look like you, Mama. I want to be pretty like you."

Marian paused at the kid's tone. Bright. Bubbly.

Fake.

"You're pretty like *you*," Marian said.

She studied the wound again. It was definitely a slice. Neat, tidy, not ragged. It looked as though it could have used a stitch or two, and her heart ached again at how she'd managed to miss something that serious. It looked worse even than the dog bite.

She finished combing through Briella's curls, then helped her pick out a soft scarf to wrap around her already drying hair. Marian stood and pushed her daughter by the shoulder to walk out of the bedroom. "You've had a rough day. I think you should try to rest in your bed for a bit. You can read or watch something on your tablet until it's dinnertime."

"Aren't you going to tuck me in?"

"You're a big girl...." Marian trailed off, thinking already of how steep the stairs would be, and how her hips would ache from the climbing. She'd be out of breath at the top. It had been months since the kid had asked to be tucked in. "Yes. Of course I will."

In Briella's bedroom, Marian tucked her daughter into bed. Tight, then tighter, the way she had when the girl was younger and would giggle about being made into a burrito. Neither of them said anything about it this time. Maybe Briella had forgotten that little joke, and Marian was too tired to make it.

She bent to kiss Briella's forehead. "Don't try to cut your hair again, okay? Let's try to keep it taken care of, and then it won't get so many tangles in it."

"I'm sorry, Mama." Briella sounded contrite, but something in the way she said the words left a sour taste in her mother's mouth.

She was placating, Marian thought. Not really sorry. Briella didn't think she'd done anything wrong, and that was the real issue, wasn't it? Briella never thought she did anything wrong. She never saw that the trouble she'd gotten into had stemmed from her own actions. She mouthed the word "sorry", but she didn't feel it.

Itching with unease, Marian kissed Briella again and, in another moment of guilt, hugged her as best she could in the awkward position of bending over the bed. She loved her daughter, hating that she had to remind herself. Hating this growing sense of discomfort. She could blame hormones, but that didn't make any of it better.

She would try harder, she told herself as she closed the bedroom door behind her at Briella's request. She paused outside the door, one hand pressed to it. Listening, giving herself a minute or so before she heaved her bulk down the stairs again.

The rap of a beak on glass. The creak of the bed. The mutter of a window being pushed up, then Briella's soft, indecipherable speech.

Marian reached for the doorknob, but at the last second, she stopped herself from opening the door. There would be a confrontation. She would yell and scold, and Briella would pretend as though she were sorry, but she would not be sorry. Marian listened a moment longer, but heard only silence broken by the hammering thud of her heartbeat in her ears.

She listened harder, eyes closed. If there was a whisper from inside or the soft, muttered caw of that damned bird, Marian didn't hear it. And, satisfied if only by the barest amount, she went downstairs, where she collapsed into her bed, exhausted, and stared at the wall for a very long time while her mind whirled.

CHAPTER THIRTY-SIX

"Do you want some iced tea?" Briella said.

Marian had switched off from the hot tea. In this late July heat, she couldn't bear it. Briella, however, had become so proud of herself for being able to operate the electric kettle that she insisted on brewing tea anyway, even if it meant putting it in the fridge to be served cold. Nobody was drinking it, really. Marian was so sick of the antinausea tea that it made her sicker to drink it than to sip seltzer water.

"No, thanks, honey."

"Are you feeling better, Mama?" Briella slid into the chair across from her at the kitchen table.

"Yes. I am." Marian smiled.

Briella nodded. "But you could get sick again anytime. The baby's still not born."

Marian had tried explaining that it wasn't the baby making her sick, not exactly, but she'd obviously not done a very good job of it. "It will be soon, though. Just another few weeks."

Briella said nothing to that, but her face gave away how she felt. Marian closed the book she'd been trying without much luck to read. She fanned herself with a catalog Dean had left on the table this morning – he'd switched temporarily back to working nights because his boss had begged him to take some shifts. With Marian feeling good – if not one hundred per cent, at least better – he'd agreed so he could get the overtime.

"Was I baptized?" Briella asked abruptly.

Marian's fanning paused, but only for a second or so. "Yes. Gramma wanted you to be, and it was important to her."

"Why?"

"Because she believed that babies needed to be baptized in case something happened to them. So they could go to heaven, in case they died." Marian didn't hesitate on the word.

"What about the babies you had that died before they could be born?"

"No. I didn't have them baptized." She had mourned their loss, those tiny, unformed children. But she had not believed them in need of baptism, or even heaven, for that matter.

"What about that one?" Briella jerked her thumb toward Marian's belly.

Marian shook her head. "I don't think so."

"Why not?"

"I don't believe the same things my mother did," she said.

Briella looked serious. "Babies are born empty. It takes them a while to get filled in with who they are. That's why you baptize them in case they die, because they haven't had time to get filled in."

"Filled in?"

"With their souls," Briella said.

Marian let the warm air wash over her with every stroke of her makeshift fan. She studied her daughter. "Are you still thinking about all of that? Even though you quit your project?"

"Just because they took it away from me doesn't mean I ever stopped thinking about it. Someday, when I'm an adult, I'll get to do whatever I want, and nobody will be able stop me."

"That's not exactly how it works," Marian said and thought of her mother.

Briella didn't crack a smile. "It should be."

A cramp rippled over Marian's belly. Braxton-Hicks. It was too soon for it to be anything else. In the next moment, the sudden pain deep inside her felt like something far more important than false cramps. The fan dropped from her hand. Breathing hard, Marian steadied herself with a hand on the table, the other between her back, where the dull ache she'd been having all day suddenly flared into sharp pain.

"Shit," she muttered as another ripple stabbed her.

"Mama?"

Marian waved a hand. "I'm okay."

"I bet you can't wait until that baby is out of you."

"That's the truth," Marian agreed, but paused to add, "Briella. This baby is not going to make me feel any differently about you than I already do. I promise you that. I know you don't believe me, and I understand why. But I want to reassure you. There are going to be huge changes, but it's not going to change how I feel about you. Or how Dean feels about you, either."

"I know it won't change how you feel about me," Briella told her in a flat voice that gave Marian a chill.

How she felt about Briella had been complicated for a long time now. Love, but distrust, fear, dislike. Affection. A fierce urge to protect her, coupled with frustration. Reluctance. None of that had anything to do with the baby. It was all about Briella.

What was motherhood, Marian thought, *but an endless stream of guilt and shame and grief for never being able to get it quite right?*

She forced herself to sit higher upright to ease the ache in her lower back. She'd get the heating pad and veg out on the couch all day, reading and keeping her feet up. She'd nap while Dean slept, let Briella rot her brain on stupid television. Except she wasn't going to get to do any of those things, because as soon as she stood, the phone rang.

★   ★   ★

It took twenty minutes to get to the hospital and felt like as long as that to get her enormous self out of the car and into the lobby, where Marian struggled to catch her breath around the tears. They'd already brought her a wheelchair and wanted all her insurance information before she could explain that she was not there to give birth, but to see her dad.

He was asleep in the hospital bed, hooked up to a bunch of wires and tubes. He looked shrunken, diminished. But when she sat in the chair next to him and took his hand, careful not to dislodge the IV running into the back of it, her father opened his eyes.

"Hi, Daddy." She hardly ever called him that, but now the endearment slipped easily out of her.

"Hi, baby girl." Her father's fingers squeezed hers without much strength.

"You don't have to talk. Just rest."

Her dad shook his head. "I'll be resting soon enough."

"Don't say that." She scooted the chair closer and gently let go of his hand so it could rest on the bed. "You're going to be fine."

His eyelids were already fluttering. They closed. Marian watched him for a minute or so, looking up when the nurse came in to check on him. Informed the doctor was in the hall, she heaved herself to her feet to find her.

"Your dad suffered a drastic fall. He's banged up. Bruised. We're watching him closely to make sure there's no internal bleeding," said Dr.

Patel, a tall woman with dark hair twisted into a bun and compassionate dark eyes. She added after a hesitation, "We haven't been able to determine if the fall was the result of a stroke, or if he's had intercranial bleeding for some other reason. It could have been from the fall, or it could have been what caused the fall. We simply don't know."

"Intercranial bleeding? Oh, God." Marian put a hand over her mouth. "That's serious!"

"It can be. But he's stable right now, not having any difficulties breathing on his own or any additional symptoms. So we're monitoring him, and if anything changes, he's here in good hands." Dr. Patel reached to squeeze Marian's shoulder and gave her belly a significant stare. "But you, miss, ought to be taking care of yourself right now."

"I need to be here for my dad."

"I understand. Of course. But you need to also make sure you're taking care of yourself and the baby. I'll have the nurse bring you something to drink. Stay hydrated. Stay off your feet," Dr. Patel admonished. She turned on her heel, but paused to return to Marian. "Has your father exhibited any strange symptoms prior to this? It might be helpful to determine if there's a precedent for anything."

"Like what?"

"Any…drug use? Of the illegal sort?" Dr. Patel looked uncomfortable. "Hallucinations?"

"Jesus, no. Nothing like that."

"He fought the EMTs when they tried to get him into the ambulance. He kept making raucous noises and flailing his arms. It took them a bit, but they figured out he was cawing like a crow. He kept trying to…fly. He was clearly hallucinating, but so far we haven't found any indications that he'd taken anything to cause them. Which leaves neurological reasons."

Marian staggered. Dr. Patel caught her by the arm. Marian fought back the faintness.

"It's a shock, I know. But it could have any number of causes," Dr. Patel said. "We're going to figure it out."

Marian pulled her phone from her purse before going back into the room. She'd missed a call from Dean and dialed him back without listening to the voicemail. He hadn't been happy that she'd insisted on driving herself to the hospital, but she'd gone fierce on him, and he'd conceded so long as she kept in touch.

"Hi, babe."

"How's your dad?"

She laid out what the doctor had told her, adding that he seemed tired but otherwise fine. She did not mention the hallucinations, the cawing, the flying. *That damned raven*, she thought. *That goddamned bird*.

Her voice broke. "I'm not sure what exactly happened yet. They don't seem to know."

"Do you need me to come to the hospital?"

"No, no," she assured him. "I'm just going to stay with him for a while. I wanted to let you know what was going on. I'll try to be home before you need to leave for work. But if I can't, can you call across the street to Amy and see if she'll take Briella until I can?"

"Of course. If you need anything, let me know."

"I love you," Marian said around her closed throat and the sting of tears.

"I know you do. I love you, too."

They disconnected, and she went back into the room. Her dad looked as though he were sleeping again, so she was quiet as she took the seat next to the bed. His hand moved at once, though, seeking hers.

"It's okay, Dad. I'm here. You rest."

He smiled faintly. "Already told you, I'll be resting soon enough. Right now I want to talk to my girl."

"Dad—"

"Hush, now," he told her, and Marian hushed. He blinked and looked at her, his mouth working while she waited for him to speak. "I'm ready to go. I want you to know that. I've been ready."

"Dad, no." Marian shook her head. Held his hand.

Her father raised the other hand to wave her to silence. "I took a fall. Misstepped heading out the back door into the yard. That brick patio came up to meet me."

"What were you trying to do in the yard?"

He said nothing for some long moments, long enough that Marian was sure he wasn't going to speak again. When he did, her father's voice was rough but not confused. He fixed her with a steady gaze, nothing uncertain about it.

"I heard your mother calling my name. Oh, I knew it couldn't be her, you know. But I thought it might be the angels. Never had them come in the middle of the day before, but then, who says angels are bound by the clock?"

Marian swallowed more tears, not wanting her dad to see her crying. "Did you see one?"

"I did. A beautiful, black-winged angel. They're not always white, you know." He chuckled, sounding so much like his healthy self that Marian flinched. "Just like people. I would imagine a black angel would come to a black man, wouldn't you?"

"Oh, Dad."

"I know you don't believe me, and that's fine. That's just fine." He patted her hand, his fingers curling to try and hold it, but not quite able to. "I wanted you to know, though. It's all going to be okay. I'm going to be with your mother very soon, and I'm ready."

"I wish you wouldn't say that, Dad. You need to stick around. Don't you want to see your new grandbaby?" Marian forced a smile. Tried a small laugh. It wasn't convincing.

Her father's eyes drifted closed again. "I'll be able to see everything about him from where I'm going. Don't you worry. We're—"

"All going to be just fine. I know," she said. "I know."

CHAPTER THIRTY-SEVEN

Marian's father died a little after six p.m. She'd been holding his hand the entire time. He didn't squeeze her fingers before he passed. He didn't open his eyes. There were no last words.

There was also no dreadful cawing, and Marian wept with grief and gratitude as she bent to press her forehead to her father's limp hand.

Death in the hospital is no unknown thing. Within an hour, the staff had laid out what Marian needed to do. They hadn't rushed her out of the room or anything like that, but they hadn't urged her to linger, either. There was compassion, but also complacency. All of them had been through this before, thousands of times.

She drove herself home. She'd already called Dean to tell him the news, and he and Briella greeted her at the front door with hugs and tears. She held them both as best she could around the enormous bulge of her belly.

"Briella," she said after they'd all wept for some ten minutes or more. "Where is Onyx?"

Briella swiped at her tears. "What?"

"Baby?" Dean sounded wary.

Marian forced a smile to her face. She put on the bright and plastic grin she'd seen on her daughter's face so often over the past year. "Where is he?"

"I don't know."

"If you called him, though, he'd come, right? He'd come to you?"

Briella looked frightened. "I don't know, Mama."

"Let's go see." Marian took Briella by the hand, tugging her toward the back door in the kitchen.

Briella dragged her feet a little but didn't totally resist. Dean muttered his curiosity behind them, but Marian ignored him. Everything had become etched in light, the outlines of every object crisp and sharp and clear. Shining.

"Call him," she said.

Briella's voice cracked as she whispered the bird's name.

"Louder," Marian said. "He'll never hear you. Tell him you have a treat for him."

"I don't want to," Briella said.

"Do it," Marian ordered.

Dean looked uncomfortable. "Babe, you're upset. Understandably. Let's just go in, maybe have some tea—"

"I don't want any fucking tea," Marian said through gritted teeth. "Call. Him."

"Onyx! Come, Onyx! Treat!"

And there, from the trees, came the bird. It flew high, then dipped into the pokeweed, yanking a sprig of the purple berries. It dropped them on the porch railing, where they hung for a moment on the edge before falling over the side. The bird landed on the railing, cocking its head to stare at them with that terrible, unblinking gaze.

"Briella," it said.

With a strangled shriek, Marian lunged for it. Her belly made her ponderous, ungainly, slow, but she had the element of surprise and a strength borne from her fury and hatred. She caught the raven around the neck with one hand, a fistful of wing with the other.

Briella was screaming. Onyx shrieked in the kid's voice and in Marian's own, or maybe that really was her own voice. She was the one ripping open her throat with the force of her fury. She was the one tasting blood.

Dean was shouting too, tugging at her, but not hard enough to pull her away. He was being too careful. Scared for the baby.

The bird twisted, pecking at Marian's hand. She didn't let go. She squeezed. She squeezed and squeezed.

Onyx stabbed at her again with its beak. The big strong wings flapped. She lost her grip on its wing. Still holding on to it by the neck, Marian groped for the glass ashtray she hadn't used in months but which remained on the porch railing. She tried to smash the bird with it, but Briella grabbed her arm.

"Mama, noooooooooo!"

The ashtray fell, hitting the porch and cracking in half. One piece stayed flat, but the other rolled down the steps. The bird twisted in Marian's grip, and she lost it.

It flew upward before diving at her face. Going for her eyes. She didn't flinch. She grabbed for it again.

This time, Dean caught her arm and hauled her back. "Enough! Damn it, Marian, enough!"

A small trickle of blood leaked from her forehead. Onyx had managed to peck her, just once. Marian swiped at the bird and threw off Dean's grip. She couldn't breathe. She was going to faint.

Dean took hold of her again and got her inside, where he sat her at the kitchen table. He put a glass of water in front of her, but she couldn't bring herself to drink it. Marian put her head in her hands.

"Mama?"

"Grampa died," Marian said. "And I am not all right."

CHAPTER THIRTY-EIGHT

Marian buried her father on a sweltering day in early August, in the plot next to her mother. She wore a black tent dress, the only thing that would still fit over her bulk. She had ankles like tree trunks. Even her nose had gained weight. She was bloated. Swollen.

Gravid.

The sickness and vomiting that had plagued her for a few months had mercifully left her, replaced by a vast and ruthless hunger she could not appease no matter how much she ate, but it was more than that. She *needed* to eat to keep up her strength. She couldn't be in bed all the time. She couldn't be frail. Since her father's death she'd gained nearly all the weight she'd lost during the worst of her illness.

"You need to slow down a little, Marian," her OB, Dr. Lopez, told her.

Marian could not slow down. She moved through her days from meal to meal, a nonstop parade of nibbling. She ate slowly but constantly. She drank only cool, clear water. No more damned tea.

It was a common enough thing, Dr. Lopez had told her, to feel out of sorts. The final weeks of pregnancy were difficult enough, but with the added stress of losing her father, it was completely normal for Marian to have some anxiety and to act on it.

It was not normal for her to attack a wild animal that had been more like a pet and try to strangle it in front of her ten-year-old daughter. Neither she nor Dean had mentioned that to the doctor. They did not speak of it to each other, or to Briella.

The raven had not come back around, not in Marian's sight anyway.

"Talk to me, baby," Dean pleaded with her in the darkness of their bedroom as she maneuvered herself into the complicated position of pillows she needed just to be comfortable.

But she couldn't do that any more than she could stop herself from eating. Or cleaning. Or fussing with the baby's room, rearranging the bedding for the crib, stocking diapers and wipes and all the things she'd been unable to do while she'd been so sick.

"You're nesting," Amy told her.

She'd stopped by with a frozen casserole for Marian to stick in the freezer for when she had the baby. Marian had invited her in to visit while the kids played outside. They'd left the back door open, which did nothing to help the heat in the kitchen, but the house was old and the air conditioning didn't work right anyway.

Marian paused in slicing cheese to lay out on the plate, along with apples and peanut butter. "Oh. God."

Nesting, she thought with revulsion. Like she was a fucking bird. The idea of it sent a shudder down her spine.

"I was the same way with Toby," Amy continued, oblivious to Marian's disgust. "Oh…please, no peanut butter."

"Shit. Sorry. I forgot. I'm so sorry. Let me wash this plate," Marian said. "I didn't use the same knife on the cheese, will that be okay?"

"Yes. It's okay. I'm hypervigilant. I just can't take any chances, you know?" Amy leaned to look through the back door for a glimpse of Toby and Briella, who were blowing bubbles. "When I was pregnant with him, I'd dream about coming home to an empty crib. As he gets older, it just seems like instead of getting easier, there's so much more to worry about. Do you feel that way about Briella?"

Marian slid into the seat across from her and pushed the plate of cheese and crackers between them. She nibbled some, which didn't relieve the hunger and didn't even taste that good. "You have no idea."

"Tell me," Amy urged seriously. "I worry so much about something happening to Toby. Jeff tells me I'm going to stifle the kid or drive myself crazy. He's even said…well, he's said that unless I can get my worries under control, we have no business having another."

Amy looked embarrassed.

"There's nothing wrong with worrying about your kid. If anything, I worry that I didn't worry enough when I should have," Marian said.

Marian could hardly describe it, could she? How it felt to look at the child you'd grown inside you and birthed in agony, sweat and blood, the one you'd cradled and bathed and loved, only to see a stranger. Worse than a stranger…something unknown.

"If something had happened to Toby like what happened to Briella, I'm not sure I'd even be okay with her playing out in the yard by herself ever again. And with what happened to the dog...."

Marian had been raising another bite to her lips, but stopped herself. "What about the dog?"

Amy looked confused. "Well...it's dead."

"What?" Marian's throat convulsed as she tried to swallow the crackers, gone dry as dust.

"Apparently Hank found it in the back yard. It was dead...." Amy's gaze twitched toward the back door again, through which Marian could see the children still blowing bubbles. "It had been...umm...attacked. Sliced up. Its eyes were missing."

Marian jerked forward hard enough to shake the table. "Oh, my God. When?"

"Earlier this morning. I was walking with Toby to the pond. We like to go before it gets too hot. You know, usually Rufus comes out. He never goes beyond the fence, of course, and we never, ever try to pet him, because you just never know...."

Amy broke off again, sending another look toward Briella. "Well. You never know about dogs, and Hank's been so adamant that nobody get into his yard. But this morning, Rufus didn't come out to greet us. I thought it was odd, but then on the way back from the pond, it might only have been about fifteen minutes, because I'd forgotten to pack bread crusts for the ducks, so we had to turn right around. So we were heading back and we saw Hank in the yard, hunched over something. I thought it was some yard waste, but it...it was the dog. Hank was crying, so I ran over to see what I could do to help, but I told Toby to stay back. I'm so glad I did, because it was awful."

A slow, rolling tension of a contraction began building low in Marian's belly. Her lower back was now aching, too. She stopped eating.

"Its eyes were gone," Amy repeated, sounding both horrified and the tiniest bit gleeful that she got to be the one to relate this story. "Something had attacked it. We think it might have been one of the coyotes that live around the power lines, but..."

"A coyote wouldn't eat out a dog's eyes," Marian said.

Amy shuddered. "Then I don't even want to think about what could have done it. Poor Hank."

"Yes," Marian echoed. "Poor Hank."

The kids tramped into the kitchen, begging for Popsicles, which both mothers approved of. Briella pulled out a twin pop and broke it in half, sharing it with Toby but giving her mother a long, steady look as she did so.

Amy waited until they'd gone back outside before saying, "She's going to be an amazing big sister. You know she's more than welcome to stay with us when you go to have the baby."

"Thank you, I hadn't thought enough about what we'd do," Marian said, then added, "when they're born, you can't imagine anything but love."

Amy gave her a curious look. "That doesn't change. Does it?"

Marian shook her head. There was still love. Of course there was, there had to be. What sort of mother didn't love her child?

"It won't be long now." Amy gestured at Marian's belly. "Are you ready for it?"

"No," Marian said. "I don't think we ever are."

CHAPTER THIRTY-NINE

The third time Marian got sent straight to Dean's voicemail, she left a string of tattered curses and a plea for him to call her back right away. He rarely kept his phone on him while at work, but he'd promised her that, this close to her due date, he would be checking it regularly. Her water had broken forty minutes ago.

By the time he called her back, Marian had her bag by the front door. All it took was her saying "it's time," and he assured her he was on the way. It would take Dean half an hour to get home. That would give her enough time to get Briella across the street and settled.

There was a light on inside Amy's living room, but because Marian had still not checked the time, she didn't know if that was a good or a bad sign. Her fingers ached as she gripped Briella's wrist. Not that the girl was trying to get away. Just because holding on to something that tightly made Marian feel as though she wasn't going to fly off the face of the earth and up in the sky.

Everything was tilting.

"They're not going to answer the door," Briella said. "It's really late. You should just let me stay home by myself."

"You're not staying alone. Babies take…oh. God." Marian waited until the pain eased. "Babies take a long time to come."

Marian rang the bell again, then knocked. A flicker of shadows in the window had her breathing a sigh of relief that was cut short by a mother of a contraction. Only when Briella let out a whimper did Marian realize she was squeezing way too hard. She let go as Amy's door opened.

Amy wore a quilted housecoat and had her blonde hair tied up in a bandanna. Marian blinked for a moment. Amy put a hand to her mouth.

"It's time? Oh!"

The contraction had eased, and in the time between it stopping and the next one beginning, everything around Marian gained an almost supernatural clarity. There wasn't a way to predict the next contraction. They'd been coming about fifteen minutes apart up until now, strong enough to hurt but not enough to knock the breath from her. Still, there was a growing tension inside her that she knew meant it was going to happen again. Harder, and harder until she couldn't stop it. The baby was coming.

This time the pressure was accompanied by a sharper pain, deep inside. It made her want to straddle, squat and push. She had to focus.

"I'm in labor."

Amy's eyebrows rose in an expression so surprised it almost seemed like she was mocking Marian with it. "Oh my goodness! Yes, of course, I told you she can stay here with us. Oh my goodness, Marian, do you need the ambulance? Come in, come in."

Briella went into the living room to settle in front of the TV. Marian bit back a groan. She could not bear the thought of showing any signs of weakness in front of Amy, who, she was sure, would have been able to labor graciously, barely breaking a sweat. Marian, on the other hand, was a mess.

"I called Dean, and he's on his way home to take me to the hospital." Marian gritted her teeth. Sweat trickled down the line of her spine and unpleasantly into the crack of her ass. Her fists were clenched, too, so she released them. "Briella. You're going to stay here with Miss Amy while Dean takes me to the hospital, okay?"

"Yeah." Briella didn't even look away from the TV.

Amy fluttered her hands. "Oh, wow. It's happening! How exciting. How long do you think you'll be?"

"However long it takes," Marian said.

Amy laughed, and Marian wanted to punch her. "Of course, of course. Babies come in their own time. Well, she'll be fine here. You go on ahead. Just keep me posted. Well, have Dean do it, I'm sure you'll be—"

"Briella, I'm leaving. Stay here."

This roused the girl, who got up to run and hug her mother. *At least she didn't smell bad anymore*, Marian thought a little wildly. She didn't have to be embarrassed in front of Amy, whose own child would never go more than a day without a thorough scrubbing. Marian kissed the top of Briella's head and caught a small whiff of sourness, but it wasn't anything nearly as bad as it had been.

Briella had muttered something that Marian didn't catch. The girl was staring at Amy with a concerned expression. Wary.

"What?"

"When will you be home?"

Marian grimaced, breathing through another long contraction. "I don't know. Soon, before you know it, with a new baby brother or sister. So be good, okay?"

"Are you going to have an epidural?" Amy asked. "I didn't have one with Toby. I was natural all the way."

Of course she'd been. Marian had decided that the moment they could put the needle in her, she'd be getting as much painkiller as she was allowed. She didn't say that now. Amy watched her all the way across the street, but Marian didn't turn back. By the time she got inside her own front door, the pad she'd put into her panties had gotten wet enough to be uncomfortable.

Dean would be there any minute. She took her time getting cleaned up. Packed a few extras in her bag. She was thirsty but didn't know if she ought to drink anything. Her stomach had stopped rumbling when the contractions began.

"Babe! Where are you!"

She went into the hallway to see Dean almost running toward the kitchen. It would have been funny if he weren't so seriously freaked out. He caught sight of her watching and turned, spinning so hard he twisted the throw rug and almost wiped out.

"Careful," Marian said. "We don't need you to end up needing a hospital stay, too."

She was in his arms a minute after that. Pressed to his chest. She let him hold her, even though another contraction was beginning its rippling agony all through her, and the last thing in the world she wanted was any kind of additional pressure on her body. She let him hold her because the sight of Dean's panicked face had shown Marian something she hadn't guessed before. Dean, for all his usual calm demeanor, was distressed by all of this, more than she was, and she had to remind herself that he hadn't been through it before.

"It's going to be okay," she told him, stroking his back.

That was the last thing she remembered.

CHAPTER FORTY

"Follow me." The ebony bird doesn't caw or squawk. It speaks in Briella's voice, but sounds much older. The way her daughter will sound when she is a woman, all grown up. "Follow me, come on."

"I don't want to go with you."

Marian wears a white nightgown, flowing. Her feet are bare. Her hair falls around her shoulders. The hem of her gown is soaked with mud and splashes of crimson that creep down the fabric from someplace in the center of her body. She is bleeding, and that blood is what mixed with the earth and made the mud.

"If you don't follow me, how will you know where to go?" Onyx tilts its head to her, that bright gaze burning.

Its mouth moves with every word. That's how Marian knows this is a dream. In reality, the bird mimics from deep in its throat. It doesn't speak, it mocks.

"I'm not going with you." Marian says this three or four times, or she tries to, but her mouth is suddenly full of something chewy and sticky like bubblegum.

She cannot speak.

Her feet are moving toward the raven, which is flying so slowly that its wings don't even flap. It hovers, moving inch by inch, with Marian so close behind she could reach out and grab it. She tries, her fingertips skimming the black feathers. The bird explodes in a cluster of darkness.

Marian screams, "I'm not going with you!"

The ground beneath her falls away, and she tumbles into nothing.

★　★　★

"Marian? Marian, can you hear me? It's time to wake up, hon."

The warm female voice was not her mother's, but it felt familiar enough that Marian wanted to answer it. She mumbled words that were meant to be agreement, but her mouth was sticky. Gummed shut. She was so thirsty it felt like she'd been sucking sand.

"Marian. Babe. Can you wake up?"

That was Dean's voice, and she struggled again, upward out of the darkness of sleep. Her eyes opened, then shut against the bright light. She tried again.

Everything hurt.

"Where am I?" Then, after a moment, she gave a panicked shriek. "The baby? Where's the baby?"

Dean gripped her arm. A woman in a pair of maroon scrubs took the other. Marian tried to fight both of them, but the pain was too much. Marian fell back into the hospital bed. She remembered Dean bringing her to the hospital and nothing much after that.

"The baby's fine. You had a healthy baby boy," the nurse said. Her strong fingers squeezed Marian's upper arm, keeping it still. "You need to relax."

That was a good thing, because now that she was fully awake, she could see the needle probing the back of her hand. She calmed herself as best she could, but wasn't able to stop the shaking. She wasn't even cold.

"You're having a reaction to the meds," the nurse said. "If you feel like you're going to be sick, there's an emesis basin right here. Okay? And if you need me, you can push this button. Otherwise, you've got some nice pain meds on a drip. You can push this button as often as you want, but it will only dispense more meds when it turns green."

"What happened to me?" The nurse gave her another squeeze, but Marian was looking at Dean. He looked as though he'd lost weight. Haggard, face drawn, several days' growth of beard. Days? "Dean?"

"You hemorrhaged. Your blood pressure dropped. We almost lost you." Dean's voice cracked and broke.

The nurse left them, and Marian waited until she'd gone before she spoke again. "I almost died?"

"Yes." Dean bent over her, and she stroked his hair. "I was so scared I was going to lose you."

"You didn't. I'm here. I'm okay. Right? I'm okay?" She shifted in the bed, wincing at the pain between her legs. Part of her wanted to reach down to feel what had happened, but she was afraid to find out she'd been torn in half or something equally horrible. It sure as hell felt like it. No C-section scar, though.

"You're going to be fine. The baby's fine." Dean's breath half sobbed out of him.

Marian stroked his head again. "What about Briella?"

Beneath her touch, Dean tensed. He looked up at her. His mouth worked, but nothing came out.

"What about Briella?" Marian repeated. Her voice sounded very far away. She was fading out again. She'd pushed the button in her hand without knowing it, she thought. She was sending herself down the rabbit hole of pain meds.

Or she was trying to pass out so she didn't have to hear something bad.

"There's been some problems," Dean said, "with Briella."

CHAPTER FORTY-ONE

There could never be enough apologies, but Marian was determined to try. Three weeks passed before she could convince Dean to head back to work. He was still on nights but hoped to switch permanently before the end of the month. She'd healed enough that she could walk across the street with the infant boy, Michael Dean Blake, strapped across her chest as he slept. She kept Briella tight by the hand.

"I don't want to go," Briella muttered as Marian rang the bell.

Marian did not look at her. When Amy opened the door, her wary look hurt Marian's heart. "Amy. Can we come in?"

"I don't think so." Amy gave a small shake of her head.

"Fair enough." Marian drew in a long, deep breath. She tugged Briella a step closer. "We have something to say."

Her nails dug into Briella's wrist until the kid spoke. "I'm sorry, Miss Amy."

Amy did not smile. If anything, her expression twisted into more distress. From behind her, Marian heard Toby's babble, but quick as a striking snake, Amy turned and pushed him out of sight.

"Better than that, Briella," Marian said.

Briella huffed and scuffed at the porch with the toe of her sandal. Marian gave her wrist another squeeze. She muttered an "ouch" but looked up at Amy. "I'm sorry I gave Toby peanuts for a snack and made him sick."

"I'm sorry," Marian said when Amy didn't reply. "Amy, I am so, so sorry."

"He's fine," Amy said. "He could have died, but he didn't. He's fine."

"Maybe we can play again sometime," Briella said.

Amy's gaze never left Marian's. "I don't think so."

Then she closed the door in their faces. Marian sagged. Against her chest, the baby stirred, rooting. It was time to feed him again.

As they turned to cross the street for home, Hank's white truck came down the street at its usual careless speed. She caught sight of his face through the windshield. His brakes came on. The truck slowed, crawling past them. He stared as it did, but although Marian raised a hand, he didn't return her wave.

In the house, she nursed the baby in the rocker next to his crib, then put him down for a nap. Sleep when the baby sleeps. That was the advice everyone had given her when Briella was born, but Marian was strangely not tired. Mikey had been sleeping four and five hours at a stretch since birth. She wasn't getting as much sleep as she needed, but she was getting enough.

She stopped in Briella's room before she went downstairs. The girl was sitting on the window seat, looking through the glass. The overhead fan swirled, sending lazy heat through the room. Marian swiped her tongue over her upper lip and tasted salt.

"School starts next week," she said. "I bet you're excited."

Briella turned toward her. Tears had slid in tracks down her cheeks. Marian went to her, sitting on the window seat and taking her small hands.

"Miss Amy hates me for what happened to Toby," she said. "She'll never forgive me."

Marian had already gone over this with her. Did Briella know Toby wasn't allowed to have peanuts? Yes, but she'd forgotten. Had she tried to hurt him? No, she would never hurt Toby. No, never.

The weeks before the night of Mikey's birth had gone blurry for Marian. She remembered the months of being so sick, death might have been a better option. She remembered the anxiety, suspicions, fears, but all of that had faded. The postpregnancy rush of hormones that could lead to postpartum depression had done the opposite for her, or perhaps it had more to do with the passing of time and the easing of her grief about her father, her ability to eat and keep down food, her return to rationality.

Briella had been nothing but sweet about the baby. Helping Marian change his diapers, bringing the burp cloths, even singing him to sleep so Marian could toss in some laundry or mop the floor. The girl had been the epitome of doting big sister.

"Miss Amy was very scared about losing Toby. If she's angry with you, Briella, we have to understand and respect that. You're right. She may never forgive you. You have to look inside yourself and know that you didn't mean to hurt him. But you can't make anyone forgive you."

Briella leaned against Marian, the girl's cheek against her mother's breasts. The pressure was a little too much. Marian's breast pads were already damp from milk. She shifted to ease the pressure and used one hand to stroke over Briella's hair. She slipped her fingers along the back of the girl's neck, but the cut there had long ago healed.

"If something bad like that happened to me, would you forgive the person who did it?" Briella asked.

"I might try," Marian said. "But I'm not sure I could."

"If something bad happened to baby Mikey, you would never forgive that person, either?"

Marian pushed the girl to look at her face, into her pale eyes. Her tone was firm. "No. I don't think I could ever forgive someone who hurt baby Mikey, even if I tried."

Her phone hummed from her pocket and she pulled it out to speak to her brother. They weren't close and had never been, but since losing Dad, they'd both been making more of an effort to reach out to each other. Keep in touch. Make amends for the silence and distance both had harbored without real reason.

Marian kept her voice pitched low as she got up and paced along Briella's worn rag rug. Moving continued to be an effort. She still had pain, and a lot of the baby bulk had not yet come off. They spoke briefly about the details for the baptism and small party after, about Desmond and his wife Theresa standing as godparents. When she got off the phone, Briella was staring.

"Who was that?"

"Uncle Desmond."

"Who's getting baptized?" Briella asked with a frown.

Marian slipped her phone back into her pocket. "Baby Mikey. Two Sundays from now."

"He is? Why?" Briella looked stunned.

Marian crossed to her so she could look out the window. Trees in the distance. A shingle or two off the roof. A single black feather caught in the corner of the eaves, or maybe only a shadow.

"Because my father and mother would have wanted that, and I lost them both, so I want to respect them," Marian said.

Briella's jaw dropped. "You don't even believe!"

Marian shook her head. "No. I don't. But it feels like the right thing to do anyway."

"He can't choose," Briella said, agitated. "That doesn't seem fair. Baby Mikey can't decide what he believes."

"I'm his mother. I decide for him, the way I decided for you," Marian said.

Briella crossed her arms over her chest and looked out the window for a moment, sullen. Then she smiled and turned to her mother. "Two Sundays from now?"

Marian nodded.

"That's enough time," Briella said.

Marian studied her. "For what?"

"To get ready."

CHAPTER FORTY-TWO

"Wish I didn't have to go in to work. I want to stay all cozy here in bed with you." Dean yawned and rolled to put a hand on the back of Mikey's head as he nursed.

Marian settled a bit against the pillows. "Wish you could too."

"Ahh, just another couple weeks and I'll be on permanent days." Dean cracked another long yawn and kissed the baby's head, then Marian's lips. "Can I get you anything?"

"No. Dinner should be almost ready. As soon as this little guy's done with his, we can eat. Can you tell Briella to wash up?"

"Of course." Dean leaned to kiss her again, lingering a little this time.

When he tried to pull away, Marian grabbed for his arm to stop him. The baby, rustled from his place on the nipple, squeaked out a protest. Marian tipped her face for another kiss. They had not yet made love since the baby's birth, but she was starting to consider it a very valid option.

"Well now," Dean said with a pleased grin. "That's nice."

Marian kissed him again. "Love you."

He shifted on the bed to sit upright, close to her. "Baby, is everything okay? I mean, are you doing all right?"

He had every right to worry about her. She'd gone through a bit of a crazy time. Stress and trauma. Marian couldn't blame him for having concerns.

"Yes. We're all—"

"Going to be fine. I know."

She blinked against a small surge of tears, but smiled for him. "It's something my dad said, and it stuck with me."

"Your dad was a smart man. And he was right. We are all going to be fine. More than fine. We're going to be fantastic." Dean kissed her cheeks, her nose, her forehead, then her lips again. "Holler if you need me."

The baby nursed. Marian dozed. The looming presence of a figure woke her, startled, enough to jerk and wake the baby, who began to wail.

"Sorry, Mama," Briella said and took a step back.

Marian soothed the baby, hushing him until he fell quiet. "What's wrong?"

"Nothing. Dean said it's time for dinner."

"We'll be right there." With a yawn, Marian roused herself to head for the kitchen.

She loved her little family. Briella in her chair, regaling Dean with stories about her new project at Parkhaven. The baby in his bouncy seat, alert and watching everything that went on. Dean, being a father. And Marian, a mother.

Her father *was* right, she thought, and for the first time in years, sent up a prayer of gratitude for her blessings.

★   ★   ★

Dean had left for work an hour ago. The baby was sleeping in his crib. She would wake him in another couple hours to nurse and change him before putting him back down, hopefully to make it at least six hours. Briella was supposed to be reading quietly in her room and going to sleep so she could keep to her school schedule, but Marian found her in the kitchen.

"What are you doing up?" Marian had come in for a mug of hot tea – not peppermint. God, no. Probably never again. But she did like chamomile and had been getting back into the habit of a mug with a book before bed.

"I was afraid of the lightning and thunder." Briella gestured to the electric kettle. "I wanted to try some of your tea. Sit down, Mom. I'll make you some."

Mom, not Mama. Well, at least it wasn't *Mother*. Marian took a seat and watched the girl prepare the mugs with the loose tea, filling the mesh strainers and adding hot water.

She'd grown again. Still lean, with petite features. Briella would always be small. But she looked different. More grown up. She would be eleven soon, Marian thought with a sense of shock, a fact she had of course not forgotten but one that had nevertheless sneaked up on her.

"Your birthday's coming up. Do you want a party? Maybe invite some friends from school?" Marian hesitated after she said it. The last time they'd tried to plan a birthday party for Briella, the bullying at Southside had come into the open.

A crash of thunder made them both jump. A moment after, both laughed. Marian tilted her head, listening if Mikey had woken, but she heard nothing.

Briella set a steaming mug in front of her. "Yeah, I'd like a party!"

"Good." Marian sipped her tea. "Oh, this is good, too."

"Is it all right if I take mine up to bed? I want to finish my book before lights out."

For a moment, Marian felt a pang that the kid was choosing to be alone rather than with her mother. But that was natural. She'd done the same with her own mother.

"You're not too scared of the storm?"

Briella paused and hugged her. "I am. But I'm too old to be scared of it."

"Maybe you're never too old to hug your mom, though, huh?" Marian let the girl go. "How about I come up in a little bit to tuck you in?"

Twenty minutes later, Marian's eyes were drooping so much she had to shake herself to keep from passing out. She heard the stealthy slide of feet on the floor above her head. Briella was awake and moving around. The ceiling creaked.

Marian sat up, rubbing at her eyes, and headed for the stairs. At the top of them, she looked to the left. The door to the baby's room was open. Briella's was closed, without even a strip of light creeping into the hall from beneath.

Marian stood still, listening. The storm had come on stronger. The hall lit briefly with blue-white light from the baby's room. Almost at once, the boom of thunder made her jump. It seemed so much closer here on the second floor.

Inside the baby's room, Mikey lay sleeping peacefully in his crib, unwoken by the storm. Fierce love burned inside her as she placed a gentle hand on the infant's back. His soft curls brushed her lips as she bent to kiss the top of his head. The milky smell of him and the softness of his breathing intoxicated her.

She knocked on Briella's door. When there was no answer, she pushed it open. The room was dim. The girl had unplugged her night-light, and Marian felt another pang at how quickly she was growing up. A flash of lightning showed the bed.

Empty.

"Briella?" Marian hit the light switch, revealing the bed's tangle of covers but no Briella. She cried the girl's name again.

Another burst of storm. The window flung open hard enough to shatter the glass. Rain and wind poured into the room. Marian screamed.

The raven flew in the window.

The lights went out.

CHAPTER FORTY-THREE

The bird was blacker than the night outside, but in the swift strobe flashes of lightning that lit the bedroom, Marian could clearly see every feather. Onyx gave her that head tilt she'd come to loathe, the one that seemed so assessing and judgmental. Marian's lips skinned back over her teeth in a grimace.

"Where is she?"

The bird didn't answer her, of course, not even with one of the few phrases it had learned to mimic. It didn't move from its perch on the window seat when Marian stalked toward it. Her fingers curled to grab it, maybe to try again to throttle the fucking thing, but she stopped herself, wary and remembering what that beak could do. In Briella's small room with its sloping eaves, in the pitch black, Marian would be at a disadvantage, even if it couldn't see in the dark any better than she could.

Another flash lit the room. Onyx croaked, like the mutter of a curse under its breath. It wasn't a word or phrase she'd heard it say before, but she recognized herself in the tone. The damned thing was mimicking *her*. Fury and disgust rose so fiercely inside her that for a moment the dizziness eased. It was back in a second or so. Her head spun.

"Where," she said again, "is Briella?"

"Briella," Onyx said. "Briella."

Gusts of wind tossed the curtains, soaking them and the window-seat cushion. Her stomach roiled, bitterness at the back of her mouth. Marian put a hand on Briella's dresser to keep herself from going to her knees.

The lights came on again, flickering and dim. Her hand hit an orange prescription bottle that fell off the dresser and rolled, popping the lid off. She and the bird dove for it at the same time. Marian caught it up in her fist. She barely had the chance to see Amy Patterson's name, with '...for insomnia' on the label, before the bird snatched at it. Marian balled her fist and punched the raven as hard as she could. It squawked and landed a few inches out of reach.

I wanted to try some of your tea. Sit down, Mom. I'll make you some.

I'll make you some.

The tea in Marian's stomach churned. She couldn't keep her eyes focused. She shoved her fingers down her throat, forcing a gag. She bent over the garbage pail, not caring if she vomited into it or onto the floor. She needed to get this out of her system, or she was going to pass out. She might even die.

The sound of Mikey's crying forced her to stand. Her nipples ached and burned as her milk began to let down. She didn't press her fingers to them to stop the flow, too disoriented, too uncoordinated. Her eyes had been closed, and she hadn't even realized it. Shit, how long had she been like that, hunched over the can with her mouth open, drool and puke hanging in strings off her lips? Tears gathered in the corners of her eyes and slid, burning down her cheeks. Mikey was crying, and Briella was still missing.

Except that it was not her baby who wailed, it was that fucking bird. This time, Marian didn't stop herself from grabbing it. Onyx took off right before she could get a grip. She snagged it briefly and was left holding a feather. The bird thumped the air with its wings, then hit the sloping ceiling hard enough to make it let out a squawk.

"Where is my daughter, you filthy piece of road-kill-eating shit?" Marian tried to scream the words, but they came out in a rasp, slurring.

More rain began to pound the roof and smack the glass as lightning illuminated the room. She could see the slashing torrent in the blue-white light. A moment later, thunder rumbled, but she heard another cry. This time, it was not the mimicking raven. It was Briella.

"Oh, God, oh no."

The kid was on the roof. Marian tugged at the sill, her fingers clumsy and thick, but determined. She yanked it up, but it stuck. She stuck her head out, but that was as far as she could get. She screamed Briella's name but could see nothing until the next flash of storm light.

Marian shoved with one shoulder, trying to get the window to open enough for her to get through it. She managed to push it another inch or so, still not enough, but now at least she could twist to see the roof in front of her. A silhouette, hunched and small. Her daughter.

"Briella! Baby, you need to come back inside, please. Come back to Mama!"

Briella turned. Marian's eyes had adjusted a bit to the darkness now. She could make out the wide, dark eyes. The curling hair, limp and straight now from the wet, hanging over Briella's shoulders and back. She wore the Parkhaven school T-shirt and a pair of shorts, and her tiny hands gripped bony knees. She wore no shoes, and Marian could see her toes crimping into the shingles.

"Come back inside!"

Marian strained, reaching, but the girl was a good six inches out of reach. Again, Marian shoved at the window, trying to get it to move just enough so that she could squeeze through it. Either it was too stuck or she was still too drugged to muster the strength, because all she did was send a stab of pain through her back and shoulders. Her breasts, swollen and leaking milk, ached as they pressed against the sill. Another retch struggled out of her, and she spat a mouthful of bile onto the roof.

Impossibly, the rain got harder. The gutters had started to fill, sending a waterfall over the edge of the roof. More rain cascaded across the faded and worn shingles, a river diverted by Briella, who hadn't moved. In the next flash of light, Marian could see her daughter's face as clearly outlined as though it were a camera's flash and her mind the film. Except nobody used film anymore, it was all digital, with chips and wires and data, and then she was fading again, her head nodding as she tried so hard to hold on to the edges of the window but found herself on her knees in front of it.

Digital chips and wires and circuits: that was how people took pictures now, it was how they lived their lives. It was what Briella had put inside the bird's brain to capture the program she'd designed to recreate herself. It was in there, inside that raven. Her girl was now inside of it. On the roof, in the rain, on a perch, crying like a baby, muttering curses, her girl had wings....

Marian bit her tongue hard enough to squirt the copper taste of blood down the back of her throat. She was not going to pass out. She was *not* going to leave her children alone. Not baby Mikey in his crib with Onyx ready to peck out his eyes. And not Briella, clinging to the slippery, rain-soaked roof in the middle of a storm. Marian was not going to abandon her babies. No.

She bit again. The pain was thin, exquisite like a burn or the first line of a fresh tattoo; it was nothing like the surging pain of childbirth she had not yet forgotten, but would, over time. She ground the tip of her tongue between her teeth until the urge to scream was bigger and bolder than the desire to let herself fall onto the floor into unconsciousness.

She stuck her head out the window again. "Briella! What are you doing?"

"I was trying to catch Onyx, but he wouldn't let me!"

"Come here!"

"No," Briella said with a shake of her head that sent strands of her black hair slapping her small, rounded cheeks.

Marian drew in the cold air. She tipped her face to the frigid rain, her eyes closed as it stung her like a thousand needles. She opened her mouth to take in the water, letting it rinse away the taste of sick and blood. She swallowed some, hoping it would make her vomit more to get the drugs out of her, although she feared they were already into her bloodstream, and she might have only a few more minutes before she could no longer fight them.

The bird landed on her back, and Marian shrieked, humping her body in an arc against the bottom of the window. It still refused to budge. She was stuck there, waiting for the sting of its beak. And where would it stab her? In the back of her neck, the base of her skull? Or would it try for her eyes?

She reached for Briella, who scooted away. The motion caused her to slip on the roof. The girl didn't scream, but Marian did.

"Stay still! Oh, God, Briella, baby, please come here to Mama. Let me bring you inside."

"Where's Onyx? What did you do to him?" Briella cried. "Did you hurt him?"

Marian wrenched her body again to get the bird off her. The weight lifted but settled again. She felt the press of its beak against her spine, and she tensed. She shook her head.

"He's fine. He's right here. I didn't hurt him."

"You can't hurt him, Mama. You have to promise me." Briella got to her feet and slipped again, ending up on hands and knees with her fingers clutching at the roof while her little toes dug in. "You have to keep Onyx safe. You have to promise me you won't *ever* hurt him!"

Marian was going to kill that bird as soon as she had the chance. "I promise, sweet girl. Just...come inside, now."

The rain had not let up, but the lightning and thunder were moving away. Briella stood upright, one foot a little higher on the roof. Marian shoved her body harder through the window, and Briella took a step toward her. She slipped, going again to her hands and knees with a cry of pain as the rough shingles tore her flesh.

With a groan, Marian tried to force her way through the small space, but without the window moving, all she managed to do was get herself wedged in place. She couldn't get a full breath without everything hurting. Again, Onyx landed on her back. The tickle of its nubbly feet sent a new nausea swelling in her that had nothing to do with what Briella had put in her tea. Marian wrenched herself around, half on her side, her arm still outstretched toward her daughter.

"You can't hurt him, because Onyx has me inside him. The way I wanted to have me inside baby Mikey, so I would know how it felt to have you love me the best."

Marian's fingers curled on nothing but the rain. She swallowed, then spat, then spat again. Sickness pounded at her guts and her head, but this time, not from the pills.

"Briella," she managed to say, "did you hurt baby Mikey?"

Briella shook her head and inched closer to Marian. "I wasn't going to hurt him. I figured out how to do it without hurting him. It wasn't going to be like with Toby or Rufus...or Grampa. But then I remembered what you said, how you couldn't forgive someone who hurt baby Mikey, and I...I worried you would find out, so I didn't do it."

It wasn't going to be like Toby or Rufus or Grampa.

Marian wanted to recoil, but she was too stuck to do anything. She tried to look into Briella's eyes, but the darkness and rain made it impossible to see anything in there. And what, she thought with a thin edge of hysteria, what would she see in her daughter's gaze, even in the brightest of lights, but nothing? Because the truth was something she had never wanted to admit but could no longer pretend she didn't know – there was a nothingness inside Briella. An empty blackness that held the place where her soul ought to have been.

"You didn't do anything to the baby?"

"No! No!"

"What did you do to them? To me?"

"I only wanted to make you sick!" Briella screamed. "The purple berries just made you throw up. It wasn't like with the pills. I thought if you were sick enough, you'd lose the baby the way you did the other ones, but I'm glad you didn't! Because I love baby Mikey, I love him! I just wanted to be inside him, so you'd love me the best! So I tried to catch Onyx, but he wouldn't let me! But I wasn't going to hurt Mikey!"

Marian did not believe it. Not for a second. Despair clawed its way up her throat and out her mouth in a low, keening shriek that sounded almost like the wind itself.

Briella slipped again and let out a cry as her outflung hand at last connected with Marian's. Her fingers linked with her mother's. She stood. A far-off lightning bolt lit her in silhouette again.

Briella's hand gripped in hers, Marian was no longer afraid the kid was going to slide and fall off the roof, not so long as her mother held her. With her body half in and half out of the window, Marian had the leverage to hold tight enough, although pulling them both back inside was going to be hard with only one hand. The rain poured over them.

Across the hall, loud enough to be heard over the storm, baby Mikey cried.

"What did you do to the dog, Briella? What did you do to Toby?"

"I had to make sure it would work before I could use it on Mikey!"

The rain was easing. The storm, passing. In Marian's fist, Briella's fingers were smooth and cold.

Those small hands had killed.

"What...what did you do to Grampa?"

Briella tugged Marian's hand, pulling herself closer to the window and safety. "I couldn't get him into Onyx, but some of Onyx got into him. I didn't want him to die. That was an accident."

"But he did die. You hurt him. You hurt all of them!"

"Not all experiments work the first time," Briella said.

"You can't do those things, Briella." Marian's grip tightened, tugging the girl closer to the window.

Briella said, "Yes, I can. If I want to."

This close, it didn't matter about the rain and the night. Only an inch or so away from her, Briella's face was easy to read. Briella's teeth chattered. Water dripped from her eyelashes and chin.

"I can if I want to," she repeated, her tone the same it had always been when she was proud and showing off to her mother what she was able to do. When she'd finished *Gone with the Wind*. When she'd painted a Thanksgiving turkey using the outline of her hand. When she'd learned to ride a bike, to tie her shoes.

When she had murdered.

The press of the bird on her back loosened Marian's grip. Marian put her other hand on top of her girl's head to feel the soaked curls. She cupped her daughter's soft cheek, chilled with the storm.

"Briella," Marian said. "Do you still wish you could fly?"

Briella smiled.

Marian shoved her as hard as she could.

CHAPTER FORTY-FOUR

The spring returned, because that's what happened when winter was over. Marian, seeking the sunshine, wrapped her baby son, now eight months old, in a blanket and hefted him onto her hip so they could both go outside into the backyard, where the grass had only just started to grow long again. Mikey chewed on his knuckles. He still hadn't discovered how to suck his thumb, and Marian hoped he never would – it was hell trying to get a kid to stop, well past the time when they should.

The new yard furniture she and Dean had put on layaway wouldn't be paid off for another month or so, but the old picnic table was still out here. She found the two pieces of the broken glass ashtray pushed together on it, empty but for the smudge of old, wet leaves. She didn't have any cigarettes in the house, but as she settled onto the splintery wooden bench and rested Mikey on the tabletop, Marian didn't even get the faintest wisp of a craving.

Some things, she thought, eventually did go away by themselves.

A flutter at the edge of the tree line turned her head. The raven, glossy and black, left its perch in a pine and circled the picnic table a few times before landing on the edge of it. It wasn't close enough to the baby to get in a peck, but it shifted from foot to foot as it settled its wings. Marian pulled the small plastic container of chili leftover from last night's dinner and took off the top. She pushed it toward Onyx.

The bird let out a rasping, muttered caw. The baby cooed and waved his hands toward the bird, but Marian kept him still and out of range. The food disappeared quickly. Onyx moved along the edge of the table, his head cocked so he could look her over with that ebony void of an eye.

"Go on," Marian said. "I'll have more for you another time."

The bird hopped, lifting itself into flight, and circled her a time or two before flying toward the trees. Halfway there, it turned and headed back. It swooped down at her, not maliciously but with obvious intent. For a heart-stopping moment, Marian thought it was going to land on her shoulder. She couldn't have allowed it. The thought made her skin crawl. She tensed, ready to scream and knock the bird away.

But it didn't land on her. It merely flew around her three times and landed once more on the picnic table. Onyx tilted his head, looking her over with that steady, unblinking stare. He cawed once. Then again.

"Goodbye, Mama."

"Go on now," Marian said again, this time in a softer, gentler voice. "I'll have more for you…"

Tomorrow, she tried to say, but her throat had closed and no words would come out. Baby Mikey started to fuss, and she gathered him close to her chest. She pressed her nose to the downy, fine hair that smelled of baby shampoo. She breathed him in, her eyes closed, hot tears tickling the corners.

When she opened them, Onyx was gone.

Marian looked at the baby in her arms and kissed his sweet, fat cheeks. She stood. She looked once more at the forest, but although she thought she heard the faint and rasping caw of a raven, she couldn't see anything but the trees.

"C'mon, baby boy. Let's go back inside." And then, with tears in her eyes but a smile on her lips, Marian added, "We're all going to be fine."

FLAME TREE PRESS
FICTION WITHOUT FRONTIERS
Award-Winning Authors & Original Voices

Flame Tree Press is the trade fiction imprint of Flame Tree Publishing, focusing on excellent writing in horror and the supernatural, crime and mystery, science fiction and fantasy. Our aim is to explore beyond the boundaries of the everyday, with tales from both award-winning authors and original voices.

·

Other titles available include:

Junction by Daniel M. Bensen

Thirteen Days by Sunset Beach by Ramsey Campbell

Think Yourself Lucky by Ramsey Campbell

The Haunting of Henderson Close by Catherine Cavendish

The House by the Cemetery by John Everson

The Toy Thief by D.W. Gillespie

The Playing Card Killer by Russell James

The Siren and the Specter by Jonathan Janz

The Sorrows by Jonathan Janz

Savage Species by Jonathan Janz

The Nightmare Girl by Jonathan Janz

Kosmos by Adrian Laing

The Sky Woman by J.D. Moyer

Creature by Hunter Shea

The Bad Neighbor by David Tallerman

Ten Thousand Thunders by Brian Trent

Night Shift by Robin Triggs

The Mouth of the Dark by Tim Waggoner

·

Join our mailing list for free short stories, new release details, news about our authors and special promotions:

flametreepress.com

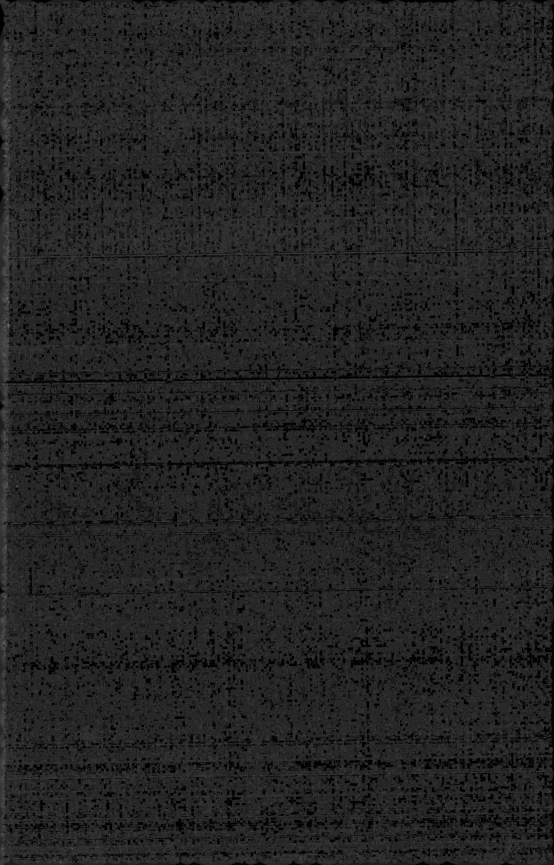